PRAISE FOR *THE BARGAIN*, BOOK ONE OF THE PLAIN CITY PEACE SERIES

"An exciting, involving novel, sensitively rendered. . . . This is clearly the first novel in a series and not all the plot strings are tied up at the end. Readers are left wanting to know more about these people we've come to care about."
—**E. E. Kennedy**
     author of *Irregardless of Murder* and *Death Dangles a Participle*

"With a blend of sweet twists, painful decisions, and unique courage, Betsie's journey delights the soul. When life brings changes and unexpected losses, *The Bargain* tugs at the heart with a deliciously fresh revelation of innocence blended with deep convictions and commitments."
—**Janet Perez Eckles**
     founder of Camino de Luz Ministries and best-selling author
     of *Simply Salsa: Dancing Without Fear at God's Fiesta*

"*The Bargain* examines a troubled time in American history—the year following the Kent State massacre—through the eyes of a young Amish girl. With deep character portrayals and a masterful plot, this life-affirming book raises as many questions as it answers. Well done!"
—**Janalyn Voigt**
     literary judge and author of Tales of Faeraven series

"Stephanie takes readers into a story that is both simple and complex. You discover that there is nothing 'plain' about the Plain life, and that none of us are immune to the desire for peace."
—**Cindy Sigler Dagnan**
     author and speaker

The BACHELOR

The BACHELOR

PLAIN CITY PEACE

BOOK TWO

STEPHANIE REED

Kregel *Publications*

The Bachelor
© 2014 by Stephanie Reed

Published by Kregel Publications, a division of Kregel, Inc., 2450 Oak Industrial Dr. NE, Grand Rapids, MI 49505.

The persons and events portrayed in this work are the creations of the author, and any resemblance to persons living or dead is purely coincidental.

Scripture quotations are from the King James Version.

Photography by Steve Gardner, PixelWorks Studios

ISBN 978-0-8254-4216-2

Printed in the United States of America
14 15 16 17 18 / 5 4 3 2 1

To my parents, Walter and Clara Morgan,
who loved me, took me to church, answered thousands of my questions,
and made sure I always had plenty to eat and plenty to read.
Thanks, Mom and Dad.

To my mother-in-law, Mary Jo Reed,
who raised a fine son and graciously accepted me into my second family.
Thanks, Mom.

In memory of Donald W. Reed,
the bravest man I've ever known. We still miss you terribly, Dad.

PROLOGUE

from The Bargain

CHARLEY WAS SOLEMN, star-lit blond hair framing his angel face. "*Mem* is sick with what Miriam Bontrager had. Sadie stayed late to help care for her, and when I brought her home, I asked her to wake you. When she told me you weren't in your bed, I didn't know what to think. How can I watch out for you when I don't know where you are, Betsie? It's not good for you to spend so much time with the English, especially alone with that boy so late, ain't so?"

"*Ach*. I thought—never mind." A quick fire of shame blazed across her cheeks, and she rushed to explain. "Michael is my friend only." Her conscience pricked like a needle through a thimble. "He's very troubled, and I was trying to help him. But don't worry, Charley. He's leaving. And he won't be back." The words caught in her throat.

Charley ducked his head. "*Ach*, that's so good, Betsie. Come here and sit by me, why don't you?" He patted the step.

She'd waited forever to be near him again, and she did not hesitate.

"Betsie, I have another question to ask you."

Her heart pounded. "What question?"

But now Charley hemmed and hawed. "*Ach*, maybe I'm no good with fancy words, but I do know where you need to be and what is best for you." He stopped to ponder, searching for a better way to put it. His face lit up with a thought. "You know it is true that you will never get to heaven if you stay with the English."

Betsie felt a quick stab of fear. "But Charley! *Mem* and *Dat*—"

"*Ach*, no." Charley groaned and cradled his face in his hands. "I told you I am a *Nixnootzich* when it comes to words. Of course I pray that your *mem* and *dat* will return soon." He raised his head. "I am trying to say that I want you to stay here. I want you for my special friend." He added, very low, "I hope one day we will have a home together. What do you say, Betsie?"

She nodded, a lump in her throat. "I . . . I'd like that more than anything."

"Then kiss me once, Betsie," he said.

Excitement fluttered through her; she'd waited a long time for this. She raised her lips and closed her eyes. His kiss brushed her mouth like a moth's wing, tentative and chaste.

He drew back and smiled, visibly relieved. "Well, it's awful late. I'd better get back to *Mem*. She needs me."

Betsie bobbed her head. "All right, Charley. See you soon." For the second time, she waved good-bye. She touched her lips as she watched Charley unhitch the horses and drive away into the darkness.

So that was a kiss, she mused as she stepped inside the door. She turned up the lamp and sat down at the scarred oak table in the kitchen. Now, now she was free to think of Charley and all the wonderful times that awaited the two of them.

CHAPTER 1

"Trouble is easier to get into than out of."

—Fannie Troyer, quoted in Betsie's journal

Betsie Troyer covered her ears as another rented moving truck roared southward past her farm, bound for Interstate 70. A white passenger van chugged in the truck's wake along State Route 42. Betsie squinted to catch a last glimpse of the Hershberger family as they left Plain City, Ohio, for Missouri.

The van slowed a bit where the road dipped in front of the Troyer farm. Betsie scanned the faces of the occupants, recognized Zeke McCoy, the English driver who regularly transported Amish passengers out west, and came to rest on Atlee Hershberger, a neighbor boy the same age as her pretty younger sister, Sadie. Oblivious to the siblings crowded around him, Atlee's dark eyes smoldered at the Troyer farm. When he caught sight of Betsie in the shadows, his hand shot up in a wave that knocked his hat from his head. He ignored the lost hat and pressed his palm to the glass. Taken aback by his ardent gaze, Betsie wiggled her fingers tentatively and quirked her eyebrows into question marks. Atlee did a double take, blushed, and slid down in his seat until only his mop of curly brown hair was visible as the van passed.

"Was I that awkward at seventeen?" Betsie grinned and shook her head as she walked to the back of her home.

The ringing blows of an ax punctuated the morning bustle. Joe

11

Miller, her neighbor across the road, must be splitting firewood in his woodlot. Betsie sighed. Joe's great-niece Katie would miss Ruthie Hershberger something awful. So many have moved away, Betsie mused as she pumped more water for her horse.

When the creak of the pump handle ceased, a sharp rat-tat on the front door caught her attention. "Now, who could that be, Judith?" In no particular hurry, Betsie caught the last dribbles of water in the priming jar and lugged the bucket to the trough. Judith, her bay mare, blew ripples across the water's surface before drinking deeply.

"Not a neighbor." Betsie fended off Judith's slobbery nuzzles. "Neighbors would walk around to the kitchen door, ain't so? Not Charley—" She pursed her lips. "Oh, Amelia, you'll shed all over my legs if you strop yourself on my ankles that way! Hush your meowing; I will feed you soon." With her toe, she gently nudged her persistent calico kitten aside. "Not Charley Yoder, because he's been here already to pick up Sadie, so who . . . ?"

Curious now, Betsie stood on tiptoe to get a better view and sucked in her breath. A familiar station wagon idled on the tree-lined driveway. She spied Gerald Sullivan, English owner of the harness shop where Betsie was an apprentice, on the front porch of her square white house. Behind him stood his daughter Sheila, shoulders slumped, brown ponytail limp, suitcase by her feet.

Betsie pushed open the gate and trotted toward the house, wiping her bare feet clean on grass damp with morning dew before she climbed the steps. A strand of wheat-colored hair strayed from her *Kapp* and tickled her nose before she tucked away the wisp.

She didn't bother to beat around the bush. "*Was in der welt?* Why have you come?"

Mr. Sullivan looked old as he hunched in the morning sunlight. "Oh, there you are, Betsie. Sorry to barge in on you unannounced. I should have figured you'd be out working hard already." He adjusted his horn-rimmed glasses and smoothed a nonexistent cowlick. "I'm sorry we're so early. Do you have a minute?"

Betsie regarded her boss with caution. Though 10 AM was early for the English, she'd been up for hours. Much of today's work she still had to accomplish on her own, what with her sister working at the bakery and *Mem* and *Dat* gone. She opened her mouth to say she was pretty busy, really. Then she caught a glimpse of Sheila's reddened eyes and her heart melted. She pulled the screen door wide and directed father and daughter to the couch while she hurried to the kitchen and retrieved Amelia's dish. She scraped both of the breakfast plates into the bowl and added some dry cat food. Returning to the front room, she scooped up her ravenous kitten with a gentle hand and deposited her on Sheila's lap.

"Want to feed her, dear heart?"

The girl nodded with a tiny smile. She sniffled as she set the dish on her lap and bent over to rest her cheek against Amelia's downy fur. The kitten vibrated with purrs and made short work of the meal before licking her chops clean and settling onto the girl's bare legs.

All the while, the pendulum of the old eight-day clock sliced away the seconds. Betsie gave Mr. Sullivan an inquiring glance. "You said the harness shop would be closed for Memorial Day. Is there something else you wanted, maybe?"

His sigh was like a great gust. "I knew you would want to help, Betsie. You're very understanding." He tried to continue, but no words came.

Betsie folded her arms and waited. The less said, the better. That was a good rule when dealing with the English. She'd learned that a long time ago.

"Mom wants a divorce." Sheila whispered the shocking words for her father, her fingers buried in Amelia's fur. "She said so in a letter that came Saturday. Dad's flying to Idaho to change her mind; the catch is, he doesn't want me to go. But I know I can help, Dad!" she burst out, her lips trembling as fresh tears spilled. "I know I can!"

Mr. Sullivan sighed and Betsie's heart went out to him as he tried to speak. "Squirt, can't you see—"

"Don't call me Squirt! I'm not a little girl anymore!" Sheila's grip tightened until Amelia ceased licking her chops to mew in protest. "Y-you're the one who drove Mom away with all your yelling! How can you get her to c-come back without me to help?"

"Easy now." Betsie reached to smooth Sheila's hair but stopped short. "You're scaring the kitty and you'll make yourself sick. Besides, it seems like your *dat* wants your *mem* to come back as much as you do."

"Of course I do, Squ— er, Sheila," he chimed in with a grateful glance at Betsie. "It's just that I need to do this on my own. I was hoping Sheila could stay with Michael until he reports for the service, but he hasn't been around for a couple of days. We left him a note, but I can't depend on him for something this important, not with his track record."

Betsie flushed. Apparently, she was the only one who knew that Michael was planning on dodging the army's draft for Vietnam. "You mean you want Sheila to stay with me for the day while you hunt for someone she can stay with?" She brushed Sheila's sleeve with her fingertips.

"That's just it. Debbie Keith and her family are out of town this week, and none of our relatives live close by." Mr. Sullivan removed his steamy glasses and rubbed the lenses with his handkerchief. "And I don't have time for a long drive. The sooner I get to Idaho, the sooner I can bring Phyllis home where she belongs."

"It sounds like I will have no ride and no work at the harness shop for a good while, then," Betsie remarked, doing some rapid calculations to figure out how she and Sadie would purchase supplies now that her money concern had become a reality.

Mr. Sullivan shook his head. "No, and I'm truly sorry about that. I've got to get to Idaho before Phyllis does something drastic. She thinks she's about to make it big as an actress. She doesn't want to hurt us, so she thinks it's best if she 'sets us free.' But I don't want to be free. I love my wife and I want her to come home." He took a deep breath. "Is there any way Sheila can stay here with you until I come back with Phyllis? To tell you the truth, she refuses to stay with anyone *but* you. If you can't help, I'm sunk." He buried his head in his hands.

No. Betsie knew the answer, plain and simple. Her sister Sadie, Charley, her Amish neighbors, bishop Jonas Gingerich, and possibly even her best friend Rachel Yutzy would advise her to refuse. The Sullivan family had caused her enough trouble already.

Mr. Sullivan raised his head when Betsie didn't answer right away.

"Look, I realize assuming responsibility for Sheila is a lot to ask. Maybe I should talk to your parents. Why don't you call them?"

"*Mem* and *Dat* aren't here . . . right now, so I can't ask them." It still hurt to admit they had left for the English world, leaving Betsie and Sadie to fend for themselves. "My sister is at work." A whisper of warning nudged at her conscience and she gave Sheila's knee an awkward pat. "Anyway, if you want Sheila to stay here, it's really my bishop I must ask for permission. It would take a while, though."

Mr. Sullivan tamped at his nonexistent cowlick. "But I can't wait! Can't you help me out just this once?"

The hurry-up English never grasped that a big decision required time, but it really didn't matter one way or another. Deep down, Betsie suspected Jonas would never grant her permission. The Troyers were already on shaky ground since Betsie's parents had left Plain City to "follow Jesus Christ," as if they couldn't do so just as well here. Now they were shunned. Betsie and Sadie had prayed that Lovina, *Dat*'s sister, could persuade Betsie's parents to honor the long-ago vow they'd made on their knees before the community. But lo and behold, Lovina now followed the same worldly teachings that had lured Fannie and Noah Troyer away from their home, their family, and the good Lord.

More than anything, Betsie knew she should follow Charley's advice: "Make up your mind to do what's right. Then do it." What was right was to avoid all contact with the worldly English—the doomed English who were far behind even the camel trying to pass through the eye of the needle on the way to heaven, if you listened to some. No good would come of allowing Sheila to stay in Betsie's Amish home. Nothing else must come between Betsie and Charley, especially now that he'd declared his intentions to her. One day, one beautiful day in the near future, Betsie would become a good, obedient wife to Charley, a wife determined to avoid the poor choice her parents had made. Betsie Yoder will be my name, she reminded herself, and Charley will be my husband. There now, it wasn't so hard, after all. She knew she must refuse.

Betsie pressed her tongue to the roof of her mouth to give the only right answer. One simple word coupled with a regretful shake of her head and she could go back to the plain, peaceful life she loved.

Saying no would have been easy had she not glimpsed pure misery in Sheila's eyes. Somehow this young girl with the pointed chin, the sprinkle of freckles across her nose, and the chicken pox scar on her forehead had worked her way into Betsie's heart despite her firm resolve to remain separate from the English. Sheila had already lost contact with her mother and brother just as she was becoming a young woman. Now her father was off on some English version of a wild goose chase.

Betsie's throat constricted—she would not cry over losing her own parents to the English, especially not in front of Mr. Sullivan. The pain of their leaving was still fresh. How could she allow a young girl like Sheila to experience this same pain on her own? She gripped her hands tight together and spoke, barely above a whisper. *"Jah. Dummel Dich."*

Mr. Sullivan raised his head and poked at his glasses. "What? I'm afraid I don't understand."

Betsie rubbed her forehead in an effort to focus. *"Ach,* I meant to say Sheila can stay with us for a little while, but hurry back." She eyed the door, worried that a neighbor, or Charley, might hear.

"Betsie, that's— I can't— you—" Mr. Sullivan stammered. He held out an awkward hand to shake, but Sheila leapt to her feet and wrapped Betsie in a fierce hug, leaving Amelia to hiss and scramble to safety under the couch.

"Ouch!" Betsie teased. "Who will you stay with if you squeeze me in two pieces?" She tried her best to laugh off her decision, but her heart pounded. What had she done?

CHAPTER 2

"The problem with a little sin is that it
usually grows into a big one."
—FANNIE TROYER, QUOTED IN BETSIE'S JOURNAL

As Sheila relinquished her hold, Betsie heard a car pull up and went limp with relief. Surely it was Michael Sullivan, Sheila's big brother, come to her rescue. In a flash, Betsie surmised that he had seen the note his father left and given up his foolish plan to dodge the Vietnam draft—foolish because even her Amish cousin Nelson had not escaped serving, although he'd been able to remain stateside at a Chicago hospital.

As far as Betsie knew, Michael hadn't told another soul that he was heading to some outlandish place called The Farm in Tennessee. Her cheeks grew warm as she recalled that he'd asked her to go along, but she'd quashed that idea. How *gut* of him, though, to come to his senses and show up at the eleventh hour, as he so often did. Now Michael could take care of Sheila until her dad returned.

She gently dislodged Sheila's grip and stepped quickly to the porch. With a grin, she craned to peer over the lilac hedge for a glimpse of the yellow jacket car she knew so well.

Her grin slipped. Parked in the driveway was a red pickup truck hitched to a horse trailer. An ominous whicker accompanied a metallic clang and the drumming of hooves. Betsie saw Judith raise her head and prick her ears with interest.

17

Mr. Sullivan loomed behind Betsie. "Oh, he's here. Good."

"Why is that truck at my house?" Betsie pointed.

Mr. Sullivan shuffled his feet. "Uh, that's my friend, Rick. He brought Fledge over. Hello, Rick!" He waved.

A man in a cowboy hat eased out of the truck cab and glowered up at Mr. Sullivan before hobbling to the back of the trailer. From her limited experience with the pony, Betsie could certainly identify with the man. The devil pony, that's what Michael had playfully called Fledge. Even Sheila, to whom he belonged, admitted that Fledge did pretty much as he pleased. A few weeks ago, Fledge had made it painfully clear to Betsie that he preferred not to be ridden.

Betsie narrowed her eyes and rubbed her backside. "You expect me to keep the pony here, too? Why can't this Rick care for him?"

Mr. Sullivan shook his head. "No one I know would touch Fledge . . . er, take him on such short notice. Your mare will tolerate another horse, right?"

"It is not Judith's manners that concern me." Betsie frowned and glanced at Sheila, who listened with anxious eyes. "Since Fledge is already here, I guess he can stay."

Mr. Sullivan patted his pockets, relief evident.

"Here you go." He pressed a wad of bills into Betsie's palm. "This should cover Fledge's feed and then some while I'm gone, especially if you supplement it by turning him out to graze." He winked at his daughter. "Remember how I cured you of saying, 'Hey!' all the time, Squirt?"

"Dad." Sheila rolled her eyes. "Every time I said 'hey,' you said, 'Straw's cheaper. Grass is free,'" she mumbled.

Betsie left the pair of them and crossed to the pasture fence, careful to keep any trace of resentment out of her manner for Sheila's sake. More ringing thumps and frantic exclamations issued from behind the horse trailer as Rick attempted to back Fledge down the ramp. Betsie marveled that he'd managed to load the pony in the first place.

"Come, Judith," she coaxed, and the mare trotted readily to hand. "Let's put you in the old cow pasture out back and we'll put that *loppich* pony closer to the house where we can keep an eye on his naughtiness."

When Judith was taken care of, Betsie called to Rick. "Turn him out here." She pushed open the other gate and stepped lively to get out of Fledge's path. The brown and white spotted pony's ears slicked flat to his skull. He bared his teeth and snapped at Rick's checkered shirtsleeve. Rick howled and jerked his arm away, leaving a triangle of fabric in the pony's mouth. With a jumble of swear words, the man hustled Fledge through the gate and slammed it shut. He glared at Mr. Sullivan.

"Never again, you hear me, Gerry? You keep that beast away from me. He kicked me good when I loaded him up, more'n once, too." He pulled up his shirtsleeve and rubbed a reddened patch of flesh. "Another fraction of an inch and he would've broken the skin." He wagged his head at Betsie. "I don't envy you, ma'am, and that's a fact."

Betsie pressed her lips together. She mustn't let on to Sheila how *ferhoodled* she felt. This mess wasn't her fault. In fact, up to this point, the girl had shown more mettle than the English adults in her life, especially noticeable since she had been "saved," as she called it.

Rick clanged the ramp shut, hopped in the truck without another word to Mr. Sullivan, and drove away. Betsie flapped her apron to dispel gravel dust as she trudged to the porch. There she took Sheila's cold hand and gave it a reassuring squeeze.

Mr. Sullivan pulled another piece of paper from his pocket. "This is the telephone number at the hotel where I'll be staying. If there's an emergency, you can leave a message with the front desk."

Amused, Betsie took the paper. She didn't bother to remind the man that she had no telephone.

"Do you have your house key?" Mr. Sullivan asked his daughter.

"Yes, Dad." Sheila pulled a leather thong out of her pocket and dangled the key.

"Then I guess this is it. Listen, if you need anything . . ." His words trailed off. "Squirt"—he gripped her shoulders—"I wish I didn't have to leave you here, but it's the only way. You know I love you. You know I love your mom. I want to bring her home so we can all be a family again." He hugged her tight.

"Michael, too?" Her words were muffled against his cotton shirt.

Betsie saw Mr. Sullivan's jaw flex. "If that's what he wants, I'm all for that." He kissed the top of Sheila's head. "I'm certainly all for that," he repeated with a brittle smile.

He headed for the car as Betsie and Sheila watched from the porch. Betsie saw tears pool in the girl's eyes as she waved good-bye.

Where she would find the courage she needed to face this long day, Betsie had no idea. And what would Sadie say when she got home from her job at Yoder's Bakery and discovered that a strange English girl had come to live with them? And even worse, how could Betsie face Charley? With trepidation, she guided her new charge into the house as Mr. Sullivan drove the station wagon out of sight.

C H A P T E R   3

"An ounce of work is worth a ton of wishing."
—Noah Troyer, quoted in Betsie's journal

"What am I going to do?" Sheila wailed. She made a beeline for the couch, flopped on her belly, and dissolved in tears. "I'm an orphan!"

Betsie bit her lip, perched on the edge of the cushion, and patted the girl's back once or twice. Michael had commented more than once that Sheila took after their mother with her flair for the dramatic.

Michael. She blew her nose and sighed. "What a *gut* thing we have so much to do, ain't so? Work will keep our minds and hearts busy."

"You mean we're going to do chores?" Sheila voice went up an octave as she sat up slowly, ponytail askew and face tear-streaked.

"It will be fun to work together. Come now, have you had your breakfast?" Betsie stood and smoothed her skirts. "And I don't mean oat rings from a big yellow box like you have at your house, mind. I mean a proper breakfast that will keep you going all morning, because you will need it before we are through."

Sheila's eyes widened and a tiny smile tugged at the corner of her mouth. "Do you think we can have pancakes? I love pancakes."

"You can have my favorite kind of pancakes. I have had my breakfast already, and so have the animals." Betsie led the way to the kitchen. *Staying busy will be best for her.* "Come, I'll show you a new way to make them. They will taste better if you help me."

21

"Really?" Sheila searched Betsie's face.

"*Jah*, that's what *Mem* always—" Betsie winced. "I mean, food tastes better when we have a hand in the making, that's what I've always heard. So now it's your turn."

"Okay, but I need to use your restroom first. Where is it?"

"That way." Betsie pointed to the kitchen door.

"I said the restroom. Hey, wait a minute! When I was really little, at my grandma's house we had to go outside to get to the bathroom. Do you mean—"

"Yes, the *briwwi* is outside, over that little rise. Here's where we keep the flashlight, but you won't need it this morning."

"Dad used to tease me about using corn cobs in the outhouse when he was a boy . . ." Sheila hinted delicately.

Betsie flopped into a chair and indulged in a hearty laugh until her arms hung limp at her sides. "*Ach*, I haven't laughed that hard in ages." She wiped her eyes with the corner of her apron. "Don't worry, *Schnickel-fritz*. The only corn cobs around here are the ones from Judith's feed. You won't even have to soften up a Sears catalog page until it's ready to use. Toilet paper is out there." Betsie indicated the sink. "When you come back, I'll dip some warm water from the reservoir on the cook-stove so you can wash your hands before we start cooking. Cold water for drinking is in a jug in the icebox if you need a drink."

"Wow, I didn't think I was gonna have to learn how to do every-thing all over again," Sheila grumbled. Her brow furrowed. "Did you feel like that when you first came to my house?"

"I felt even worse. You learned a lot of useful information at your grandma's house. Now off with you."

Betsie swung the bucket and headed for the pump. She frowned when she saw Fledge moping near the driveway. The minute Charley and Sadie saw the pony, they would demand an explanation. How in the world could she explain that *loppich* Fledge without immediately revealing Sheila's presence?

Quick as a wink, a solution popped into her head and she left the bucket by the pump. She opened the gate and hurried alongside the fence into the barn, where she selected a couple of ears of field corn.

Then she stood near a vacant loose box, shelled off some corn kernels into the feed box, and waited.

The rattle of corn worked wonders. Greedy Fledge poked his head around the door. Betsie shelled the other cob and let the pony see the grain drop into the feed box. Fledge stomped and stretched his neck, nostrils flared.

"Come, Stubby-Legs. You know this tastes delicious, come along." She held her breath as the pony minced past her into the stall and lipped at the corn.

"Got you." She eased the door shut, penning him in. "That ought to keep you busy for a while, and in the meantime, maybe I can think of how to tell Sadie and Charley about you and Sheila."

Back at the pump, Betsie primed it with the ready jar of water, filled the bucket and the priming jar, and met Sheila on the way to the kitchen door. The girl's face was a study.

"What do you do if you have to go when it's raining?" Sheila asked. "Or snowing, even?"

Betsie shrugged. "I hurry. And now it's my turn." She drew a corn cob from her apron pocket and waved it suggestively, smiling as Sheila laughed. "Let's wash up now." While Sheila stood at the sink, she tied an apron around the girl's waist. Quicker than a flash, she set out a deep bowl and a fork.

"Good thing I haven't had my second cup of tea yet. The stove is still pretty hot." With a practiced hand, Betsie filled a battered teakettle with water from the pail and clapped the lid tight. With a whack she set the kettle to the left side of the hob, the hottest part right over the firebox, and opened the bottom damper. She held her hand above the hob for a second and poked a couple of sticks of wood into the firebox to make the fire a bit hotter before brushing up the stray bits of bark that marred her spotless floor.

Betsie pitched the sweepings into the fire and slammed the door.

"Whew, I thought Grandma's kitchen was hot on Thanksgiving, but I'm roasting worse than the turkey." Sheila wiped sweat from her forehead.

"Follow me to the icebox, then. We need eggs and milk." Her bare feet scuffed as she moved to open the door.

"Is there really ice in here? Ahh." Sheila savored the cold air that rolled off the metal shelf.

"It's hiding in the compartment underneath. Here, hold out your hands. One, two, three brown eggs. Whoops, don't drop them, now! I'll carry the milk." Betsie grabbed the bottle and pressed the door shut.

Over on the hob, the water hissed as the fire crackled. "Now, regular pancakes, I would have to mix up twice if we wanted some tomorrow, too. But Pancake Casserole goes together easily, plus we can heat up another serving tomorrow if we like. So take those eggs and crack them into this bowl." Betsie indicated the crockery and waited.

Sheila gaped. "But I haven't cracked an egg in ages! My mom cooks TV dinners, remember? Or she did before she left." Her lip trembled.

"Here, I'll do the first one. You watch me and it will come back to you." She smacked the middle of the shell firmly against the rim of the bowl. A deft movement of her hands and the yolk and white slid out to rest in the bottom of the bowl, pretty as a picture. "Your turn."

"But what if I break it?" Sheila hedged, hands behind her back.

Betsie chuckled. "The eggshell is supposed to break, *Schnickelfritz!* How else do we get the egg out?"

"I meant the bowl." Sheila managed a sheepish grin. She picked up the egg and rapped it gingerly against the rim. "Nothing happened."

"Try again, dear heart. You'll soon get the hang of it."

This time the shell cracked. Awkwardly, Sheila pulled it apart. Bits of brown shell showered into the bowl. Betsie mustered her patience, fished them out with a clean spoon, and watched as Sheila successfully cracked the third egg.

"You see? Much better! All it takes is practice." Betsie poured in the milk and set Sheila to whipping the eggs and milk together with the fork. She assembled the other ingredients and Sheila measured and mixed well.

"We make a good team! What's next?"

"Let's see." Betsie wasn't used to narrating her recipes. "*Ach,* I forgot the smoky links. Wait here while I get some from the freezer."

"My grandma had a freezer, too! Can I come and see? Besides, I think I'm done mixing. At least my arm is worn out. Don't you think an electric mixer would be easier?"

Betsie rested her fingers briefly on Sheila's shoulder and was rewarded with a look of pure gratitude. "Maybe it would be easier, but it's not our way. Follow me, now."

Mercy, I must be getting soft, Betsie thought as she hurried down the steps ahead of Sheila. A few weeks ago, she'd shied away from all physical contact with the touchy-feely English.

"Ooh, it's cool down here." Sheila ran a finger along a row of canning jars that gleamed like jewels in a mine. "You guys did all this?"

"*Mem* and me and Sadie, *jah*." Sorrow filled her heart as she thought of this year's garden and the lonely prospect of canning without *Mem*.

"You know what? I believe God does like it when we grow our own food. I've been at Grandma's when she canned peaches, and man, it's a lot more work than buying a can of peaches at the store, but the taste is worth it!"

Betsie retrieved a packet from the freezer, the insides rimed with frost. She shivered and let the lid slam.

"Hey, wait a minute! I hear the motor running. How come you can have electricity for this and nothing else?"

So many questions. Betsie massaged her forehead as they climbed the steps. "It's gas-powered."

In the kitchen again, she plopped down the package of smoky links. "Now we'll pour the batter into a greased casserole, slice these over the top, and bake for twenty minutes." Maybe she could forestall some questions? "Hold your hand right here." Betsie guided Sheila's hand to a few inches above the hob.

"Ouch!"

"I know the fire's hot enough when it's too hot to keep my hand there for long. Twenty minutes or so and you will be sitting up to a hearty breakfast. Though it'll be lunchtime soon!"

She slid the pan into the oven and glanced idly out the window at the barn where Fledge was hidden. She dug a finger under her *Kapp* and scratched where a hairpin poked. The more she thought about training Fledge, the better she liked the idea. Sheila could help; the girl could certainly use some confidence. Training Fledge could be good for all of them. She would talk to Charley about it.

Betsie stilled. Or maybe not. The less said to Charley about the English and their lazy ways when it came to training horses, the better. She would have enough trouble on her hands explaining why she'd taken in an English girl without asking bishop Jonas Gingerich, upholder of the *Ordnung*, for permission.

CHAPTER 4

It would be a lot easier to do the right
thing if I had only myself to please.

—Betsie's journal

Steam billowed from the kettle spout. Betsie found a dish towel and
grabbed the handle. She poured a stream of boiling water over the tea
ball in her cup. She paused and looked at Sheila. "Want some?"

Sheila shook her head and sat at the scarred harvest table. "May
I have some milk instead? Man, is my arm tired from doing all that
mixing. Mom has an electric mixer; she used it once to make a box
cake for Dad. I know you Amish don't have electricity, but it was hard
to imagine until I actually did without it. I miss it already."

Betsie hid a smile. "Of course you can have milk. And once we get
your breakfast on the table, I want to talk to you about some plans I
have for Fledge." She poured a glass of milk and handed it over. "We
can wash these dishes while I tell you." She thumped a plastic washtub
in the sink, poured the rest of the boiling water in, added cool water
from the bucket, and squirted in dish soap, swishing her hands to
make it bubble up.

"Just like at Grandma's house!" Sheila grinned and swigged her
milk. "Wow, that's cold." She smacked her lips and wrinkled her nose.
"And thick. I don't think I like it. Very much." She put down the glass.

Betsie sighed. "You have a milk mustache." A stealthy movement caught her eye. "Amelia, stay off the table!" she cried, but it was too late. The calico kitten leapt to Sheila's lap and stretched to lick her creamy mustache, expression rapt as she rumbled with purrs. Sheila giggled, her troubles forgotten for the moment.

"Well, I guess we know who will drink the rest of the milk. Go ahead and pour the milk in her bowl over there." Betsie felt lighthearted, free . . . and needed. If only Sadie and Charley could understand.

A rap at the door called her back to the present. "Now who could that be?" She dried her hands on her apron and crossed to the door.

"Mattie." Betsie pushed open the door, her heart thumping wildly. "Why aren't you at the bakery? Has something happened to Sadie? Or—to Charley?"

Mattie Yoder shook her head and stepped inside, her beady stare raking over the kitchen and coming to rest on Sheila. "*Guder mariye*, Betsie. No, Charley and Sadie are watching the bakery. I drove over to see you."

I know better than that. Betsie composed herself. "It was so good to hear that you recovered quickly from your illness. Now, what can I do for you?" She glanced at Sheila, who was looking Mattie up and down with wide eyes.

"Could you check to see if you have any of that canned sweet pickle mix Fannie used to trade with me? I had a customer ask for some yesterday." Mattie leaned against the wall, one foot tucked behind her knee like a stork.

Betsie started to comply but Sheila's eyes widened in alarm. She stepped back and rested her hand on the girl's shoulder. "We were just down there and I didn't see any, but you're welcome to check for yourself, Mattie. Sell what you want and I'll take the price out in trade." With a nod of her head she indicated the cellar door.

Mattie replied with a sour smile. She pushed away from the wall and tugged on the door until it opened with a protesting creak. "I'll tell Charley to fix that," she informed Betsie, and then she disappeared into the gloomy maw of the doorway, her dress draping her body like a shroud.

"She gives me the creeps." Sheila mouthed the words with a shiver.

Betsie gave her a reassuring pat and suddenly realized the girl hadn't understood a word of the conversation since she and Mattie had spoken in *Deitsh*. "Don't worry. She's my friend Charley's mother. She wanted some of our canned goods for her bakery."

"Then why did she look so—" Sheila's anxious whisper broke off as Mattie's steps echoed and the woman emerged from the cellar bearing two quart jars filled to the brim with bright green.

"You found some. I'm glad you got what you came for," Betsie said, but she knew why Mattie had really come. Someone—Joe Miller?— must have reported Sheila's arrival this morning. Already the gossip grapevine was in full swing, with Mattie being the worst offender.

"*Jah*." Mattie stopped square in front of Betsie and Sheila. "So this is the English girl I've heard tell of."

Betsie forced a smile. "Yes, this is my friend Sheila," she replied in English.

"And what did Jonas have to say about her visiting with you?" Mattie continued in *Deitsh*. Her eyes glittered with spite.

Betsie flushed. *I'll cross that bridge when I come to it.* "That's between me and Jonas. I hope your customer likes *Mem*'s pickle mix." She herded Mattie toward the door.

Mattie's lips crooked into a smile of satisfaction. "Well, I'll be going."

Betsie watched Charley's mother stalk to her buggy and drive away. "Well, that's that," she said with a shaky laugh. "I guess we can expect a visit from our bishop mighty soon. But first," she said with a wink, "That pancake casserole you made smells so delicious I can't resist. Let's eat."

"Ugh! How many more chores, Betsie? I'm so hot and my muscles are sore." Sheila rested her chin on the broom handle.

Betsie checked the clock and her heart plummeted. Soon Charley would drive up behind his fast-stepping horse to bring Sadie home from her job at Yoder's Bakery and she would have to break the news about Sheila.

"Tell you what. How about you rest a while? I'll show you to your room." Plenty to choose from, now that *Mem* and *Dat* are gone. Betsie set her chin. Gone temporarily, she reminded herself.

Sheila yawned and rested the broom in the corner. "Okay, only do you think I can watch TV first? Just to wind down."

Betsie folded her arms and raised an eyebrow. Sheila glanced at her and reddened. "Oh. No electricity. I forgot."

"You will get used to it before long," Betsie told her. "I have lots of books and we can get more at the library soon. There are always mail-order catalogs; they are fun to look at. Maybe another time when you aren't so tired, we could even play some board games of the evenings."

Sheila yawned again and looked at Betsie with watery eyes. "Sounds fun," she murmured. "Can I take the kitty up with me?"

Had she overdone it with work? Betsie was only trying to keep the girl's mind from her troubles. Well, it was too late to mend it now. A good rest would work wonders. With Sheila napping, Betsie could get the approaching confrontation with Sadie and Charley over with.

"*Jah*, that's a good idea. You can keep Amelia out from under my feet while I finish up our dinner. Here you are, dear heart." She handed over Amelia and picked up the suitcase.

After they clomped upstairs, Betsie led Sheila to the room that had been Lovina's until recently. *Gut* thing Betsie had kept it neat, hoping against hope that her aunt Lovina would prevail and bring Betsie's parents home as she'd set out to do. Instead, the room was just another empty one along the hallway where her bustling Amish family had once slept.

"Here you are." Betsie led the way to the dresser. She put Sheila's suitcase beside it. "You can unpack later, maybe. See?" She pulled out a drawer in the nightstand beside the bed. "Here is a flashlight to find your way if you need to—"

"Nuh-uh." Sheila shook her head. "I'm not going out there in the dark."

Betsie smiled and turned down the pinwheel quilt. "Although I'm sad for you, what with your *mem*, *dat*, and even your brother Michael gone for a while, can I tell you a secret?"

Sheila snuggled into the bed and nodded, already half asleep.

"I'm glad you're here." With a timid hand, Betsie smoothed the hair from Sheila's forehead and turned to go.

"I love you," Sheila murmured drowsily. She didn't stir after that.

"I love you, too," Betsie whispered. She eased the door shut and lingered in the hall, out of sorts. Tears stung the corners of her eyes as she realized she really did love that *Schnickelfritz*. But how could that be? Sheila was an outsider. Do I belong here with my people? Or am I more like the English, talking of loving and such? She crossed the hallway to her bedroom, eased open a drawer, and drew out her notebook, the one she'd taken along to the Sullivans' home.

At first, Betsie had used the notebook to record instructions and tips for her cousin Nelson as the Sullivans taught her how to make harnesses and such. When Nelson's time of service in the Chicago Army hospital ended, he would reclaim his business from Gerald Sullivan and Betsie would turn over the notebook. At least, that had been the plan.

She fingered the dog-eared black cover. As the weeks passed, the notebook had become more than an instruction book. Thoughts, impressions, and observations of her time with the English crowded the pages in the back, in stark contrast to the all-business section at the front. She relished setting her thoughts down, creating pictures with words, and making sense of an English world that, to her Plain way of thinking, often made no sense at all. She read her entry about Michael introducing her to an English ice cream sandwich. Why call it that when there was no bread in sight? She smiled. It was rather similar to the Amish calling two cookies with a cream filling a whoopie pie.

Betsie drew a deep breath and light-footed it downstairs to the kitchen. She deposited her notebook on the table before lifting the lid from the potato soup to give it a quick stir. She wrapped a clean towel around her hand, unhinged the door of the warming shelf, and raked the steamy loaf of bread into a basket. Only when she'd covered the loaf with the checkered towel did she sit and draw the notebook toward her like a magnet. She fished a pencil from her pocket, flipped toward the back, and smoothed the rumpled page where she'd left off.

Evening sunlight bathed the kitchen by the time Betsie heard the familiar clip-clop of a fast-stepping horse. She jumped up from the table so quickly that her chair teetered and crashed to the floor. *Ferhoodled* for sure, she chastised herself as she righted the chair.

Quick as lightning, she ladled hot soup loaded with carrots, onions, macaroni, and diced potatoes into three bowls and set them on the table. Her hand shook as she attempted to slice the bread. A steadying deep breath helped some, and she managed to arrange the slices prettily before setting out softened butter and delicately pink apple jelly.

By the time she had three glasses filled with cold water, the kitchen door opened.

"*Ach*, Betsie, I forgot you would be home all day. How good supper smells! The way my feet hurt after working at the bakery, I know I couldn't stand up long enough to cook anything. It is good to have you home." Sadie hung her bonnet on the peg and plopped into a chair with a groan. She nudged off her shoes, tugged to loosen the stocking ends, and wriggled her toes.

"Eat up, then," Betsie urged. If Sadie's mouth was full, she couldn't scold when she heard about Sheila. As much. "Where's Charley?"

Sadie blew on her soup. "He worked out a trade with Sawmill Joe over the way—fresh baked goods for some lumber he needs. He's storing the lumber in our barn."

Betsie's breath came in anxious puffs. "Charley's in the barn?"

Sadie eyed Betsie before crumbling a slice of bread into her soup. "*Jah.* I told him it was all right. The barn's as good a place as any, ain't so? That way the lumber will stay dry in case it rains. Why gasp about it like a fish out of water? Now let's pray so I can eat."

Dutifully Betsie took her seat and closed her eyes, but her silent prayers did not concern the food or blessings for which she was grateful. They ran more like *Please, please, please let Sadie and Charley accept Sheila.* Surely the good Lord would understand.

Sadie sighed as she always did when she finished her prayers and Betsie scooted her chair back to stand. "Go ahead and eat. I'm going to ask Charley to eat with us as thanks for all his help while we wait for *Mem* and *Dat* to come back."

Sadie caught her sleeve. "Do you truly believe they will come back, Betsie?" Worry showed in her sister's round blue eyes.

Betsie's heart filled with tenderness. Though she was seventeen and very independent, Sadie still needed her parents. "I've been praying and you've been praying, Sadie. The good Lord hears us. I know He will bring *Mem* and *Dat* home, so make up your mind to believe it, as I have." Betsie sighed. "So many of our neighbors have left us behind." She quelled irksome thoughts of Sheila, now as alone as Betsie and Sadie. "Like our brother Eli and the others who settled out in Missouri, or cousin Nelson, serving his enlistment in Chicago." She chuckled. "That Atlee Hershberger sure is a character. When his family left this morning, Atlee waved and made sheep's eyes at me."

Sadie sputtered, her face growing bright red as she choked on a spoonful of soup. Betsie thumped Sadie's back helpfully as her sister's eyes streamed with tears. Gradually Sadie regained her breath and took a long sip of water, watching Betsie over the rim of her glass. "*Denki, Schweschder*," she croaked at last. "Hershbergers are gone, you said?" Her lower lip trembled. "Atlee's gone," she whispered.

"Yes, they left right after you did. Are you sure you're all right?" Betsie asked as Sadie dabbed her eyes with a handkerchief.

"Don't worry about me," Sadie sniffed as she stared into the depths of her soup bowl. "I'm fine." Betsie squinted at her sister. She hadn't realized how much Atlee had meant to Sadie. Resisting the urge to pull Sadie into an English-style hug, Betsie sighed and vowed she would be more grateful that Charley wasn't leaving her.

"Well, I'll go invite Charley to stay and eat, then. I'll be right back." *Jah*, I'll be back, right after Charley finishes blowing his top. She winced. The English expression said it all.

The lengthening shadows of the late spring evening couldn't hide the questions in Charley's gaze as he advanced toward her, his stride measured and sure. As he emerged from the deep shade, he took off his hat and slicked sweat from his forehead. The clouds parted and a shaft of sunlight illuminated his golden hair before he replaced his hat. Betsie's knees weakened.

They met by the pump. "Betsie, have you bought a pony?" His tone indicated this wasn't the best idea.

Her cheeks grew hot. "No. That is, I didn't buy him. He is . . . boarding here for a while, though."

"He will eat you out of house and home, by the looks of him. Do you think it's a good idea to board a horse, now that your *Dat* is gone and you have so little money coming in? After all, you can't earn enough making harnesses to support yourself and Sadie, not with that English hippie never around to teach you how to work." He scratched his bare chin. "Maybe taking in a couple of boarders isn't such a bad idea, now that I think on it more. Will you pump me some water so I can wash up a little?"

He held his hands under the pump and waited. At least 'that English hippie' would have said please, Betsie thought, but she knew he was right. Michael wasn't much of a hand to work. She and Charley made a good team. She watched as the water splashed over his capable hands, hands that could drive a horse, build a barn, or pick up a fifty-pound sack of feed with ease. Hands that could encircle her waist and draw her near to him—oh, if her cheeks flamed any more, she would have to stick her head underneath the stream of water to cool off.

"Your *mem* pays Sadie for her work in the bakery and *Mem* and *Dat* left plenty of canning and stores, so we are all right for a while yet," she reminded, not ready for him to go. "Maybe you would like to come in and have a bite, Charley? I made that potato soup you like, the one with the macaroni."

He swiped his wet hands over his face and nodded. "That sounds good. I will eat a little, but my mother has cooked a good dinner for me and I promised not to spoil my appetite here."

Betsie struggled to keep a pleasant expression on her face. Outfoxed by Mattie Yoder again, yet Charley didn't seem to realize anything was amiss. He had vowed to reverse the old pattern of dominance that his mother had established from the day her husband died, when Charley was barely a month old. Mattie had reigned supreme ever since. She had never remarried and Betsie was pretty sure she knew the reason why. There was something sour and off-putting in Mattie Yoder's manner—she always seemed to be lurking, eavesdropping, waiting for a slip—yet Betsie would be the first to admit a grudging admiration for this lone Amish woman who not only managed to support her son, but to flourish in a man's world.

Best of all, Yoder's Bakery gave Sadie a place to put her considerable baking skills to good use, Betsie reminded herself. At the moment, Sadie was the only wage-earner. How long could they hope to survive on her sister's income? Betsie fell in beside Charley, new worries eclipsing the original ones.

And then Sadie screamed.

"Was in der welt?" Betsie cried, but Charley had already bolted for the kitchen door.

CHAPTER 5

Look out how you use proud words.
When you let proud words go, it is
not easy to call them back.
They wear long boots, hard boots; they
walk off proud; they can't hear you calling—
Look out how you use proud words.

"PRIMER LESSON" BY CARL SANDBURG,
QUOTED IN BETSIE'S JOURNAL

"SADIE! WHAT'S WRONG?" Betsie burst into the kitchen behind Charley and skidded to a halt. She saw her sister, backside jammed against the countertop, a heavy saucepan clutched in one hand. Sheila stood in the kitchen doorway, one hand to her chest and eyes wide as saucers.

Charley confronted the girl. "Who are you? What are you doing here? Answer me, why don't you?"

Betsie stepped forward. "Charley, she doesn't understand *Deitsh*."

Charley flicked a glance at Betsie. "You know her? Does she have something to do with the pony in the barn?"

"*Jah*. This is Sheila Sullivan, the daughter of the harness shop owner." Resolutely Betsie crossed the wood floor to stand by her friend. "She will stay with us until her parents return."

Sadie's color rose as she spewed a torrent of *Deitsh*. "What? Haven't

I had enough to deal with for one day? You have no right to make such a decision! The bishop warned us about *Mem* and *Dat*, and now you allow this English girl to stay in our house. What will Jonas have to say about this, I wonder?" Sadie gave Charley a push. "Go ahead, tell Betsie this girl can't stay here, Charley!"

He shook his finger at her. "Betsie, you know—"

Betsie could feel Sheila's shoulders quaking under her arm. "Wait, Charley." She folded a tearful Sheila in a hug. "Are you all right?"

Sheila tried to sniff back tears. "I smelled dinner and I was hungry, so I tiptoed downstairs and yelled, 'Boo!' to surprise you, but I scared her instead"—she pointed at Sadie—"and she screamed, and I told her I was sorry like a bazillion times but she waved that skillet like she was going to bean me, and then you guys barreled in the door. I couldn't understand a word anyone said, but I do know one thing. They don't want me here. Why don't they like me, Betsie? Did I do something wrong?" She knuckled away tears.

"Of course not, dear heart," Betsie comforted while glaring at her sister and Charley over her shoulder. "Sadie was startled at your practical joke, that's all, and that's my fault. Tell you what," she went on, "how about I fix you up something to eat? See, I made potato soup, and here's the bread you smelled. Try some apple jelly on it while I dish up your soup. Sit down now." Betsie cut two slabs of bread for Sheila before ladling up another bowlful of soup. "It's still quite hot, so take care. I will get some water." She paused. "What's wrong? Why aren't you eating your bread?"

Sheila took a deep breath and looked at Betsie, her expression sweet and reverent. "Will you pray with me while I ask the blessing?"

"*Jah*, it is good you remembered that." Betsie avoided Charley's accusing gaze, rested her hands on the back of Sheila's chair, and bowed her head.

"Dear Lord," Sheila prayed, "thank You for this good food. Help Dad find Mom fast so I don't have to stay here long, not that I don't want to stay, but I don't want to be a bother. Please keep Mom and Dad married and let us be a family again. Take care of Michael and let him know we love him and You do, too. And Lord, thank You for

Betsie because I love her. In Jesus' name we pray, Amen." She spread jelly on her bread and took a healthy bite.

The simple prayer restored a measure of peace to Betsie's heart. "You hear why I allowed her to stay," Betsie said in her own language to Sadie and Charley. "Tell me, what else could I have done? Charley, you lost your father very young. We're without our own parents for a time, Sadie, and it's a heavy burden for us, although you are seventeen and I am nigh on twenty. Think how hard it must be for a young girl like Sheila, not yet twelve." She paused. "She has no one but me, but us. Do you really suppose the good Lord would have me turn her out into the streets? Our hearts are not made of stone, are they, Charley?" She smiled at him to belie the sting of her words.

"It's true that it was hard growing up without my *dat*," Charley conceded as he folded his arms and lifted his chin. "But open your eyes and ears, Betsie," he went on in *Deitsh*. "Look how she is dressed, in heathenish short pants and a shirt that barely covers her middle. She prayed, yes, but how did she pray? Out loud, that's how, making public her talk with the good Lord. These are not our ways."

Betsie stiffened, but Charley pressed on, oblivious. "Seems to me that this girl does not come from such a good family if the father is chasing after a mother who left and she doesn't know where that fancy brother of hers is. And what kind of influence have they been on you? You've made it very hard for Bishop Jonas. Your *dat* urged him to grant you permission to board with these Englishers; that is commonly known. Jonas shouldn't have granted that permission, to my way of thinking, even though I know you are only trying to help your cousin with his business. But, Betsie! Recall to your mind why Nelson is gone from home in the first place. Is it not the English and their Vietnam War? No good comes of associating with the English. That we know, yet you have taken this English girl into your home. What will the result be?" Charley lifted his palms, fingers splayed.

Betsie rounded on him like a mother bear protecting her cub. "Oh, so you know better than our bishop, Charley? My father and mother left, too. Does that mean I am from a bad family? As far as Nelson being in Chicago and Michael in—" She checked herself. She'd almost divulged Michael's secret and the near-miss rattled her. Anger sparked. "As far as wherever they may be, at least I know where they are not, and that is tied to their mother's apron strings."

Sadie sucked in her breath with an audible hiss. Betsie, dimly aware that Sheila had left the table to sidle up and tuck her cold hand into Betsie's own, watched as Charley's color suffused to a mottled red. The thought of her harsh words choked her. She wished she could unsay them, but it was too late. With great dignity, Charley exited the kitchen. Sadie followed hot on Charley's heels without a backward glance.

Sheila broke the silence, her tone subdued. "Who are those people, Betsie?"

"Sadie is my younger sister." Betsie retrieved her notebook from the table. "And Charley Yoder is my . . . boyfriend. At least, he was."

CHAPTER 6

"Be ye not unequally yoked together with unbelievers: for
what fellowship hath righteousness with unrighteousness?
and what communion hath light with darkness?"
— 2 CORINTHIANS 6:14, QUOTED IN BETSIE'S JOURNAL

BETSIE YAWNED AGAIN. Oh, how little sleep she'd gotten, wishing she'd
kept her big mouth shut. Only after she'd vowed to make amends with
Sadie by fixing an extra-good breakfast in the morning had she fallen
into a fitful sleep.

But when Betsie arose, she'd found her sister's bed already made up
and her breakfast dishes draining. She'd muttered under her breath
while the leftover pancake casserole warmed in the oven, hashing over
what she would say to Sadie later. And what of Charley? She recalled
her parting words to him and closed her eyes in shame.

It took her until the middle of breakfast to realize that fretting would
not resolve the situation. She plunked her fork on her plate, carried it
to the sink, and scoured the dishes like they were her own guilty conscience. As the morning progressed, she tackled the kitchen counters,
swept the floors, and used the washboard and washtub to scrub dish
towels, dishcloths, and a couple of soiled aprons. After a good rinsing
and wringing, she backed through the kitchen door with the full basket
on her hip, hurrying to finish yet another chore before Sheila awoke,
only to blunder smack into Charley.

"Whoa, Betsie." His strong arms steadied her as he retreated a step. "Doing the wash, I see."

She studied his face and detected a warm twinkle in his blue eyes that made her heart skitter like a drop of water on a hot griddle. "Yes, and if you hadn't saved me from dumping this basketful in the dirt, I'd be doing the whole wash over again. *Denki.*" She dropped her gaze. "Oh, Charley, last night I didn't mean—"

"All that is past." He released her and steepled his fingers briefly. "I understand why you would be angry at yourself. Here, give me that basket of wet wash. I will carry it for you."

She relinquished it and fell into step beside him. Why had she agonized? Of course someone wonderful like Charley would realize she hadn't meant what she said about the apron strings. She'd simply blurted out the first mean remark that came to mind, much as Charley had done when he first rejected Sheila.

"*Ach*, I am happy we have this chance to talk. You are right, I am angry with myself. I mulled it over after you left last night and now I see—"

"Wait. I have something to say. You were right about me and my *mem.*"

Betsie stopped in her tracks. "I was?"

He nodded and shifted the basket. "The day that Jonas pronounced the shunning of your parents, I promised you that I would assume the responsibilities that *Mem* has taken upon herself, such as speaking with Jonas if necessary, but it's been hard to do." A pleading look came into his blue eyes. "You see, because she's taken the man's part in our home for so long, she takes too much responsibility upon herself. I'm sure she didn't mean to push me aside, and I don't believe for a minute she meant to cause you so much trouble. It's just that she tries so hard to follow the *Ordnung*, ain't so?"

"Oh, Charley." She smiled up at him, relieved. "What a help it would be if you kept your *mem* from interfere . . . I mean, if you took over as head of the household. Then I wouldn't have to worry about what she might say about Sheila."

"Oh, I didn't talk with Mem until she'd already told Jonas about the girl. He says he will be over to talk with you soon."

Betsie's jaw dropped. "Talk with me?"

"*Jah*, now you see why you cannot have the girl staying here, of course. It is not our way, Betsie." Charley set the basket down with a thump and hung on to the wire clothesline with one hand like he was ready for a long chat.

"What?" Betsie said loudly enough to startle a pair of mourning doves into whistling flight. "That is not what I meant at all. How can you say she doesn't belong here?" She hung up the clothespin bag and shook out a dark blue dress with a snap before pinning it upside down to hang by the skirt. "Sheila is so young. She still needs a mother's help."

Charley drew himself up. "You are not her mother, Betsie."

"I know that! But I am all she has." She snatched a damp apron from the basket. In the midst of pinning it up, she recalled last night's taunt about apron strings. She bit her lip, finished the task, and stole a glance at Charley's chiseled profile. "Charley, I don't like it when everything is upruffled between us. I know what a good man you are. Do you really believe I should turn Sheila out of my house? I have so much room here now that *Mem*, *Dat*, and my little brother Abijah are gone. It didn't seem right to say no."

Charley stared across the road at a field hazy with early morning mist. "I suppose the child is not responsible for the bad actions of her parents. And maybe"—Charley looked into her eyes—"maybe it is your job to show her kindness. But Betsie, you must think. Talk with me before you make a decision next time. You know," he lowered his voice, "someday soon, we will make a home together and we must be in agreement about how we run it."

Betsie closed her eyes with a shiver of delight. She was on the verge of nodding when Charley continued.

"After all, what would everyone say if I decide one way to handle a matter but you hold out for another? How would it look if my own wife didn't agree with me?" Charley chuckled.

Betsie blinked. Yes, how would that look?

He brushed her cheek tenderly with his knuckles. "You know I want you for my wife, Betsie. Recall my advice and talk to me when you have a difficult choice to make. I will advise you, taking into account the *Ordnung*, of course, and together we will make the choice that best sets us on the way to heaven. And now I have kept you from your work long enough, and I have my own to do. Just think about what I said."

As he set off for the barn, Betsie longed for the day when they would do all their work together. She finished hanging up the rest of the wash, pondering how tenderly he'd touched her cheek.

Later that morning after Charley had left, Betsie watched as Sheila skipped along the pasture ahead of her, the girl's high spirits miraculously restored after a good night's sleep.

"I'm sorry I slept so late this morning! After I read my Bible and said my morning prayers, I made believe that yesterday was a bad dream. But then I thought of how we'd carried candles up to bed and blew them out when it was time to go to sleep and I felt a little better. I'm pretending like I'm living in the olden days!"

Sheila tiptoed backwards and grinned at Betsie, who covered her mouth and yawned. She didn't have the heart to admit that the candles had been an old-fashioned prank, an attempt to rib Sheila after she yelled to surprise Sadie. The oil lamp would return to its rightful place tonight.

"Watch out where you're going," she said. "You don't want to step in something you shouldn't."

Sheila giggled. "That's so gross, Betsie!" She held her nose and mimicked shaking off her tennis shoe.

Betsie, still smarting from Charley's advice, managed a wan smile as they entered the barn. "That's my Judith." She waved a hand at her mare. "She's a *gut gaul*. You two will get along fine."

Judith snorted and pawed at the straw in her box. Dust rose and Sheila sneezed. "*Goot gall*? What does that mean?"

"Good horse. I'll wait here while you fetch her some water. Can you work the pump the way I showed you earlier? Don't forget to pour some in the top to prime it first and then refill the water jar."

"Gosh, just like *Little House on the Prairie!*" Sheila sped out of the barn with the bucket.

Betsie peeked into Fledge's stall; he was lying down, nose pointed toward the back wall. Not a speck of feed remained in his trough.

She scratched behind Judith's ears while she waited. Had she really done wrong, as Charley said? How she longed to talk over matters with *Mem* and *Dat*, but they were far away in Belle Center, living their new English life, free to worship the good Lord.

"I'll ask them in a letter, that's what." She rubbed Judith's satiny neck as the mare snuffed at Betsie's pockets. "No apple this time, Judith. Yes, I will write a letter and I'll ask when they're coming home, too. Enough is enough."

A surprised squeak interrupted her reverie. "Are you talking to your *gaul*, Betsie?"

Betsie pulled her mouth into a wry grin and took the bucket from Sheila. "What if I am? Judith never scolds me. Did you have any trouble with the pump?"

"No, it was easy!"

Out of the corner of her eye, Betsie saw Sheila flap her shirt to dry it. "It was?"

The girl gave up and wrung the wet fabric out with a grin. "Okay, I admit it sure is a lot easier to fill a bucket at my house. Turn the spigot and water comes out!" Her eyebrows drew together. "Betsie, does God really like it better if you pump your water instead of getting it out of the faucet? And if you use candles instead of electric lights?"

Betsie had to laugh. "*Schnickelfritz*. It must seem strange to you, but we don't mind working hard to get the results we want. The easiest way to explain it all is this: we have church rules called the *Ordnung,* and these rules are what dictate the way we do things. These rules protect us from the careless ways of the world." She nodded, pleased with her impromptu answer. *Thank the good Lord I was able to answer a difficult question so well.* "In fact, I've heard Jonas, our bishop, say that following the *Ordnung* to the letter keeps families together."

"But it didn't work out so well for your family, did it? Anyway, I guess I'm going to have muscles like Superman by the time Dad and Mom come for me." She flexed her arm to demonstrate. "Do you think it'll take a long time until they get back, Betsie?"

"You are as big a *Wonnernaus* as I am." Betsie tugged on Sheila's ponytail. "I was just wondering the same thing about my parents. I wish they had never left."

Sheila sobered. "Why did they leave? Can't they do that here? Follow Jesus, I mean. When you're Amish, you go to church and everything, right? And read the Bible and pray? What else did they need? Jesus paid it all, like the hymn says. All churches believe that, right?"

With each question, the weight on Betsie's shoulders increased. She leaned against the rough wall. "A while ago, you asked me these same questions. Do you recall what I told you?"

"Uhh . . ." Sheila twirled the end of her ponytail, lost in thought. "You said your church teaches it differently than mine. I mean, I get that churches have some differences, but the stuff I'm talking about is pretty basic, you know?"

Careful to conceal her exasperation, Betsie was suddenly inspired. "Maybe soon you can go to the service with us and see for yourself. Would you like that?"

Sheila nodded until her ponytail bounced. "That would be so fun! But what I really want to know is—"

"Here is what I know." Betsie straightened. "Whenever there is work to be done, your talk gets faster and faster. Don't you think Judith and Fledge might be hungry and stiff after a long night in the barn? They can't let themselves out, so we must be kind and do it for them." She softened her reminder with a smile.

"Oh, gosh! I forgot all about Fledge. Where is he?"

Betsie motioned with her head. "In that stall. I don't guess he likes being shut up, so he is sulking. He will get up once he sees Judith go out. Horses are herd animals and prefer the company of others to being alone." She caught Judith's halter and stilled as the import of her words hit home.

I let Sheila stay here because I didn't want her to be alone, she realized. *But there was more. I guess I didn't want to be alone, either.*

Now that there was no prospect of work at the harness shop, a lonesome parade of weekdays marched across the calendar with not much to fill them but chores until the next visiting Sunday. Sadie worked long hours at the bakery, but she talked with plenty of people during the day. Why should she want to chat with her sister when she got home? Especially a sister who had brought an English girl into the house, in direct opposition to the *Ordnung*.

How she yearned to talk with Rachel Yutzy. She couldn't call on the phone like an Englisher to see if her best friend was busy. Anyway, Rachel most certainly was busy, what with her own late fall wedding to plan and a household to prepare. Charley came by when he could, but he was usually busy working the farms where he sharecropped. The truth was, with so many members of Betsie's family gone, each new day would offer mostly empty hours without Sheila to fill them.

"Stand back in case she gets frisky." She led Judith to the back door which led directly into a fenced pasture. "Whoops, there she goes!" Judith's hooves clattered as she lunged for freedom. Her dark hide gleamed in the sunlight.

A plaintive whinny sounded as Betsie and Sheila watched the mare's antics. "I told you so," Betsie nudged Sheila. Fledge's nose poked over the half door. "What's the matter, Stubby-Legs? Do you miss your girlfriend?"

"Can we let him out, too?"

"Yes, but he must do it our way." Betsie sorted through the tack hanging from the pegs on the far wall. "*Ach*, here is a good lead rope. You will snap this to his halter and lead him out."

"You want me to do it?"

"He is your pony, ain't so? Just snap it on and then I will stand by the front door. Hold on tight, now," she cautioned.

Sheila looped the lead rope around her hand and braced herself. "Okay, I'm ready. I hope he doesn't drag me."

But Fledge, ever contrary, minced toward the barn door and daylight like a perfect gentleman.

"He's not even like the same horse!" Sheila patted his neck and led him out.

"You be careful anyway. I doubt he has forgotten the mean tricks he knows. Time and hard work are the only cure for a *loppich* pony like him, but he will learn."

"What does *loppich* mean? And where should I lead him?"

"Naughty. Let's put him in with Judith. I suspect she can teach him more in five minutes than we can in a day."

Betsie led the way to the outside gate. Fledge lifted his head and neighed a greeting. Judith merely flicked an ear as she ripped up choice spears of tender green grass with her strong teeth.

"Whoa, Fledge!" Sheila dragged her heels. "He's going to pull me into the pasture head-first, Betsie!"

"Oh, no. He mustn't do that. We are in charge, remember?" Betsie crowded Fledge's spotted rump against the closed gate and leaned into him while he nickered a one-sided conversation with Judith. "He must learn to stand until we are ready." After a few seconds, he calmed down. Betsie unsnapped his lead a split second after she swung open the gate and the pony bolted.

Betsie and Sheila watched as Fledge neighed again and circled wide around Judith in an extended trot, a pony's version, anyway. The mare paid him no heed.

"Oh, I hope he doesn't hurt her!" Sheila nibbled at a hangnail.

"Don't worry, dear heart. Judith won't let him."

Fledge's agitation grew as Judith continued to ignore him. Impatient to be noticed, he sidled up to the mare and shoved his nose in the same clump of new grass.

The next instant, Judith snapped at him. Fledge pinned his ears and bared his teeth, but Judith was too quick for him. She wheeled and nipped him smartly on the rump.

Fledge squealed again and raced down the pasture, bucking and pitching all the way. He shied at the fence and twisted to see if Judith followed, but she cropped peacefully at the grass clump, oblivious.

Betsie and Sheila laughed. "I told you Judith could take care of herself," Betsie said. "He will learn."

"Oh, my aching sides," Sheila wheezed. "Did you see how surprised he looked when she stood up for herself?"

"Jah." Betsie rubbed her chin with her forefinger. "I sure did."

CHAPTER 7

"One lie brings the next one with it."

—FANNIE TROYER, QUOTED IN BETSIE'S JOURNAL

SHEILA RUBBED HER bicep and groaned. "I think I know why you call them Monster Cookies," she groaned. "That dough was so stiff after we added the oatmeal and the M&Ms that my muscle feels like it's been stomped on by Bigfoot."

Betsie sighed and wiped sweat from her forehead with her sleeve. Two days had come and gone with only sullen silence from Sadie and little more from Charley. Things needed to change and food was usually a good peace offering. Betsie and Sheila had cooked and baked until the table was spread with Sadie's favorite dishes. But it was getting late. There were four places prepared and only two were occupied.

"I guess your sister isn't coming home for dinner tonight, Betsie. And neither is Charley. It's just like Michael's surprise birthday dinner when we got it all ready and he never showed up." Sheila frowned and squinted at the tea towel calendar with the red cardinals imprinted along the top. "And would you look at that? Tuesday was the first of June, Michael's real birthday, but we don't even know where he is." Her brown eyes filled with tears and she put down her fork. "I'm not hungry anymore."

Betsie swallowed a tasteless bite and patted Sheila's hand. "I am sure Michael is fine . . . wherever he may be. As for Sadie, could be the bakery got extra busy and she had to stay later. Or maybe Mattie ran out of flour or some such and it put them behind. It's hard telling . . . wait, I think I hear them." She strained her ears. Sure enough, a horse clopped into the driveway.

"I'm glad I was wrong!" Sheila's eyes sparkled with excitement. "Here they come. I can't wait to see their faces!"

The kitchen door opened. Sadie hung up her bonnet without a glance at Betsie and Sheila. Then she sailed through the kitchen and stomped up the back stairs.

Sheila let out her pent-up breath. "She's still mad, all right. At me."

"No. She is angry with me, but she will get over it in time." But Betsie was beginning to have her doubts.

The door opened again. "Hello," said Charley. He put an oblong brown-paper package on the countertop before handing Betsie a bottle and a cardboard carton. "I brought you some milk and eggs."

"*Denki*, Charley, that was kind of you. I must find a way to earn some money so you don't have to think of us all the time." She stowed the items in the icebox with a pleased smile.

"Oh, I don't mind." He smiled back before he acknowledged Sheila with a cordial nod of greeting.

"Hi! We baked your favorite cookies. Want one? Or do you want the special dinner we made first?"

Charley's ruddy complexion deepened. "My mother cooked another big meal. Sadie and I ate with her." He patted his stomach.

Sheila's face fell. "Oh. I get it. I mean, my window was open this morning and I overheard you and Betsie fighting again. I couldn't understand your language, but I can guess you don't want to have anything to do with me. Just like my mom and dad. I'm always in the way."

Betsie grasped Sheila's hand and pleaded silently with Charley.

"You know," he said as he walked to the table, "it seems like there is one little corner inside that isn't quite full yet. And this"—he picked up a lopsided monster cookie studded with colorful candies—"is just what I need to fill it." He took a bite and smacked his lips with appreciation. "Now that hits the spot. Maybe I can take some home for later? *Mem* didn't make any of these at the bakery today."

Gratitude filled Betsie's heart. Charley could be wonderful with children when he tried. "Sheila, can you fetch a napkin from that drawer? Bundle up some cookies for Charley to take home. Give him a good number."

"Sure!" Her face lit up with joy.

While Sheila busied herself with the cookies, Betsie impulsively squeezed Charley's hand. Startled, he nodded and picked up the package.

"Here is your mail." He raised an eyebrow. "It is postmarked Tennessee, but there is no return address. Who do you know there?"

It was Betsie's turn to be startled. She knew she was blushing. "Tennessee?" She handled the package like it might bite her as she noted the tiny precise handwriting she knew so well. "Oh, of course! It must be the . . . the horse-training book I sent away for. I've been expecting it." The fib made her insides churn.

"Now, what use would you have for a thing like that?" He thumbed the brim of his hat and scratched his head.

Betsie glanced at Sheila, still busy counting cookies, before answering Charley in rapid *Deitsh*. "Well, you see, I thought maybe I could make some money breaking horses to drive. Then I could sell that horse for more than I paid and buy another. If training horses to drive proves too difficult, I can still earn money by selling them green-broke." Yes, that sounded fine. She almost believed it herself. "So, really, it's a good thing that I have Fledge to practice on." She plunged ahead. "I want to teach him to pull a pony cart."

Sheila returned with the knotted bundle of cookies, her expression wary. "Here you go. You weren't talking about me again, were you?"

"Of course not," Betsie scoffed. "Didn't you hear me say *gaul*? Tell Charley what that means, if you remember."

"Horse!" Sheila's eyes danced.

"Very good. I will enjoy these cookies," Charley told her. He wagged a finger at Betsie. "Training horses to drive is hard work, Betsie," he cautioned, careful to speak in English. "And even dangerous at times."

"We will be careful. Maybe you could help us out." Betsie bestowed her most winning smile.

"You show good sense to ask for my help," he said with a nod of approval. "We will take the training a step at a time." He paused. "Unless your book says different."

"My what? Oh, this here." She clutched the package to her chest. "I'd already forgotten about it. What a *Glutzkupp* I am."

"You are not a dunce, Betsie." Charley opened the door. "You think more than any girl I know. *Gut nacht*, Sheila." He raised his eyebrows in a question.

"Even I can guess what that means. Good night!" Sheila waved happily. "He's awfully good-looking," she sighed after Charley had gone. "But he's kinda bossy, too."

Betsie studied a table knife and polished a water spot with her apron.

"What's this?" Sheila prodded at the package. "Hey! That's Mike's writing. Why in the world would he send you a book about horse training?"

"Shh!" Betsie cast a wary glance toward the stairs. "I don't really know what kind of book it is, or even if it is a book."

"Oh, I get it. You didn't want Charley to be jealous of Mike, so you told a fib. It feels like a book." Sheila traced the postmark, puzzled. "But what's he doing in Tennessee? I thought he got drafted." She turned enormous eyes on Betsie. "Do you think he burned his draft card like those guys on the news? Betsie, is my brother in trouble?"

CHAPTER 8

I love opening letters. Letters bring faraway friends near.
—BETSIE'S JOURNAL

BETSIE QUAILED AT the thought of Michael being arrested for draft-dodging. She could almost see his lanky body being thrown into a dark prison cell, deprived of the freedom he prized so much. Sheila certainly suspected something was going on, but Betsie couldn't face lying anymore this evening. Butterflies fluttered in her stomach and she carefully folded the damp towel, casting about for a way to distract Sheila's thoughts about her brother.

"I have an idea."

"What?"

"First, let us see how fast we can put all this food away so it doesn't go to waste. I don't think we'll have to cook for a couple of days except to pop these dishes in the warming oven," she added ruefully. "When that's finished, we will clean up the kitchen. And when we're through, we will take this package into the front room and open it. Maybe there is a letter inside that will answer all your questions." Betsie offered her hand. "Is it a bargain?"

Sheila shook hands dutifully. "I guess so, but let's hurry! I can't wait to see what Mike says."

When the work was finally completed to Betsie's satisfaction, she led the way to the couch, package in hand.

Sheila snuggled up next to her. "I can't stand it. Rip it open!"

"No." Betsie ran her fingers along an edge and loosened the tape, careful to keep the brown paper intact. "I can turn this paper inside out and use it the next time I mail a package. Waste not, want not." Her smile was sad. Frugal *Mem* was always in her thoughts, even though she was far away.

"I don't want to wait. Do you have to fold that paper right now?"

"*Schnickelfritz*." Betsie set the wrappings aside and examined the thick cloth-bound book. A white envelope was tucked inside the front cover.

"You were right—it's a book!" Sheila tilted her head sideways to read the gilt lettering on the spine. "But not a book about *gauls* or training them. A poetry book." She wrinkled her nose.

Betsie slid out the letter. "No doubt you are more interested in what your brother has to say."

She drew a couple of sheets of lined notebook paper from the envelope and held them toward the light to make out the handwriting. Sheila scrunched so close that she practically sat in Betsie's lap.

"He says, 'Dear Pippa.'" Betsie tried unsuccessfully to restrain her smile as she read his familiar nickname for her. "'Well, I made it. I'm at The Farm in Tennessee. I didn't include a return address on the package because I don't have one. The USPS has yet to assign an address to an abandoned school bus in the middle of nowhere.'"

"Mike's living in a school bus on a farm?" Sheila squeaked.

"'But first things first,'" Betsie read on. "'If you're worried about my welfare and draft-dodging, don't be. After talking with you, I reported. The first thing they do when you report is take your height and weight. I was 6'2" and tipped the scales at 127. I completed all the rest of the rigmarole and stepped up to the last military man in line, a real hard-bitten type. He looked over my packet and told me that I failed the physical.'"

"Failed?" Sheila whispered.

Betsie moistened her dry lips and continued. "'Tell you what, I almost keeled over. I asked him why I failed, and he told me I was eleven pounds underweight and therefore didn't meet their qualifications. I asked him what that was supposed to mean. He told me I'd get a letter with all the details, but that basically I have a six-month deferment to overcome my physical disqualification. Then he pointed me toward the exit and barked, "Next!"

"'Can you believe it? It's a good thing I didn't eat your good cooking every night, Pippa. If I had, I would have been on the next plane to Nam for sure.'"

"But I don't get it," Sheila interrupted. "If Mike didn't have to go to war, why is he in Tennessee?"

It was a good question. "Let me read some more and maybe we'll see. 'So I got to thinking about my lucky break. I couldn't see fattening myself up like a blue-ribbon hog so they could ship me off to the slaughterhouse. The more I thought it over, the better life down at The Farm sounded. No government and no draft, ever. Live off the land and be kind to Planet Earth. Grow your own food. Everyone shares everything. The way I see it, living at The Farm is the next best thing to being Amish like you, so that's where I headed.'"

Betsie licked her thumb to turn the page over and resumed reading. "'I'd kept in touch with a buddy of mine who knew someone who lived at The Farm. My buddy said he'd heard you had to take a vow of poverty when you arrived, so I decided to pack the bare minimum and that meant leaving the Super Bee at home. Besides, it seemed like more of an adventure to stick out my thumb and hitchhike south, so that's what I did. Hitchhiking was an experience unto itself; maybe I'll tell you about that part next time. Anyway, when I arrived, that vow of poverty was a lot more thorough than I expected. I wasn't even allowed to keep this poetry anthology to myself, so that's why I mailed it to you for safekeeping.'" Betsie rested one hand on the book. "'I think you'll like it, Pippa.'"

"Most likely I will," she mused as she opened the book. "I certainly enjoy reading Emily's book of poems when I get the chance. Emily Dickinson, I mean," she corrected herself. Eagerly she perused the table of contents. This book appeared to be a collection of poems from many, many authors, some from the *Biewel*, even.

"Very romantic, huh, Betsie?" Sheila wiggled her eyebrows and heaved a contented sigh.

Betsie slowly became aware that she was tracing the gilt lettering on the book's spine with a reverent fingertip. She flinched like she'd touched a hot coal and cast the book aside.

"It is very practical, that's what I think, to send this book to me for safekeeping. Now, tell me, do you want to hear what your brother has to say, or do you maybe want to make up your own stories?"

Sheila regarded Betsie with interest. "No, that's okay. Sorry, I'll let you finish."

"*Gut*, because we are going to train Fledge tomorrow and it's getting late. Anyway, I'm almost done. 'So here I am, sleeping in an abandoned school bus. I put a blanket and a pillow in the aisle and that way I have plenty of room to stretch out. You've caught me sleeping on the floor of the harness shop enough times to know this arrangement suits me fine, except one of the bus windows is stuck open. I'll need to find some way to block the rain, but otherwise, I'm all set to have the adventure of my life. I'll write more next time, that is, if you don't mind hearing from me. And hey, if you want to write back, you could try addressing a letter to me in care of General Delivery, Summertown, Tennessee. I'm dropping a line to Sheila, too, so next time you see her, let her know I'm thinking of her. She's a good kid.

"'Well, time to hit the hay since it's getting too dark to see. I need to rig up some kind of lighting system, too, I guess. But for now, I can't wait to get up in the morning and start my new life, free to live how I want to. I want you to know that I haven't felt this good in a long time, Pippa, all things considered. Take care. PS I'm sorry I won't be able to train you in the harness shop after all. PPS If you think of it, tell my dad that I'm okay and not to worry.' He signed it 'Michael,' see?" Betsie showed the page to Sheila.

"I guess the letter to me will go to my house and I won't get it for a long time. I miss him," Sheila said softly. "Can I send him a letter, too? He doesn't know Mom wants a divorce, or that Dad went after her."

"Of course, that is a good idea. See that lap drawer in the desk over there? You will find paper, envelopes, and stamps. Also ink pens." Betsie thought of the dark bus and smiled. "Right now, you and your brother are almost Amish, ain't so?"

"Hey, that's right. We sure will have a lot to talk about." Sheila brightened. "Betsie, are you going to write to Michael, too?"

Trust forthright Sheila to cut to the heart of the matter. Was it a good idea to correspond with a person who'd garnered Charley's deep distrust from the moment they laid eyes on each other? Yet Betsie had always reassured Charley that she thought of Michael as a good friend, nothing more. Surely he would understand if Betsie wrote a letter or two to a friend. There was no harm in that.

Then why did you lie to Charley about the package? Betsie pursed her lips.

"*Jah*, sure." She tossed off her answer carelessly. "It will be good writing practice for me, ain't so? After all—"

"Wait, what was that? Did you hear something?" Sheila watched the staircase with big eyes as Amelia arched her back and hissed.

"What did it sound like?" Betsie hastily scooped the book and the letter under the brown paper.

Sheila listened for a moment and shrugged. "Kind of like a squeak, but maybe it was only Amelia mewing. I hope it wasn't a mouse. Anyway," she yawned hugely, "I think I'll go up and write that letter to Mike now."

"Turn up the gas lamp like I showed you if you need more light while you write. I will check on you in a little while to see if you need anything."

"Thanks, Betsie! I feel a lot better since we heard from Mike, don't you?" She launched herself at Betsie's middle and hugged her tight. "Goot knock."

"*Gut nacht*, dear heart." Betsie watched Sheila scramble up the stairs to a chorus of squeaks from the old treads. It is foolish, the way Sadie is avoiding a harmless girl like Sheila, she mused as she tidied up. First thing in the morning, I must talk with my sister.

CHAPTER 9

It's difficult to cast off pride when someone as
handsome and capable as Charley chose me.

—BETSIE'S JOURNAL

"I DON'T WANT TO talk about it." Sadie jostled Betsie aside and made a beeline for the door. "Charley's already here anyway."

"But you didn't eat your breakfast!" Betsie protested.

"I'll get something at the bakery."

The screen door slammed shut behind her sister. A tear welled up in Betsie's eye. As she reached for her handkerchief, she caught a glimpse of Charley as he alighted. He leaned toward Sadie and spoke cheerfully to her and then he jerked his thumb toward the open wagon. Sadie smiled brightly until he left her side. Then she glowered straight ahead.

Betsie dabbed her eyes and blew her nose. As she patted her front hair, she saw Charley emerge into the sunlight with an armload of pony-sized harness. An image of him easily tucking Fledge under one muscular arm intruded on her thoughts. Rattled, she composed herself before pushing open the door.

"I thought maybe you could use this," he called, harness buckles jingling with each step. "Today should be a dry day. I'll hang all this rigging over the fence here so it will be ready when you need it for your training."

"*Denki.* You are good to help us." Her voice caught.

Charley rested his boot on the bottom step, concern in his eyes. "Is everything all right, Betsie?"

It was all she could do to muster a nod. "Must be a storm is brewing later, maybe. Stormy weather always turns me broody."

From the corner of her eye, Betsie saw Charley rub his chin and squint at the powder-blue sky. She caught his glance at Sadie, who sat stiff as a poker in the wagon. When Charley looked back at her, Betsie dropped her gaze to her shoes.

"Maybe this will cheer you up." He delved into a pocket. "Here is a note from Rachel Yutzy to you. She dropped up to the bakery early this morning and asked if I would deliver it when I picked up Sadie."

Betsie took the envelope with her name written in Rachel's sprawling hand and broke into a smile. "A letter! This is just what I needed, Charley. I can't wait to read it." Charley flashed a grin and Betsie's heart soared. *I can't believe the good Lord let Charley choose me.*

"I'll be off, then." He touched a finger to his hat. "Leave the harness to hang on the fence this morning so the pony can see it's no threat. Then try to buckle it on him in the afternoon, but don't force him— take it slow. When he gets used to the feel of it, ground drive him. That means holding the reins and walking a few feet behind to get him used to going where you want. Before long, we ought to be able to hitch him up to a cart." He grimaced. "I guess I will have to borrow that, too, when the time comes. Be careful, now. If I get some time, I'll drop up this afternoon to see how it's going."

Betsie's smile widened. "It'd be real nice to spend some time together, Charley. I'd like that."

He gave a pleased nod and headed for the wagon. Betsie watched him swing into the seat with an easy grace that belied his rugged frame. As he drove the wagon across bone-jarring ruts, Sadie scooted closer to Charley to make herself heard above the racket, and Betsie frowned but quickly lifted her chin. *He's coming back to me. Charley always comes back to me.* Oh, what a blessing it would be to work with a considerate, faithful man like Charley at her side. Betsie breathed a prayer of thanks to the good Lord and returned to the house, her hot words with Sadie all but forgotten.

CHAPTER 10

"Take My yoke upon you, and learn of Me;
for I am meek and lowly in heart: and ye
shall find rest unto your souls."
— MATTHEW 11:29, QUOTED IN BETSIE'S JOURNAL

"WHY DO THEY PUT so many buckles on a pony harness?" Sheila grumbled. She tucked the tag end of leather through a loop as Betsie watched.

"Leave one of them unfastened and you will likely learn the reason soon enough," Betsie said. "We are almost done. I'm surprised he's tolerating it so well. Maybe Judith really is a good influence." She scratched under Fledge's creamy forelock as she supervised Sheila's progress. The pony snorted companionably.

"There." Sheila stood back to survey her handiwork. "Did I get them all?"

"*Jah*, you did very well. And see? I don't think he minds wearing a harness at all. I wonder if the owner before you broke him to harness."

"Search me." Sheila shrugged.

Trust an Englisher to buy a driving pony when a riding pony was what he really wanted, Betsie thought darkly. "I wouldn't be surprised if that's the reason you've had so much trouble with him." She reached to put pressure behind the backband. The pony shifted his hindquarters and laid back his ears. "I thought so. He has a ticklish spot there.

No wonder he doesn't like to be ridden." She felt like a very accomplished horsewoman.

"Now you tell me!" Sheila made a comical face and rubbed her behind. "What's next?"

"Since he's doing so well, I don't see why we shouldn't do as Charley suggested. We take these reins and ground drive Fledge around the pasture so he can get used to going where we want him to go. I will walk well behind him instead of hitching him to a cart." Betsie picked up the reins and draped one over each hand with her thumbs pointing toward Fledge's rump. "Stand over there out of the way in case he doesn't like this part. Get up, Fledge!" She flirted the reins and held her breath.

Fledge stepped out at a sedate walk. Betsie followed, her head held high. What a knack she had with horses! A daydream of a successful career as a horse trainer filled her mind as she shadowed Fledge down the pasture. She imagined a corridor of box stalls filled with spirited Standardbreds for driving, powerful Belgians for plowing and hauling, and sleek ponies gentle enough for children to drive. Yes, and every horse wore a halter she'd fashioned in the harness shop. As she walked past the stalls in her daydream, the horses nickered a welcome. Fifty—no, a hundred pairs of brown eyes followed her every move with adoration . . .

"I can't believe it, Betsie! He's doing great!" Sheila called.

Betsie couldn't stop smiling. She took deep breaths of fresh spring air and rejoiced at the caress of sunshine on her cheek. Oh, it was good to be alive on such a beautiful day. Her heart swelled with hope.

Fledge shook his head and neighed at Judith, who lazed in the shade at the far end of the pasture. Betsie came out of her reverie and flapped the reins to keep the pony's mind on business. He threw his weight against the breastplate with renewed vigor.

"Easy, Fledge." Betsie kept her voice steady and full of authority. The pony responded with a jog trot. She pulled the reins tight across his back and dug in her heels. "Whoa!"

Instead of slowing to a stop, Fledge swished his tail and broke into a lope. Betsie felt like her shoulders were being wrenched from their sockets as she sprinted to keep up. It was difficult to pull back on the reins with nothing to brace her feet against.

"Can't . . . hold on . . . much longer . . ." she panted. "Whoa!" Fledge stopped. Betsie tried to, but she stumbled and caromed off the pony's muscular rump. She staggered, tripped over a rock, and sat down on her *Hinnerdale* with a bone-jarring thud, still clutching the reins. Disoriented, she flopped backward into the silky grass with one arm across her eyes.

Presently Sheila came panting up to stand beside her. "Betsie! Betsie! Are you okay?"

She moved her arm and squinted at a fine view of Sheila's knobby knees. "*Jah*, I think so." The successful horse trainer daydream popped like a soap bubble.

"Maybe we should have waited for Charley," Sheila said, her voice thick with laughter.

Betsie propped herself up on one elbow, winded. "Here, hold this." She pushed the reins into Sheila's hands and scrambled to her feet with a rueful glance at Fledge. "I can't let him think he's the winner. Two of us are better than one. Together we will drive him back to the barn and unhitch him. Only then can he go visit with Judith. Get up, Fledge!" Betsie didn't try to keep the edge from her voice. Her backside smarted too much.

The training session concluded, they cleaned the tack and curried Fledge, then Betsie remembered Rachel's note. Sweet, roly-poly Rachel: childhood friend, wader of creeks, skipper of stones, snitcher of doughnuts, and keeper of Betsie's confidences. She needed to see her friend immediately. "How would you like to go visiting?"

Sheila's eyes sparkled. "Instead of chores? Sure!"

Betsie led Fledge to the side door and turned him out. "*Ach*, tired of Amish ways so soon?" she teased. She puckered her lips and whistled. Judith whinnied and cantered toward Betsie.

"Yeah. Everything is ten times harder than at home. I mean, you don't have to train a car to take you where you want it to go," Sheila explained. "But going places is always more fun than chores, no matter where you live."

"All right, we will go. My friend Rachel Yutzy sent word by Charley to come over. You will like Rachel. She is always cheerful, never troubled. She talks a blue streak, too, like someone else I know."

Sheila grinned. "I can't wait! Hey, what are you doing with that other harness? I thought we were done training for the day."

Betsie paused with one hand on Judith's trappings. "Now, how do you suppose we will get to Rachel's house—fly? Help me buckle Judith's harness on her. And do not worry," she responded to Sheila's look of disgust. "Once we get her harnessed and hitched up, Judith is the one who will be doing the work."

"Okay," Sheila said. "But you have to admit it would be easier to stick a key in a car and drive there."

Betsie recalled driving Michael's Super Bee into the barn to hide it on the night he left for Tennessee. She'd experienced an overwhelming sense of relief when she switched off the engine. "I guess you don't want to help me drive the buggy, then."

Sheila clapped her hands together. "Really, Betsie, I can help? But I'm not old enough to drive without a license!"

"*Schnickelfritz!* You don't need an English driver's license to drive a buggy," Betsie said with a laugh. "Buckle that up good, now."

After they parked the buggy in the yard, Betsie and Sheila stopped to freshen up at the pump. Betsie tried to ignore the tender spot near her tailbone as she sidestepped the splashes of water that Sheila deflected her way.

She cupped her hands under the spout for a drink as Sheila pumped. Instead of raising the water to her mouth, she lobbed it at Sheila and the water caught the girl full in the face.

Sheila gasped and wiped her streaming cheeks. "Ooh, that's cold! I haven't had this much fun since we helped Mike wash his car. I miss him, Betsie, don't you?"

"Mm-hmm," she answered noncommittally. "And that reminds me, if you have finished your letter to your brother, run and fetch it. Later, we will stop by the post office in town to mail it. And would you mind bringing my letters from the counter and my bonnet from the peg?"

Sheila's eyes crinkled in a smile. "I'll be right back!"

Betsie sighed and shook her head. What would Rachel and her family make of an English girl dressed in short-legged pants with pink patch pockets that rode low on her hips?

Sheila emerged from the kitchen door, black bonnet swinging from one hand and envelopes clutched in the other. "I wrote one to my dad, too," she explained as she climbed in beside Betsie.

"*Denki.*" She shuffled the mail together and tucked it into her pocket.

"I didn't see a letter to Michael."

"No. Charley wouldn't like it. Get up, Judith."

Sheila rolled her eyes but settled back to enjoy the ride. Fledge trotted along the fence as they passed, plaintive whinnies expressing his distress at being left behind. "Too bad, Stubby-Legs," Betsie told him. "Judith is a good Amish *gaul* who works when I ask her to, so now she gets to stretch her legs and see new places. Don't run away from me next time and maybe you will have more freedom, too." She checked for cars and carefully guided Judith onto the road.

Sheila puckered her eyebrows. "What do you mean, Betsie? Judith is working and Fledge is goofing off in the pasture. He's the one who can do whatever he wants."

"Looks to me like what he wants is to go with Judith, yet there he stays, locked up on the wrong side of the fence." Betsie indicated Judith's head. "See how proudly she carries the bit. It is an honor for her to serve us and she knows we expect her best effort. She in turn trusts us to care for her and provide everything she needs. She is not anxious about anything because her only wish is to please me, even though she could have refused."

"You know," Sheila mused, a quizzical expression on her face, "I've heard something a lot like that before, but I can't remember where. May have been in one of those Laura Ingalls prairie books." She shrugged. "Hey, you promised I could drive, right?"

"Watch how I do it now and you can help me drive home. We will take the back way from Rachel's later to stay off this busy road. It's longer but safer," she said as a green car zoomed past. "Hurry-up English," she muttered.

Soon Betsie pulled off the road into a drive that led to a house ringed with honey locust trees. A few chickens swirled out of the buggy's path as it rolled past the rainbow of flowers that Rachel's mother lovingly tended. She paused on her knees to greet them, deadheaded blooms in her hand, as Betsie and Sheila tied Judith in the shade.

"*Ach*, Betsie. Rachel is waiting for you out back." Naomi Yutzy sighed and dabbed her eyes with an apron corner.

"Naomi, is something wrong?" Betsie stooped to see her face, usually so full of fun. "What's upset you so?"

"It is the good Lord's will. You'd better go out back and talk with Rachel." Naomi shooed them on their way without so much as a glance at Sheila or her English clothes before resuming her gardening with another heavy sigh.

CHAPTER 11

"Marry in haste, repent at leisure."
—WILLIAM CONGREVE, QUOTED IN BETSIE'S JOURNAL

THOROUGHLY ALARMED at Naomi's behavior, Betsie grabbed Sheila's hand. "Come along."

She led the way to the back porch. There in the shade of the honey locusts sat Rachel on the porch swing, a pad of paper on her lap, pencil dented with tooth marks.

"Oh, there you are, Betsie," she said listlessly. She removed her steamy spectacles and polished them on her dress.

Betsie caught her friend's wrist. "Rachel, your eyes are all red and puffy. Tell me what's wrong. Your *Mem* wouldn't say. You two are frightening me!"

"Maybe I shouldn't be here." Sheila shifted uneasily.

Betsie jumped at the interruption but Rachel only stared at her lap. Betsie crooked a finger at Sheila and they retreated a few steps to stand in the yard.

"I noticed Katie Miller, the little girl who lives near me, on the rope swing when we drove up. See there?" Betsie pointed to the little girl dragging her bare feet slowly through the dirt beneath the swing. "That's Katie. Her great-uncle has business here, maybe, and he has brought Katie along. Now she has some time to play, but no one to play with. Katie is younger than you, but she will keep you company while I talk with my friend, okay?"

Sheila gaped. "But what should I say? I can't just walk up to an Amish girl and—"

"Why ever not? Amish girls don't bite. Besides, I happen to know that Katie's best friend Ruthie Hershberger moved to Missouri on Monday and Katie will miss her sidekick. You go help her feel better. Off with you, now." Betsie gave Sheila a little push, her mind occupied with Rachel's troubles. "Tell her you are my friend and everything will be all right. My kitten Amelia came from Katie's house," she prompted when Sheila's footsteps dragged again. "The Yutzys likely have a whole barnful of kittens you two can hunt for."

Sheila stopped behind a tree trunk and peeked at Katie, whose bonnet hid her face as she teased the kitten in her lap with a white clover blossom.

Sheila glanced back at Betsie, woebegone. "Do I have to?"

"Yes, you will have more fun with Katie than with Rachel and me," Betsie encouraged. "I will come for you as quick as I can, but by then you won't want to leave." She watched Sheila trudge in Katie's general direction before rejoining Rachel on the porch.

The swing chains rattled as she sat down next to her friend. "Rachel, out with it. What's happened? Why are you acting this way?"

Wordlessly, Rachel pushed her pad of paper into Betsie's lap. "See for yourself."

"Can a piece of paper upset you so?" she teased, trying to cheer her up, but Rachel would not meet her eye. A chill ran down her spine. Alarmed, she read a few lines to herself, stopping short when she spied her own name.

"*Glutzkupp*," she admonished. "Is this some kind of joke? Why have you written my name and Sadie's? I know my own name well enough. Stop this right now and . . . why, there is your name at the top, across from Sam's," she noticed, naming Rachel's *Bo*. "And here is Charley's name, across from mine. It's almost like you're making a—"

Rachel snatched the pad away and hid it behind her back. "I can't bear to hear you say it out loud. Don't you see, Betsie?" She searched Betsie's eyes. "I am planning our wedding, mine and Sam's."

Betsie stared before she burst into laughter. "*Was in der welt* do you mean by frightening me half to death, Rachel, as if you are not happy about such a thing? Of course you are planning your wedding, because fall is coming faster than we think. *Ach*, you had me so worried. I think I will just go home until you are out of this mood."

Piqued, she vacated the swing, but Rachel caught her dress and pulled her to sit down once again. "Betsie, listen once and don't stop me from talking or I won't be able to finish." Tears sparkled on Rachel's cheeks. "I don't want to tell you this, but I must." She closed her eyes. "Sam Hochstetler and I are not getting married in the fall. We are marrying in two weeks."

Betsie recoiled before she could stop herself. "Oh, no! Rachel, not that," she whispered, cold with horror. "Don't tell me you and Sam are going to have a—"

Rachel's eyes popped open and a fiery spark kindled. "Shush. Get your mind out of the muck. There is no chance of such a thing between Sam and me. You should know better." Two bright spots of color appeared high on her cheeks. "Besides, for me and you, this may hurt worse even than that. Oh, Betsie, Sam's *dat* has sold his land for a good price. His family is moving from Plain City to Missouri, like so many others who have emigrated in search of cheap land, and I . . . and we must . . ." She gulped and grasped Betsie's hands. "Do you understand?"

A sinking feeling settled in her stomach as Betsie realized what her best friend didn't have the heart to say. "But no, Rachel! You can't marry Sam in a hurry-up wedding and move to Missouri with his family! That is not our way. This can't happen. You mustn't let it. What about your *mem* and *dat*? Your sisters and Levi?"

Rachel fumbled for her handkerchief and removed her spectacles to dab at her eyes. "*Mem* is beside herself, and some days she and *Dat* are of half a mind to emigrate along with the Hochstetlers. Why, the English developers have been all up and down our road, offering fancy prices for farmland that they intend to subdivide and build up to sell on speculation. I'm surprised you haven't had any offers for your land, you being right there on State Route 42 and all."

"*Dat* refused to talk with them. He sent them packing, which is exactly what Sam's *dat* should have done." Betsie leapt to her feet, fists clenched. "You must stay here, Rachel. You can't leave Plain City!"

Rachel threw up her hands. "Sam would give me no peace until I agreed. He is talking it over with Jonas Gingerich this very minute." A more contented air came over her. "What a good thing Sam and I have already completed our questioning and are ready to make our kneeling vows and join the church this Sunday. Times are changing for everyone, Betsie. Besides, your own brothers Eli and Abijah are already in Missouri, so why shouldn't I leave Plain City and live out west, too?"

"Because I don't want to lose you!" Betsie shouted. Shocked at her outburst, she clapped her hands over her mouth, shook her head, and backed away slowly until she fetched up against the porch railing.

Rachel's smile was warm with affection as she crossed to stand beside Betsie. "I don't want to lose you, either, but I do want to go with Sam. I don't want to leave *Mem* and *Dat*, but Sam and I want to have *Bopplin* of our own, and we need our own farm where we can feed our children so they grow healthy and strong. Yes, as I said, times are changing. If we stay here, we expect any day to see the yellow monster machines that churn up acres of good farmland and spit out flimsy houses for the English until there are more of them than us. The price for land continues to go up, up, up, and where will it all end? Mark my words, one day Columbus will swallow up Plain City, you wait and see."

Betsie burst into laughter and plopped on the swing beside her friend again. "*Ach*, Rachel, that is not possible! Why, it takes nearly an hour to get to Columbus from here, and that's by car." Measuring distance sobered her. "What am I going to do without you, my dear friend?"

"We will write to each other, of course," Rachel replied stoutly. "I want you to know that I am praying every day for your *mem* and *dat* to return," Rachel said. "And also Lovina, your aunt." Rachel caught her rosebud lip between her teeth. "So many from your family have gone away. How glad I am that you have"—she lowered her voice to a whisper with a hint of her old sparkle—"Charley Yoder to take care of you one day soon, yes?"

Betsie felt the heat steal across her cheeks. "I can't believe you said that out loud."

Rachel held up her hand. "Then don't answer me. I know that I am right, though you may laugh at me as you did about Columbus. Wasn't Sam the one who gave you the note from Charley when he first asked to drive you home from a singing?" Rachel winked and picked up the pad of paper. "I will tell you something. If I weren't marrying Sam, I would be after Charley. He is a fine-looking man, in case you haven't noticed. Now, I want you and Sadie to be my *nayva hokkah*. Will you do it?"

"I can't speak for Sadie," Betsie hesitated. "I can barely speak to Sadie at all these days. But of course I will be your attendant. I will sew my dress, and hers, too, if she agrees, just as soon as you choose a color. Is there anything else I can help you with?"

Rachel's smile broadened. "I knew I could count on you. *Mem* is helping me sew my dress, but as we get closer to the day, I'll send word by Charley when I need your help."

"You're getting married, Rachel." Betsie sighed. "This day was bound to come, but it's happened so much sooner than I expected and you will be so much farther away. What will I do without you to talk to, sing with, quilt with, can with? We've been friends for so long."

Rachel's eyes widened. "Why don't you and Charley move to Missouri, too, once you marry? Your brother and my sister are already out there, and now Sam and I will be. What's keeping you here?"

Pain pierced Betsie's heart. "I can't leave, at least not until we get *Mem* and *Dat* back home. Then . . ." She thought of Sheila, the harness shop, Michael. It all seemed like part of another life, and just as soon as Sheila's parents returned, all that had happened in Hilliard would be firmly in the past. "You know, one day after my parents return and when all this is settled with Sheila's family, maybe I'll speak to Charley about moving. Then you and I will be an inseparable pair again."

"Yes! We can raise our babies together, just like we always dreamed, lots and lots of babies. Oh, it will be wonderful!"

A lump rose in Betsie's throat. She craned to find Sheila and Katie

Miller, but the pair was nowhere to be seen. "I'd better go before I start to blubber like one of those *Bopplin*. Where did those girls go?"

"Sheila, is that the English girl's name? I saw her and Katie wander over by our barn while you were yelling before. There they are." Rachel paused, eyebrows raised. "Tell me the truth. Do you really think it was wise to take her into your home? My lands, when I saw those short pants with her mosquito-bitten legs sticking right out!"

Betsie raised an eyebrow of her own. "I imagine our clothing seems pretty strange to her, too. She needs me, Rachel. Charley thinks so, too, although he didn't at first. You know how it hurt me when my parents left. If I can spare Sheila even a tiny bit of that pain, I will."

"*Ach*, you are so good, my friend. If anyone asks me whether you've lost your mind, I'll say your soft heart took over." Rachel watched Sheila and Katie. "Despite her clothes, the Englisher looks like a sweet girl."

"She is. In many ways, she reminds me of the best friend I ever had. But now I am losing you."

Rachel removed her eyeglasses and wiped them carefully. "Don't speak of it. We'll see each other again. And maybe it will work out that you can at least come out to Missouri to visit us, and Susan and Eli too."

"We'll see." Betsie mustered a smile. "Now let's get back to your wedding! Come now, give me something to do. I can't imagine having a hurry-up wedding like this."

"Let's see." Rachel scratched her nose with the worn pencil eraser, oblivious of the gray smudges it left as she consulted her list. "We can always use more dishes for the wedding meal. Pack up all you can loan to me. Cutlery and glasses, too. Tablecloths . . . oh! Don't forget pitchers, dish towels, serving bowls, platters—"

"How about the kitchen sink?"

"Ouch, Betsie, that's an old joke." Rachel pulled a wry face. "Tell you what, just for that, I will ask you to make me some of your banana cream pies. I never tasted better. Get along with you, now, and take care of your little girl," she said with a wave.

A change has come over my friend, Betsie thought as she hurried to the barn. Already Rachel seemed more grown up, as though merely talking about being yoked with Sam Hochstetler had a good effect. Oh, how she would miss the girlish Rachel of her youth, because in two short weeks—

Betsie stopped in her tracks, clasped her hands hard together, and closed her eyes. *Please, please.* Rachel and Sam, married in such unseemly haste? Why, it was impossible. Surely the good Lord would remind their bishop of that.

Her breathing slowed and she lifted her chin. A smile tugged at the corner of her mouth. What had happened to her and Rachel was certainly shattering for the two of them, but it barely created a ripple in the tide of time and Amish customs. Nothing much had changed among the People for hundreds of years, and nothing much would change now if Betsie could help it. Then and there, she made a vow to reunite her loved ones and live peacefully among them in Plain City until the end of her days. With that, Betsie turned and walked toward the barn to find Sheila.

CHAPTER 12

"A great deal of what we see depends
on what we are looking for."
—NOAH TROYER, QUOTED IN BETSIE'S JOURNAL

BETSIE STEPPED INTO the cool shadow of the barn, her heart at peace, until a strident voice broke in on her thoughts.

"I don't care what my *mem* told you, Katie! *Youens* can't go up in my barn loft and that's the long and short of it. Now go away and leave me to my work."

"You might be older than me, Levi Yutzy," another voice piped, also in *Deitsh,* "but you can't boss me around that way. Naomi told me I can hunt for Snowball's kittens and I mean to right now. You try and stop me from going up that ladder."

Amused at the spat between her youthful neighbors, Betsie peeked into the barn. She saw Levi planted like a sturdy tree at the foot of the ladder, the handle of a manure fork clenched in one fist and a paper bag shiny with grease spots doubled up in the other. He towered above Katie's green dress and black bonnet, but there was an obstinate set to the girl's back as she stepped by him and curled her bare toes around the bottom rung of the ladder. Levi scowled down at her.

Betsie watched Sheila, who shifted from side to side. "Katie," she hedged, "I can't understand a word you two are saying, but I don't want to see Snowball's kittens, honest. Can we go find Betsie?"

72

"*Jah*, better listen to the English girl, Katie," Levi smirked. "She shows better sense than you. She doesn't want to see what's up there."

Katie snapped to attention. Even from her remote vantage point, Betsie could tell the girl had thought of something. "Huh. Did you tie two cats together by their tails again, like the last time I was here?" She advanced a couple of rungs up the ladder, fearless. "Boys who do that are meaner than snakes. I'm going to tell Naomi on you. Or maybe you got something hidden up there. Something you ain't supposed to have. Is that it?"

Levi's face turned paper white beneath his battered straw hat. "You keep quiet! You don't know what you're talking about." He brandished the manure fork at her and Katie squealed as smelly debris spattered her dress.

Enough was enough. Betsie stepped into the barn. "Oh, there you are, Sheila. I am ready to go home. Hello, Katie! Listen, did you hear that? Joe is calling you. Run along, now. I'll maybe bring Sheila across to visit you some time soon."

"No, I didn't hear. Good-bye, Betsie. Good-bye, Sheila. I'd like to have you drop up to my house sometime." Katie stuck out her tongue at Levi and flounced out of the barn.

Betsie watched Levi as he truculently kicked up dust with the toe of his shoe.

"Ready to do some driving, Sheila?" Betsie asked without turning toward the girl. "I will be along to the buggy in a moment. I want to have a word with Levi."

"Okay! Hey, Katie," Sheila hollered, "I get to drive! Wait up and you can watch me!" Sheila sped off to catch up with her new friend.

When they were alone, Betsie raised her eyebrows and gazed pointedly at Levi. It was a look she remembered her *mem* using on her older brother. Levi kept his eyes on the ground as he moved away from the ladder and let the pitchfork clatter to the floor. He twisted the paper bag tighter shut and ignored her, but Betsie bided her time and kept silent. At length, Levi sneaked a look at her and she wiggled her fingers at him. His eyes widened and then narrowed with wariness.

"Don't you want to tell me what you have hidden in the loft, Levi?"

Betsie asked, but he didn't take the bait. Time to stop beating around the bush, she decided. She crossed the floor and bunched the folds of her dress in one hand. "Shall I climb up and have a look for myself?" Her shoe touched the bottom rung.

Levi lunged at her. "No, Betsie!"

The greasy paper bag ripped and several oatmeal raisin cookies plunked to the floor. Betsie stooped to retrieve them and offered them to Levi, who snatched them from her hand with a scowl and shoved them in his pocket. "Then tell me what is up there, Levi. Shall I help you?" She gave him a knowing look. "Are you going to eat those cookies while you listen to a transistor radio, maybe?"

"A radio?" he echoed, his voice sliding up the scale. He rubbed the back of his neck and nodded slowly. "*Jah*, a radio. How did you know?"

Betsie smiled. "It's not so long since my older brother hid a transistor radio in our loft and I don't mind telling a tale on myself. Once when he wasn't around, I listened to that radio, too. But do you know what I heard?" She held up a finger and leaned closer. "Some English church program about telling the truth. So you can imagine I didn't want to listen anymore."

She watched the boy to see what effect her words were having. He flushed and hung his head. Good. She continued, her tone kindhearted but firm. "Don't try to fool your parents, Levi. Get rid of whatever you have hidden up there as quick as can be and you'll be able to look your *mem* and *dat* in the eye and tell the truth again. After all, you may hear something far worse than a church program on the radio, like English music on WHOA, even . . . or-or so I've heard." She turned to take her leave but added, "I must say I'm surprised at you, Levi. You never acted ugly like this when my brother Abijah was around."

A hoarse croak startled her and she swiveled to look over her shoulder. "Are you all right? You're not choking on one of those cookies, are you?"

Levi, his face flaming, thumped his chest and coughed weakly. "A dry crumb got lodged. I'm all right now." He ushered her to the door. "Good-bye, Betsie. I will do as you said. Only, you won't say anything to my parents, will you?"

She shook her head. "Not so long as you take care of this matter right away. Can I trust you?"

Betsie offered her hand and Levi pumped it solemnly. "I will take care of it tonight," he said as he walked with her to the entrance.

"Good. Your family has enough upset to deal with, ain't so?" Betsie smiled sadly at him and exited the barn.

As she settled into the buggy beside Sheila, Betsie took stock. An hour ago, she'd had a best friend who lived close by, one with a younger brother the same age as Abijah. How everything had changed in the course of an hour! With every second that passed, the prospect of Rachel Hochstetler, a remote stranger in a faraway state, was fast eclipsing the dear girl named Rachel Yutzy whom Betsie had always known. For that matter, Levi Yutzy, with his peach-fuzz chin and rebellious ways, called to mind that her own baby brother must be growing up fast, far across the wide Mississippi River.

"Betsie? Do I get to drive now?"

Sheila's question snatched her back to the present. "*Ach*, so you think you are grown up, too?"

"Grown up is the last thing I want to be," Sheila vowed fervently. "All I want to do is drive for a while, but if you changed your mind—"

Betsie hooked one arm around Sheila's shoulders and gave her a brief squeeze. "No, I didn't change my mind." She placed the reins in the startled girl's hands. "Why don't you try going to the end of the driveway? I'll hold the ends like this, see? But you are the driver. Later I'll take over so we can mail our letters at the post office." She watched Sheila for a moment. "That's the way! Work with Judith instead of trying to control her and you'll do just fine."

She settled against the seat back and wished she could apply such sage advice to her own life, but she couldn't shake the feeling that her friends and family were slipping through her fingers like sand through an hourglass.

CHAPTER 13

"Among the long black rafters
The wavering shadows lay . . ."
—"The Bridge" by Henry Wadsworth
Longfellow, quoted in Betsie's journal

Hours later, Betsie awoke with a start. A haunting memory of a nightmare alarm clock lingered. The clock's human hands had grabbed her throat. She'd struggled against the choking hold until she couldn't resist anymore. Just before she lost consciousness, a bell like the one in the harness shop dinged and she'd awakened. She shivered and released a pent-up breath. It hadn't really happened. It was only a nightmare. Gradually her pounding heart slowed.

On the verge of falling back to sleep, she heard a ringing neigh, followed immediately by another. Fledge. Drat that *loppich* pony. But something had disturbed him and she supposed she had better make sure everything in the barn was settled. Quickly she pinned her dress over her nightgown, grabbed a flashlight, and padded downstairs to the kitchen.

When she reached the door, she fumbled in the darkness for one of her *Dat*'s knobby walking sticks, shiny with use. She held it by the middle, the heft of the thicker end reassuring. Just before she stepped outside, she remembered Abijah's old letter about the pet rat snake he'd hidden in the barn. With a shiver, she slipped her bare feet into a worn pair of work boots that rested on the mat in front of the door.

Outside the air was muggy and thick clouds swirled past a waxing moon. Betsie swatted at a mosquito that buzzed near her cheek and squinted as she shuffled over the grass to the barn. Fledge was quiet now. In fact, she didn't hear a sound. What could have alarmed him in the middle of the night?

Her heart leapt strangely and she stopped short. Once before, someone had visited her farm in the dead of night. Mightn't he do the same again?

She picked up her pace until she was fairly running through the whispery grass. Of course he wouldn't drive his car here. He'd hitchhiked all night to get here from Tennessee, she told herself, maybe so he could surprise me. But now I can surprise him and he can take Sheila home and everyone will be at peace.

She slowed at the open barn door, more certain with every step that she was right. At the threshold, she stopped and nearly laughed aloud. Hadn't Michael played plenty of practical jokes on her? Well, this time the tables would be turned.

Silently she slipped through the opening and stood for a moment as her eyes adjusted to the darkness. Gradually she made out the dim outline of a tallish person standing by Fledge's stall, a hand clamped over the pony's muzzle to quiet him.

Betsie stifled a giggle. With speed born of pure adrenaline, she brandished the cane and rushed toward Michael.

"Now I've got you!" Her gruff voice echoed in the dark. "What are you doing in my barn?" she demanded.

Her effect on the person in the shadows was electric. He emitted a piteous shriek that wavered oddly between treble and tenor and dropped like a stone to his knees.

"Don't hurt me!" he begged in a welter of frightened *Deitsh*.

The hair on the back of Betsie's neck brushed up. This person was not Michael, come to make her troubles vanish in an instant. The familiar unkempt fluff of hair at the back of the man's head made her pause.

"Abijah?" she whispered. The cane slipped from her numb fingers and crashed to the planks. "Can it be?"

"Don't make me go back to Eli's, *Mem!*" he pleaded. "I'll do anything if you will only let me stay here with you and *Dat!*"

"Oh, Abijah." If only her brother knew. Betsie fumbled in her pocket and brought out the flashlight. "It's me. Betsie. I-I was trying to teach somebody a lesson." She flicked the switch and held out a hand to help him up. "My goodness, but you have stretched out since I saw you last! You are taller than I am." No wonder she'd mistaken him so easily for Michael, but now her light picked out holes in his green shirt and clumsy patches on his broadfall trousers. She made her voice stern. "How did you get here?"

"Can I have something to eat before I tell? I'm awful hungry." His brown eyes pleaded like a puppy's.

Betsie's heart melted. "Hasn't Susan been feeding you enough?" She looked him over with a critical eye. "You are all arms and legs with no meat on your bones and no mistake. Come with me. After you eat some, you must tell me how you got here, though."

"How about I tell you now and then I can eat a lot and go to bed, *jah?*" he mumbled through a huge yawn. "For one thing, Susan is a stingy cook, but mostly I ran off because Eli wants to start a woodshop and he wanted my help running it. He didn't want me to ever come back home, even though his broken leg was almost healed up by the time I got to his house. I helped in the woodshop and I was good at it, but I didn't want to make furniture for the rest of my born days. Eli wasn't even paying me nothin', just room and board. So I got a ride with Zeke. You know, the English driver who took the Hershbergers out west? I heard from Atlee Hershberger that Zeke would soon be on his way back to Plain City, so I asked if I could ride along. He said yes. Really he said, 'Sure, son, you can ride shotgun with me. I had it pretty rough as a youngun, myself.'" Abijah grinned. "He didn't charge me nothin' except I was supposed to wake him up if he got sleepy and started driving off the road, but he didn't. He bought me a hamburger, too."

"That was kind of him, but—"

"So can you hold off telling *Mem* and *Dat* I am home until later in the morning so I can sleep for a while yet?"

Running away. Hiding out. Huge problems, but they paled in comparison to what Betsie had to tell him. "Bije," Betsie said gently. "Walk now with me. I have some sad news to share." And as brother and sister linked arms and walked out of the barn together, a slow rain began to fall.

Raindrops pelted the kitchen window later as Abijah lounged in his old place at the table. "I can't believe *Mem* and *Dat* moved out weeks ago," he said, his expression dazed. "I could have left Eli's so much sooner."

Betsie stopped in the middle of pouring another glass of milk. "That's a funny way to say it, ain't so? You mean you should have left sooner so you could try to bring them back, just as we still try to do. *Ach*, I am so tired I don't know what I am saying."

"Finicky old Betsie," Abijah teased. "You always fussed about the right words when you tried to help me with my school lessons. I don't miss spelling or grammar one bit, but I sure do miss the times we talked about nature and animals. If only . . ." A faraway look came into his eyes, but then he roused himself and held out his glass. "If only I could have some more milk."

"That is easy enough." She shook the last drops from the bottle. "That's all the milk we have until we get more from Yoders'." She smiled. "Maybe we will keep a milk cow again, now that you're home. Also I lost count of how many times I refilled your plate. It's been a while since I've seen such a *gut* appetite."

"It's because you are such a fine and generous cook, *Schweschder*," Abijah said with a crooked grin. He wiped his mouth with the back of his hand and slapped his belly. "Ah, I feel better already. And now for my bed."

"Well, you know where it is." Betsie watched him through bleary eyes. "I reckon I ought to get another hour or so of sleep, if I am able. Some of us won't get to sleep as late as others," she reminded.

"Only one time is all I ask. I know every tub must stand on its own bottom. At least that's what Eli's woman drummed into me at least twenty times a day." He scowled at the memory.

"You mean Eli's *wife*, Susan? Well, our own dear *Mem* says the same," Betsie said mildly. "I wish she and *Dat* were here to welcome you home proper."

"*Ach*, so do I. But since they are not, it looks like I am the man of the house." He pushed back his chair and stretched. "*Gut nacht*, Betsie."

He ambled up the stairs on his spindly legs, leaving Betsie with an unsettled feeling. Wasn't Abijah the least bit sad that their parents had left the Amish?

"I must ask Charley to talk with Abijah," she murmured as she settled into her bed a while later. "Charley will know what to do." She rolled over and closed her eyes, grateful for the patter of raindrops that drowned out her misgivings.

CHAPTER 14

"We are seldom aware of what's cooking
until the pot boils over."

—FANNIE TROYER, QUOTED IN BETSIE'S JOURNAL

IT WAS STILL DARK when Betsie awoke again, though a faint gray light hinted that the rain had let up. Oh, it would be muddy working outside today.

Betsie flipped back the quilt and dressed slowly, groggy from a lack of sleep. After she picked up her notebook, she shuffled into the hall and was surprised to see Sheila's door ajar. Curious, she poked her nose around the corner and smiled.

There sat Sheila in the middle of her bed, fully dressed. The gas lamp flared in the damp breeze as she turned the page of a book.

"My, aren't you up bright and early! The Plain life must be agreeing with you," Betsie commented.

"If you can't beat 'em, join 'em," Sheila agreed. "You don't mind if I read my Bible and pray awhile before I come down, do you?" She displayed the cover and Betsie recognized *Good News for Modern Man*, the book Sheila had gotten from her Sunday school teacher.

"No, I don't mind. Myself, I like to have some quiet time with my thoughts before I start my day," Betsie told her. "Come down when you are ready. I have a surprise for you."

"Your surprises are always good ones, Betsie." Sheila returned to her reading, a happy smile curving her lips.

Nearly an hour later, Betsie pushed the pot of oatmeal to the right on the hob to keep it warm. Eggs scrambled with water instead of milk would have to do. Betsie was grateful for the leftovers she and Sheila had stored, but how long would her icebox and storage cellar hold up under Abijah's famished onslaughts?

She sat down and stroked the table's satiny planks. Thoughtfully she pulled her notebook toward her and picked up the green pencil with "Sullivan and Son Harness Shop" imprinted in gold letters. Actually, all that remained was "Sullivan and Son Har" since she'd sharpened the pencil to a stub.

What might Michael be doing right now? She'd been so sure that he was the intruder in the barn, although it would have been a shock to see him again. Not as big of a shock as discovering her younger brother, though.

She shook her head. Abijah—what was going on in that head of his? Busily her pencil scratched as she tried to set her scattered thoughts on paper. Steam from the teakettle fogged the kitchen window as the minutes passed.

"Hey, get away from my door!"

Footsteps thumped on the floor above Betsie's head and she heard a door slam. Sheila's voice came again. "Betsie, help! Someone's watching me!" A doorknob rattled. "Hey, let me out of here! Betsie!"

Betsie clapped a hand to her head. "It's all right, Sheila, I'm coming!"

Why had a surprise seemed like such a good idea? Betsie rushed up the stairs to find Abijah leaning backwards and holding Sheila's door shut, a smirk on his face. When he saw Betsie, the smirk vanished, replaced by a look of earnest worry.

"There you are, sister. I've trapped an English girl in our house and she's reading some heathenish book. She even knows your name. I will keep you safe, don't worry." He straightened a bit.

The doorknob rattled and Betsie caught a glimpse of Sheila's ruddy face as she strained to pull the door open. "How dare you say that about my Bible? You open this door right now and let me out!"

"All right, I will if you say so," Abijah said. A rakish grin spread across his face.

"No, Abijah!" Betsie bellowed.

But Abijah let go and the door flew open. Betsie caught a quick glimpse of Sheila's wide open eyes and mouth before the girl landed on her *Hinnerdale*. Betsie rushed to her side.

"Are you all right, dear heart?" she asked tenderly. "You aren't hurt, are you?"

"Th-that was plain mean!" Sheila sputtered. She closed her eyes and took a couple of deep breaths. "You know what, Betsie?" the girl continued in a quiet voice. "I was reading in my Bible about forgiveness, and this would be a good time to practice it." She leaned to look past Betsie at the culprit. "So I forgive you, Elijah," she said sweetly. "I know you didn't mean to hurt me."

Abijah's eyebrows shot up. "My name is Abijah," he growled. "And maybe I did mean to hurt you. You think you're smart, don't you? Sitting there so lazy and reading a book, but you don't belong here, English girl. Go home and take your fancy book with you."

"Abijah! You ought to be ashamed—" Betsie began, but Sheila cut her off.

"You need the Bible more than you think!" She waved the book at him. "God is the only one who can change somebody as mean as you, so I'm not going to try. But I am going to pray for you every day, and that's not all. I'm going to ask God to save you. So there!" Sheila's mouth moved like she was going to stick out her tongue, but instead she folded her hands and closed her eyes. "Dear Lord, please save Abijah—"

"Betsie, she's praying out loud! Stop her!" Abijah tried to shoulder past as Betsie struggled to hold him at bay.

"*Was in der welt?*" Sadie stormed into the room. "Can't a person get ready for work in peace, Betsie?" She glanced at Abijah's back and sucked in her breath. "Why is this man in the English girl's room?" She spun Abijah to face her.

"Sadie, it's me," he said.

Sadie stopped in mid-scold. "Can it be my brother?" She grasped his hands. "Oh, Abijah, I can't believe how you've grown! Why aren't you at Eli's?"

He glared at Sadie. "Because Eli wanted to keep me there forever as cheap labor! I got a ride home with one of the truckers who had just moved Hershbergers out there. And I won't go back."

"I found him in the barn last night, Sadie," Betsie broke in. "Look, breakfast is ready. Come down and eat with us. All of us," she said, gesturing to Sheila, who had finished her prayer silently and now stood beside Betsie. "Then Abijah can tell you his story." She glared at her brother. "But not before he makes things right with my friend. That is no way to greet a guest in our house. *Mem* and *Dat* did not raise you to act so. I invited Sheila to stay with us until her parents return, and while she lives here, she is free to worship the good Lord as she pleases."

A knowing look came into Sadie's eyes. "Charley sure would be angry at you if he heard you say that," she reminded in *Deitsh*.

Betsie ignored her sister. "While I was working for Sheila's family, she was very kind to me, but have you been kind to her today? No. She is a girl and younger than you. So what do you have to say for yourself?" Betsie planted her fists on her hips.

Abijah locked eyes with Sadie for an instant, and then he looked from Betsie to Sheila, who met the cold fire of his gaze calmly and without guile. He drew himself up. "I hope you ain't hurt too bad," he grunted. "I was only fooling, but I guess the English can't take it very well. And now I'm a-going to see if Levi Yutzy wants to go fishing and have a fish fry for breakfast." He stalked to the stairs, put both hands on the railing, and vaulted easily to the landing. Then he clomped down the rest of the steps and out of sight.

CHAPTER 15

I can't figure out what's happened between
Sadie and me. We used to be so close.

—BETSIE'S JOURNAL

"SO I SNEAKED INTO the barn, Sadie, ready to protect the horses. Imagine my shock when I found our baby brother hiding there. Although he's not such a baby anymore, what with a fine crop of peach-fuzz on his chin." Betsie chuckled. "He begged to sleep late this morning, all the way to seven o' clock. At Eli's he'd been milking the cows at four."

She fanned herself as she took her place at the table. Oh, so muggy! What a pity that her seat faced away from the slight breeze that wafted through the open door. She counted her blessings just the same, grateful that Sadie consented to take breakfast with an English person even if she was pointedly ignoring the girl. She breathed a prayer of thanks to the good Lord.

"*Jah*, I wish I could have seen your face," Sadie agreed. "But tell me, Betsie, wasn't it awfully risky to venture out to the dark barn in the middle of the night? There could have been a robber out there, you know. Or maybe you were expecting someone?"

Betsie glanced sidewise at her sister, who smiled slyly as she buttered a slice of bread. *Did I talk in my sleep about expecting to see Michael in the barn? If so, Old Owl Ears must have heard me.*

Taking a deep breath, Betsie steadied her voice, willing herself not to break the shaky truce that Abijah's return had created. "I wasn't expecting anyone. I wish Abijah hadn't run off to Yutzys' this morning, what with their whole family getting ready for . . . I mean . . ." She hesitated.

"Getting ready for Rachel's wedding, *jah*, I know. Well, don't look so surprised that I heard already," Sadie went on. "You know Sam and Charley are friends. Let's see, Charley told me yesterday morning that Sam asked him to be a *nayva hokkah*. Didn't he tell you yet? Well, maybe he will say something today. I wouldn't worry."

"I'm not worried. Charley will tell me as soon as he gets a chance. Besides, I already heard it from Rachel." She pushed back her chair and crossed to the stove. "Anyone else want more tea while I'm up?"

"No, thank you, Betsie," Sheila said.

Sadie shook her head and speared a bite of eggs. She raised them to her mouth but suddenly tipped her head and glanced out the door. "Charley is a bit later this morning, ain't so? And I don't know how you can drink hot tea when it's like an oven in here," she groused as she resumed eating her eggs.

Sheila looked up anxiously. "Will you listen to me recite the Bible verse I'm trying to memorize? I need to practice saying it for the next time I see Abijah."

Sadie stopped in mid-chew and looked at Sheila like the girl had suddenly sprouted from the wooden chair. "Now, that will certainly do some good." She scooted her chair closer. "I'd like to hear it."

Betsie raised her eyebrows "You would?"

Sadie swallowed the bite of egg, nodded, and folded her hands in her lap. "Of course, don't be silly. Go ahead, Sheila, and don't be bashful. Speak up good and loud." She glanced toward the door again.

"Okay, here I go." Sheila closed her eyes. "'For God so loved the world that He gave His only begotten Son, that whosoever believeth in him should not perish, but have everlasting life.' John 3:16." She savored the words. "I love that verse. I was thinking a lot about it just before I got saved."

Sadie's eyes widened. "Got saved from what?"

Betsie cast a scowl at her sister, but Sadie took no notice.

"Saved from sin, of course. Oh, yeah. Betsie did tell me your church says it differently. At my church—better yet, in the Bible, it says you're saved when you accept Jesus' sacrifice for the forgiveness of your sins. The whole story is right there in that verse. It's really special because you can be sure, you know? 'That whosoever believeth should not perish, but have everlasting life,' it says. And I want Abijah to have everlasting life for sure," she said through gritted teeth, "even if he was mean to me for no reason."

"You're very kind to him after the way he treated you, Sheila," Betsie began, but she stopped. Sadie was smiling like a cat that got into the cream. As she watched, her sister pushed back her plate and tied on her bonnet.

"I have to go to work now," Sadie informed Sheila. "But thank you for sharing about being saved. It sure was interesting to hear." She smiled in the direction of the door and raised her voice slightly. "Right, Charley?"

CHAPTER 16

" . . . be sure your sin will find you out."
—NUMBERS 32:23, QUOTED IN BETSIE'S JOURNAL

BETSIE'S HEART PLUMMETED. Charley stood on the step. Sheila waved at him and resumed her breakfast.

"Sadie, wait for me in the buggy," he directed in *Deitsh*. "Betsie, I would have a word with you," he said with a crook of his finger.

Betsie joined him outside, her gaze downcast. "What is it, Charley?" she asked, even though she had a good idea.

"Why are you listening as Sheila speaks of being saved?" he asked. "What she says goes directly against what we believe. You must be more responsible and stop her, Betsie, especially since your parents fell under the same delusion," he cautioned. "I have been plenty lenient in allowing her to stay here without consulting Jonas. Must I go to him after all?"

"No, don't!"

"No? Once you seemed happy when I told you I would be the one talking to our bishop from now on, and not my mother."

Betsie took a deep breath. "Jonas knows by now that Sheila is here, Charley. The Yutzys knew about her already. Word spreads quickly, even without a telephone." She shrugged. "Surely she is allowed to believe as she pleases. Unless maybe you think she should join the Amish?" she teased gently.

Thunderclouds gathered on Charley's brow. "Must I remind you that this is no laughing matter? Either see to it that there is no more proud talk of being saved, or I will speak with Jonas, because in our community, the only 'saving' that needs to be done is to save you from yourself and the error of your ways." He stepped closer and lowered his voice. "You know I care about what happens to you, Betsie. It seems you are becoming more like the English every day."

Betsie made an impatient gesture. "I didn't seek the girl out! She was brought to me, I believe, under the guidance of the good Lord."

"I see." Charley folded his muscular forearms into a formidable barrier between the two of them. His eyes were like blue ice. "And was it 'the guidance of the good Lord' that brought you an English book of poems and a letter from this girl's brother?"

Betsie caught her breath. *Sadie.* She must have told Charley what she heard when she listened on the stairs that night. It appeared that the truce between them was entirely one-sided.

Betsie felt a muscle in her cheek twitch. Oh, how confrontations *ferhoodled* her. She balled her fists against her hips to keep her hands from shaking. "I didn't seek out a letter from Michael, if that is what you mean. How can I control who mails letters to me? The book is here for safekeeping, not for a present. Yes, Michael is the one who wrote to me from Tennessee. But there he will stay, so you don't have to be jealous of him."

Charley's eyes widened. He was so startled at her boldness that he backed up abruptly and would have toppled down the steps if Betsie had not reached to steady him. She clung to his work-roughened hand.

"Charley, you are the one who I want to marry. Don't let's argue this way. Can't you trust me to do what's right?" Betsie pleaded.

"I thought I could." He withdrew his hand. "But now I am not so sure. Tell me, Betsie, will you try to keep Sheila from talking about being saved?" He waited for her answer.

"I will do my best, Charley."

With a slight nod, he turned to go, but when he reached the driveway, he turned again. "Will you promise not to answer the letter you received?"

Betsie searched his face, aware that he had taken to heart her half-serious jab about jealousy. "I haven't answered him and I don't mean to. You are the one I care about."

His eyes softened. "That is good to hear."

She rubbed her forehead as he walked away. "Wait! Charley, I meant to tell you first thing that Abijah has run away from Eli's and he's not little any more, quite stubborn, in fact. Things didn't go so well and he ran off angry a while ago." She skimmed down the steps to stand in front of him. "*Dat* would have been able to handle him, but I need your help. Abijah said he was going fishing with Levi Yutzy. After you drop Sadie off, can you drive to the covered bridge on Axe Handle Road and talk with him? Bije will listen to you. I know he will. Everyone at church respects you, whether young or old. Can you talk to him for me? Tell him we must work together and not quarrel?" She looked up into his handsome face.

Charley flashed his teeth in a smile. "*Jah*, of course I'll take care of it. You can count on me."

"That's a load off my mind," Betsie sighed. "*Denki*. And Charley . . . if I do get another letter from Tennessee, even though I never asked for one . . . I won't so much as open it. I promise."

"You've made me very happy. I wouldn't ask if I didn't care so much for you. You know that, Betsie."

"*Jah*. I do know," she whispered.

She waved as he and Sadie drove off together, her sister's bonnet hiding her face. Betsie leaned against the maple tree and slid to sit at the base, her chin tucked against her chest. Surely if she kept her promise not to write to him again, Michael would forget all about her, especially since he was meeting new people and learning a new way of life. His letters would simply stop, and that would be the end of it.

Although . . . she was taking care of Michael's sister, Sheila. For Michael's parents. And Michael was her teacher, in a way. He'd taught her a bit about making harnesses, more about good writing and poetry, and a lot about how to be a good, if somewhat unconventional, friend.

But Betsie knew from experience that for each of Michael's good qualities, two or more poor ones tipped the balance the other way.

Charley—rugged, trustworthy, reliable, hard-working Charley—was as near to perfect as a Plain man could be. In fact, there was no physical comparison between the two men. Was she even supposed to think about how Charley looked? But she couldn't help it. Even Rachel Yutzy, her loyal friend, had pointed out Charley's fine appearance. And . . . how could she forget? Charley was Amish and Michael would never be, so that settled that.

Lost in thought, Betsie stood and wandered to the driveway, barely registering that her hemline drabbled through grass damp from last night's rain. Listlessly she pulled a few straggly weeds behind the mailbox post, checking for car and buggy traffic before she stepped into the road to weed the front. As she straightened, she noticed that the mailbox was hanging open. She pitched the weeds in the ditch, wiped her hands on her apron, and started to slam it shut.

To her surprise, a letter lay on the bottom of the box. Betsie squinted to make sure there were no spiders and drew out the envelope, her heart pounding as she read the Tennessee postmark. Another letter from Michael?

Her first thought was that Michael must be awfully bored to write another letter so soon. Her second was that she knew she was going to open the letter, despite her promise to Charley.

She ripped open the envelope, fingers trembling as she drew out and unfolded a single sheet of notebook paper. The message was brief.

"Dear Pippa, Just dropping a line to say I mailed a package to you yesterday. When you get it, would you please reply right away? I could really use a friendly ear. Yours, Michael."

Betsie frowned. Michael's anxiety fairly crackled off the page. She flipped the paper over, but there was nothing more to read. She flexed the envelope to peek inside, instinctively moving away from the road as the familiar rumble of a moving van approached from behind. Her damp skirts flapped with the van's passing as she stared at the paper.

"'I could really use a friendly ear,'" she read aloud. "Why, I wonder?" Betsie mused.

"What are you talking about?"

Betsie's heart practically leapt into her throat. She whipped around and there was Charley. The van that passed must have drowned out the sound of clopping hooves and buggy wheels, because Charley had already pulled off the road and now stood at his horse's head.

"Charley! You scared me," she chided, her voice shaky. She lowered her hand and nestled the letter and the envelope amidst the folds of her skirt. "I thought you were going to find Abijah and talk to him for me."

His gaze was direct as he walked toward her. "I stopped by Yutzys' and Naomi told me to try the duck pond instead of the covered bridge. I am on my way there now. You can depend on me, Betsie." He glanced toward her hidden hand. "But can I depend on you? Have you already broken the promise that you made just a few short minutes ago?"

Betsie opened her mouth to deny it, but she couldn't. She nodded her head, hot and cold all at once, and handed the letter to him.

Charley took it without examining the contents and stared at the ground, his jaw muscle twitching. When he looked up at her, she read longing in his eyes, but duty was there, too. Suddenly he ripped Michael's letter down the middle, realigning and shredding the paper to bits. Disgust was written on his face as he hurled the fragments, which sprinkled the ditch in a white shower. Then he climbed into the buggy and drove on without so much as a backward glance.

CHAPTER 17

"I'm so glad we're going to church together, Betsie!"

Betsie glanced at Sheila. The girl's smile lit up a hazy Sunday despite the dark smudges under her brown eyes.

She forced herself to respond pleasantly as they walked past many buggies toward Sol and Ellie Beiler's barn. "I'm glad, too."

It was useless to ask Sadie and Abijah to chime in with reassurance. Stony silence radiated from the pair of them as they brought up the rear.

Not that it had been silent the night before. Sheila had asked to go to church with the siblings and that had led to a fight that escalated like a barn afire. Long after Sheila had climbed the stairs in tears, Sadie and Abijah continued to berate Betsie for even entertaining the notion of an English girl going to meeting with them. They'd objected to her English clothing nearly as much as they'd objected to her foreign beliefs.

Finally Betsie, beside herself with anger at the suggestion that Sheila be left alone while the three Troyers went to the meeting, stormed that Sheila was going with them and that was the end of it. Then she'd dug out an old dress for Sheila to wear, since the single dress she'd packed was most certainly a miniskirt. True, *Mem's* old dress nearly dragged the ground when Sheila put it on, but the length would partially hide her knees socks and bare knees, not to mention her grubby tennis shoes. The only other concession was to arrange the girl's hair in a lady-like bun instead of the ever-present ponytail. The fringe of hair Sheila called her bangs would have to remain.

Even after all the turmoil, it was good to be here for worship. Sheila adjusted her knee socks, which promptly sagged to her ankles again. "I hope you don't get in trouble for bringing me," she fretted.

Betsie ignored Sadie's scoff and took a steadying breath. "Don't worry, dear heart. Imitate me. Keep your eyes open and your mouth shut. I will help you as much as I can. What's important to remember is that we are worshipping the good Lord, so no talking or fidgeting. If you have questions, ask me at home later. If you do all those things, there will be no trouble." She wished she were as sure as she sounded. Sheila nodded, her eyes huge.

"I told you we were going to be late," Abijah growled as he pushed past them to join the group of single men, including a somber Charley. He ignored her, although he certainly had a smile and a nod for Minerva Beachy.

I shouldn't have opened Michael's letter after I told Charley I wouldn't. I don't want to lose him. Chastened, Betsie turned away in time to intercept a guilt-stricken glance from Levi Yutzy as he fell into line behind Abijah. In a flash, she knew what Rachel's brother had been hiding in his haymow the other day—not a transistor radio, but Abijah. She watched as her self-assured brother took his place with the single men, unmindful of his old Sunday trousers that flapped an inch above his ankles.

Sadie nudged her impatiently and Betsie stumbled forward. Goodness, the women were already filing in, each in her proper place as was fitting. Thank the good Lord there was no time left for questions from the other ladies, although plenty of looks were cast askance at the English girl. Filled with gratitude, Betsie guided Sheila to the women's side of the barn, which had been freshly whitewashed and swept clean of all dirt and cobwebs to accommodate the service, since Sol's house was not large enough. She grimaced to see an open seat directly in front of Mattie Yoder, but she indicated the backless wooden bench with a sigh and Sheila sat obediently, reverent and ready for worship. How different this meeting was from the English revival she'd attended with Sheila. The girl fidgeted a bit and Betsie nudged her with a knee, a silent reminder to sit still. Sheila nodded and leaned forward slightly to gaze at the men, seated separately from the women. When the men removed their hats as one, Sheila shouldered Betsie and nodded toward Charley's blond head. Betsie merely raised her eyebrows. The girl mouthed a silent, "Oh, yeah," and faced forward, hands once more folded devoutly in her lap.

The slow, almost mournful singing began, of course without accompaniment. Behind them, Mattie struck a particularly sour note and Betsie winced when Sheila clapped her hands over her ears. A vigorous nudge and down came the hands. A long while later, the first hymn ended and the second one, *Lob Lied,* began. Betsie saw Sheila's eyes widen at the prospect of more songs that lasted just as long as the first, but thankfully the girl held her peace.

At last it was time for the solemnity of congregational prayer. Betsie knelt and Sheila immediately followed suit. With her eyes dutifully closed, Betsie couldn't observe her charge, but she could feel that not a muscle moved. Prayer time she understood.

When the first sermon began, the sonorous high German of the *Biewel* scriptures seemed to lull the girl. Gradually her head drooped, snapped to attention, and drooped again until it thumped against Betsie's shoulder. The rap of skull on shoulder blade sufficed as a wake-up. Sheila straightened, blinked like an owl, and rubbed her head before focusing her bleary eyes on the pulpit. She reminded Betsie of the poodle in *Tom Sawyer,* the dog that wandered into the church service and drowsily sat down on Tom's pinch bug. *Ki-yi!* He'd sailed down the aisle and back again, a "woolly comet," in Twain's words. She bit her lip to restrain a smile.

This would never do. What must the good Lord think of her? Ashamed, Betsie composed herself and glanced at the candidates for baptism, seated on the first row as they listened to the morning's second sermon. Rachel hunched in an attitude of submission like the other candidates. The speaker droned on, drifting through the story of

Noah's ark, the children of Israel crossing the Red Sea, and then every New Testament story that mentioned water and baptism. The barn rustled with weird echoes that made it difficult to hear the preaching. Betsie had to admit that if she didn't know practically by heart how the service progressed, she'd be as lost as Sheila must be right now, especially during the parts conducted in high German.

But who was she kidding? Poor Sheila would even be lost during the parts in *Deitsh*. And was she imagining it, or was Jonas staring right at her? But she had no time to dwell on the bishop, for Sheila nudged her again and mouthed, "How much longer?"

She held up two fingers in her lap. The peace sign, Michael had called it. Maybe the familiar gesture would give Sheila peace.

"Minutes?" Sheila's smile was glad.

Betsie gave her head a slight shake and Sheila's eyebrows raised until they disappeared behind her bangs. "*Hours?*"

Her nod was almost imperceptible but Sheila wilted like a potted plant in a dry spell. Why had she fought to bring this oh, so joyful girl to a solemn, lengthy service conducted in a foreign tongue?

At last, Rachel and the other candidates knelt and responded to the familiar questions. Was it Betsie's imagination or was there more emphasis on the fourth and final question, the one where the candidates promised to obey the *Ordnung*? Surely it was more important to focus on Jesus. Wasn't it?

She watched as the candidates knelt. Jonas cupped his hands above each candidate's head and a deacon poured a dab of water for baptism from a cup he'd filled from a small pail. As Jonas released the water to baptize the first person in the name of the Father, the Son, and the Holy Ghost, Betsie noticed that Sheila brightened for the first time. After baptism, Jonas raised each man to his feet to administer a handshake and the kiss of peace, at which Sheila wrinkled her nose. His wife followed suit with Rachel and the other women.

Finally, the service was over. Once everyone migrated outside, Charley nodded coolly at Betsie from across the yard before he scooped up an adoring Jakob Beiler and swooped him high in the air while Sol and Ellie beamed to hear their small son's giggles.

Like *Mem* always says, babies know when someone loves them. Oh, what a good father Charley will make. Her heart warmed. She eagerly tracked Charley's progress as he made his way in her direction.

"Yes, it sure is a hot one," she heard him say. He and Sol Beiler shook their heads as they searched the brassy sky for signs of relief.

"Hey, Charley!" Silas Yutzy caught Charley's eye before he could stir another step, and both were soon engrossed in a conversation about trimming a work horse's overgrown hooves. Betsie noticed that although Silas was older, he listened with respect to what Charley had to say, thumping him on the back when the conversation ended.

Just look at him, she thought with approval as she and Sheila filled their plates with good food. Each person rated an equal share of Charley's time and attention. Young or old, congenial or ornery, he made them all feel special. Someone like Michael, a rebel if Betsie had ever known one, couldn't possibly compare.

When at last Charley was close enough to touch had she dared, she started to say hello. But before she could greet him, pretty Minerva Beachy trod on Betsie's toe as she swooped in between.

"Oh, Charley, I baked a batch of those Monster Cookies you like," Minnie cooed, batting her lashes over her brown eyes. "Come find me after you eat and maybe I'll share some."

"That's mighty thoughtful of you, Min. Maybe I'll do that." The two of them detoured around Betsie and strolled toward the tables, chatting and laughing.

Betsie inclined her head. Apparently Min had noticed Charley's appearance, too. In fact, she mused, all the unmarried girls were watching Charley's every move like a pack of ravenous wild dogs. She frowned as she located a seat for herself and Sheila.

"Mmm! These are those special church sandwiches you told me about the first day I met you, huh? So good!" Sheila took a huge bite and watched the crowd happily.

Betsie nodded absently and reached to swipe a blob of peanut butter spread from the corner of Sheila's mouth. "That's right."

"And you know what?" Sheila brandished a fork. "I can't stand regular pickles, but these pickles are yummy. What kind are they?"

Betsie noticed that Ruthie Miller, Katie's big sister, stared at Sheila as she chattered away in English. After sending Ruthie an apologetic smile and a helpless shrug, she dug into her own pickles. "They're bread-and-butter pickles, dear heart. There's lots of sugar in them, so they're sweet, like you."

Sheila grinned. "Aw, heck. Hey, lookit! I see Katie!" She crammed the rest of her sandwich in her mouth and chewed mightily before speaking again. "I can't believe I know someone here. Can I go say hi, Betsie?"

Pleased that the girl was taking the initiative this time, Betsie said, "Of course. You don't have to stay with me. You'll be safe. When you want to find me again, I'll be waiting under this mulberry tree. See? The leaves are shaped a bit like mittens."

"Oh, I know what a mulberry tree looks like. Grandma Sullivan had one in her yard and we used to sit in the shade but it got torched when her farm house burned down. I'll see you, Betsie! Hey, Katie! Katie Miller!" Sheila waved with great energy and hitched her too-long skirts as she sprinted to catch up with her new friend.

Slightly relieved at the prospect of a break from the eternal font of enthusiasm that was Sheila, Betsie poked Ruthie. "How is your newest quilt top coming along?" she asked innocently.

"Oh, coming along quite nice." Eager to talk about her new pattern, Ruthie took the bait and Betsie smiled to herself. If Charley could greet neighbors and make small talk, so could she.

She listened with only half an ear and an occasional nod as Ruthie held forth for a good ten minutes.

"Now, I also pieced a Broken Star in jewel tones on a black background, so the colors glow. But you'll have to decide for yourself which one you like better when I invite everyone over for a quilting—"

Somebody nudged Betsie and grabbed her sleeve.

"Come quick," Rachel was hissing in her ear. "It's Sheila. Mattie's got a hold of her. Something about her behavior in church."

"I must go, Ruthie." Her heart in her throat, Betsie leapt from the hard bench and sprinted to where a crowd congregated near Ellie Beiler's purple petunias, the bright splash of color carefully planted and trained to look like water cascading from the mouth of a tin bucket that glinted in the sunlight. On tiptoe, Betsie glimpsed Sheila, eyes wide as she cowered against the siding, trapped by Mattie Yoder.

"I saw you with my own eyes, fidgeting and falling asleep during the sermon. Can you deny it?" Mattie prodded at the girl with a bony finger.

"No, but I—"

"What? Such sass, talking back to your elders that-a-way. And just look at your hair."

"What's wrong with my hair?" Tears welled up in Sheila's eyes as she brushed her bangs aside, but Mattie showed no sympathy.

"Chopped off in the front instead of letting it grow long to give glory to the good Lord, that's what's wrong with it. Don't think a hand-me-down *Kapp* can hide your scorn."

"I love God." Betsie heard Sheila's voice low and clear as she pushed her way through the crowd to reach her side. "And I love Jesus."

She was close enough now to catch the hiss as Mattie inhaled a shocked breath. "I never heard the like. A girl like you will not go to heaven. Do you want to know why?" Mattie loomed over Sheila, her thin lips pulled into a grim smile.

"Mattie, stop!" Betsie cried. Trapped behind a couple of strapping youth who were enjoying the show, she looked wildly about. Where was Charley? Why didn't he control his mother as he had promised?

But it was too late. "It's because you're English, that's why. And there's not one thing you can do about that." Mattie planted her hands on her hips, her face radiating satisfaction that she'd done her duty.

Betsie surged forward to sweep the girl into the protection of her arms, but Sheila shook her head. Pale and trembling, she faced Mattie.

"Y-you were r-right about everything you s-said." She straightened, her freckles and chicken pox scar standing out in vivid relief against her ashen skin. "Everything except this: Jesus loves me. Even if I die this very minute, even with all you say I've done wrong, He loves me and I *will* go to heaven because He paid the price and I'm saved from my sins. I'm sure of that."

Marveling at Sheila's bravery, Betsie glanced at Mattie. Speechless for once in her life, Charley's mother glared at the girl who had dared to stand up to her. Then she turned and pushed through the throng, her dark attire flapping like buzzard wings.

We'll get that visit from Jonas now. I'm sure of it. As anger smoldered, Betsie scanned the faces in the crowd and was gratified to notice a few dear souls who clearly sympathized with the English girl who'd suffered Mattie's venomous tongue-lashing, among them sweet Ellie Beiler, her usually cheery countenance troubled. At Ellie's side stood Katie Miller, fists doubled and black eyes snapping sparks at Mattie's back.

Stony faced, she guided a trembling Sheila toward their buggy. There they found Rachel, tears rolling down her cheeks as she paced forlornly back and forth. Sam shifted from his left foot to his right as he watched, powerless to comfort his intended.

"I'm sorry, Betsie. I tried to get Sheila away from there, truly I did, but Mattie was too much for me. I'm so sorry." Rachel wrung her dimpled hands.

"It's not your fault, Rachel. You're a wonderful friend and you did what you could. Go to Sam, now. Look how worried he is about you. We all know no one can stop Mattie once she gets going." Not even the one who promised me that he would. "Come, Sheila, let's go home."

CHAPTER 18

"The more you know, the more you know
you don't know."
—FANNIE TROYER, QUOTED IN BETSIE'S JOURNAL

"WHY DOES SHE hate me so much? What have I ever done to her?"

Betsie guided Judith along the road for home with a tearful Sheila huddled tight against her side. "She's a difficult person to get along with, dear heart. Even her own son has trouble with her. Please don't take it so hard."

"I can't help it. No one has ever said anything that mean to me before." Sheila rubbed her eyes with grimy fists. "I want to go home," she whispered.

"Finally," Abijah muttered.

"What did you say?"

He straightened. "I said *finally*. She don't belong here and you know it, Betsie. Now she knows it, too. Send her home before Jonas gets a hold of her is what I would do if I were you."

"Stop talking about me like I'm not even here. For your information, there's no one at home to send me to, but guess what?" Sheila leaned toward Abijah, who crowded into Sadie, who shoved him back toward Sheila. "I changed my mind. No mean old witch is going to scare me away. I'm staying. And guess what else?" She smiled and batted her eyes. "I'm going to pray for you every day, *Bije*. And you can't stop me. So there." She stuck out her tongue.

"You tryin' to catch flies with that tongue, like an old green frog?" Abijah retorted, and Sadie giggled.

Instead of replying, Sheila folded her hands and closed her eyes. "Dear Lord, please forgive and save Abijah from his sins so we can both live in heaven forever 'n' ever, amen." She smirked and settled into the buggy seat.

"The good Lord won't answer a prayer like that."

"Sure He will. You wait and see, Sadie. And don't worry, I'm praying for you, too."

With that, the girl hummed a happy tune that caused Judith to swivel her ears. Betsie thought she recalled the chorus from the revival in Hilliard, something about flying away by and by. She grinned. Whatever else people said about Sheila's faith, it had sustained the girl during some very tough times.

Dawn the next morning found Betsie ensconced in the dimly lit kitchen, where she'd been waiting for nearly an hour after tending to the horses. She'd written in her notebook by candlelight first. It was nice, she decided, having time to sort out her thoughts on paper before breakfast.

Next, she'd debated on how to start a letter to Michael. "Hey" was how he'd always greeted her, but that didn't sound right. "Dear" . . . well, Michael wasn't her dear. But how silly. Every letter she'd ever written had begun that way.

"Dear Michael, How are you? I am fine." No. She ripped out another sheet. With her pen poised, she pictured Michael as she'd last seen him: loaning her a denim jacket that smelled like him, *stroobly haar*, bell-bottom jeans. She recalled his smile, with one side of his mouth quirked upward like he knew everything she was thinking. She remembered the sparks she felt when he touched her hand and said good-bye . . .

Dear Michael, This is to let you know that your sister is safe
with me until you or your parents come home. Sheila's doing

very well and I like having her here with me. My sister Sadie—
remember her?—is still adjusting to having an English girl in
the house, but she's coming along.

Betsie nibbled the pen cap. "Coming along" was an exaggeration
and no mistake.

Did I ever tell you about my little brother Abijah? I call him
little, but he's fourteen and near as tall as you. He was in
Missouri helping our brother Eli, but he ran away and hitched
a ride home. He and Sheila didn't get along so well at first and
they still don't, but your sister is praying about it and it will
all work out in time.

If I live long enough, she wanted to add, but didn't.

It's fine that you sent me the book of poems for safekeeping.
I haven't had time to read it yet because *Mem* and *Dat* are
still gone (please pray they come home) and I am mother and
father both to three young people, but I look forward to reading it. I know if you like the book it will be good, because I
really like the Emily book. As she says, "There is no Frigate
like a Book to take us Lands Away, Nor any Coursers like a
page of Prancing Poetry" but you know that. Emily didn't
let anyone tell her how to write, that's plain to see, what with
capital letters every which way. Speaking of somebody telling
someone how to write, I probably shouldn't be writing to you
at all, because Charley wouldn't like it, but I figure this letter
I'm writing is more of a business letter, not a personal letter,
so he won't mind.

I hope you are enjoying life at The Farm. It doesn't sound
like someplace I'd want to live, but we are not much alike,
ain't so? Except I'm starting to enjoy writing. I write in my
notebook every day like you said I should, the same notebook
you gave back to me after reading what I wrote.

Betsie squirmed. Writing a letter to Michael was complicated enough without reminding him of her descriptions of him and life in the Sullivan house. Memories of him snatching away her notebook, holding it far above her head and out of reach, bopping her one, even . . . did he think he was a caveman, clubbing her like hairy old Alley Oop in the funny papers she'd once seen? Her fingers itched to cross out everything after "like you said I should," but she didn't want to start over again, so she let it stand.

> Sometimes I wonder what it would be like to write poems or even books. I like to read, after all, but I know there's more to writing than that. Being a writer like Laura Ingalls Wilder or Mark Twain or you is something I dream about if I have a spare minute or two—when your sister is not asking me questions, that is. She's a great hand to ask questions!
>
> It's no use for an Amish girl like me to dream about writing books, though. It's enough for me to work in the harness shop until I get married, or I could be like Sadie and work in a bakery, or I could even teach school. But after I join the church and marry, my work will be raising and feeding my family and helping my husband with the farm work. All my friends have the same dreams. And so do I, I guess. There will be no time for writing books once I marry.
>
> I hope this letter finds you healthy. I can't imagine how you are getting along without your yellow jacket car. I am getting along without it fine, but

But what, Betsie?

> I miss you

There, she'd owned it. No matter how much he'd teased her, she still enjoyed talking to Michael. He was a good friend, but she'd never admit it to Sheila. No, the girl was already convinced that Betsie plus

Michael equaled a match made in heaven. A broad smile covered her face at the very idea. *I miss you . . .*

*I miss you*r teasing. Be careful down there in Tennessee.

She signed her name and popped the letter into an envelope.

She huffed out the candle and dashed through the dewy grass to deposit the letter in the mailbox and put up the flag. As she entered the house, the stairs creaked and she slipped into a chair. A moment later, Sadie's silhouette tiptoed through the shadows toward the pantry.

"Guder mariye, Schweschder."

"Oh!" Sadie jumped, one hand over her heart. "Betsie, what are you doing in the dark? I thought you were still in bed."

"I pulled the covers over my pillow so you would think so." She patted the chair next to her. "I need to talk with you, sister. Sit with me."

Sadie crossed her arms and scowled. "The talking you should have done was to ask me first if that English girl could live in our house. And I would have told you no, just like I told you not to take her to the service. But you didn't listen to me, and Mattie Yoder sure lit into her. At least, that is what I heard."

"Anyone who would pick on a child is not worth the breath it takes to mention her name. Although Sheila is English, she is more like us than you think. She's lost her parents, too." Betsie clasped her hands together. "Deep down, we are the same as her, Sadie. She needs a home until her parents return. Can't we share ours with her? We have plenty of room and she's awfully sweet."

"Sweet or not, it makes no difference." Sadie's blue eyes flashed. "Have you forgotten what Charley said? 'Have nothing to do with the English.' Well, I don't call what you have done 'nothing.' Why do you completely ignore what he says to do, Betsie? If I were you, I'd listen to a man like Charley instead of rejecting his good sense and making a fool of yourself into the bargain. Did you even think about how much trouble we are going to get into with the bishop when he finally drops up? Or do you ever think of anyone but yourself?"

Betsie clapped both hands to her head. "But Sadie! How is it thinking of myself when I'm trying to help a much younger girl deal with the loss of her parents? The awful pain I feel when I think of *Mem* and *Dat* grows with each day that passes, and I know you feel it, too. Wouldn't the good Lord want us to ease Sheila's burden if we are able?" she pleaded.

Sadie sniffed. "I don't presume to know what the good Lord thinks of an English girl's problems. And anyway, would you help this girl out if it weren't for that fancy brother of hers? Writing letters to the likes of him—"

"I knew it. It *was* you we heard that night." Betsie narrowed her eyes. "You were eavesdropping when I read the letter to Sheila."

"So what if I was?" Sadie flushed an unbecoming red.

"I'll tell you so what. Michael and I are friends only." An image of his quirky smile tugged at her heart. She banished it. "I needed to let him know his sister was in good hands. But why am I explaining this to you? You don't need to stick your *Wonnernaus* in my private business."

"*Wonnernaus!* Someone must keep watch over your wild ways, now that *Mem* and *Dat* aren't here."

"Wild ways?" Betsie sputtered. "Do you know who you sound like, Sadie? Mattie Yoder, that's who, and you will become a nasty cackling hen like her if you continue to harden your heart this way."

She covered her mouth, aghast at the words that had popped out. "Sadie, Sadie. I didn't mean it. We must not be at each others' throats. We have more important work to do, like praying together to bring our parents and Lovina home."

"The good Lord will not answer our prayers as long as that English girl is in this house. That's what I think." Sadie's back was as stiff as a fence post. She snatched her bonnet from the peg and settled it into place. "And now I must go. Charley is here to drive me to the bakery. We are fortunate he still drops up to help us out, what with *Mem* and *Dat* shunned and your foolishness. Plenty of girls would like to marry him. Minnie Beachy would snatch him up in an instant."

"Sadie, wait!" Betsie followed her sister out the door, but it was too late. She watched Sadie march across the grass to the waiting farm wagon. Charley helped her sister into the wagon and drove away without so much as a wave good-bye. Betsie's eyes smarted. *Mem* and *Dat*, I don't know how you did it. Whatever made me think I could raise three *Yungi* when I am yet one myself? I never realized what a lot of patience and skill it takes to raise children who obey the *Ordnung* and are a credit to their parents. Would that the good Lord would teach me how.

Betsie flipped irritably through her notebook and slapped it shut. How fruitless to outline the harness business for Nelson! The handbook she wanted would contain every scrap of *Mem*'s homespun wisdom and every one of *Dat*'s favorite *Biewel* verses. She craved their guidance to help her smooth things over with Abijah and Sadie—and yes, Charley, too. Even Sheila, with all her "and a little child shall lead them" faith, would benefit from Noah's and Fannie's loving guidance, if only they were here.

"What an opportunity I missed. I should have written down every word they said when I had them here," Betsie mourned. Still, there was no use crying over spilt milk, one axiom of *Mem*'s that she did remember. She crammed the notebook into a drawer and slammed it shut.

"That's the way, Betsie!"

She whirled to see Abijah grin his approval.

"What do you mean by that?"

"Enough of books and such. Who needs learning? Not me, that's for sure." He crossed the kitchen, peeled back a checkered napkin, and palmed two biscuits from the breadbasket. He crammed one in his mouth and sprayed crumbs as he declared, "Enough of chores, too. I'm going to Levi's. Ah, ah," he cautioned as Betsie drew herself up to protest. "You are not my mother. So I can do what I like."

He smiled like an angel and was about to chomp the second biscuit, but Betsie snatched the bread from his hand and flourished it under his nose.

"If you don't work, you don't eat. We must train Fledge today and I need your help. Go out and hitch him up for us. And watch out, he bites and kicks." She bit into the biscuit with gusto.

Abijah watched Betsie chew and swallow. Then he shrugged, walked nonchalantly to the counter, lifted the napkin again, and stuffed several biscuits into his pockets. Betsie moved to block the doorway, arms folded and lips pursed.

"Do you think you could stop me, *Schweschder*, if I truly wished to go out that way?" Abijah asked with a scornful laugh. "Lucky for you, the old maple tree that scratches against my window is plenty close enough for me to shinny down whenever I want to leave this house."

He backed toward the stairs with a nasty smirk. The next instant, he lost his footing and sprawled backward, slamming his shoulder against the doorjamb. He looked wildly around him.

"Did you enjoy your trip?" Sheila grinned as she withdrew her foot.

Betsie covered her mouth with one hand and attempted to keep her eyes grave.

"What do you think you're doing, Froggy?" Abijah's voice cracked with indignation.

"I hope you aren't hurt too bad," Sheila said sweetly. "I was only fooling, but I guess the Amish can't take it too well." She mimicked Abijah's earlier apology in triumph.

Abijah's brows drew together. He opened his mouth and scolded Sheila with *Deitsh* words that scorched Betsie's cheeks. She was glad that the girl didn't understand the words, although there was no mistaking the gist.

"I don't care what you say about me," the girl flashed, hands on hips, "but you should be nicer to your sister. Betsie does all the work around here. At least Sadie earns her keep, but you know what? I haven't seen you do anything but loaf." She glanced at Betsie, flushed, and squared her shoulders. "Look, I know I shouldn't have tripped you or criticized you. That's not the way Jesus wants me to act. I really am sorry for what I did. Let's call it even. Shake?"

Betsie willed her brother to take the proffered hand, but his arms remained pinned to his sides.

"Oh, you think it's that easy?" He shook his head. "Well, maybe I am lazy, but I do know what Jesus wants me to do, and that's to join the Amish church. And when I do, at least I will have a living hope of going to heaven someday."

Betsie cringed. "No, Bije," she whispered under her breath.

Sheila's features softened. "Honest, Abijah?" she asked eagerly. "That's great! My prayers are working! Look, let's be friends. I've been praying for that, too."

"You pray?" The boy snorted. "Your prayers are useless. You think you're so smart with your fancy books and going to high school someday, but you don't you know anything. Listen to me and I will teach you a lesson." He put his hands on his hips and leaned toward her. "I stand by what I said before. Nobody English can ever go to heaven. Ever." He spun on his heel and ascended the steps two at a time.

"Sheila, dear heart." Betsie gave her shoulder an awkward pat. "Don't pay him any mind."

"But he said the same thing Charley's mother said to me at church. Is that what you believe about us?" Sheila flung herself into a chair and Amelia jumped up to touch her nose to the girl's face. "About me?"

Betsie hung her head. "Some do. But don't worry—no, let me finish," she said when Sheila tried to protest. "I've never met anyone so young whose faith I've been more sure of than yours. That is truly what I believe."

She watched as Sheila wrestled with her reassurance. It was easy to see that, though mollified, the girl was still deeply troubled.

"I have an idea. How would you like to visit your friend Debbie?" Betsie asked suddenly, thankful for the inspiration. "Didn't your *dat* say they were on vacation last week? They should be home by now, and as long as her parents are willing, I believe Debbie would be glad to see you. What do you think?"

Sheila's eyes blazed like twin stars. "Honest?" She hugged Betsie. "If I get to come back here and stay with you afterwards, that would be great! I want to be here when my dad comes home, even if it means giving up time with Debbie, and boy, do I miss her! Wait a minute. How will we get in touch with Debbie? You don't have a phone, remember?"

"*Ach*, I've been needing to go into town to the fabric store since I must sew my own *nayva hokkah* dress to help Rachel out. There are pay phones in Plain City, you know, and you will be placing the phone call, not me," Betsie informed her. "If you can recall the Keiths' phone number," she couldn't help teasing.

Sheila laughed. "Are you kidding? I could dial it in my sleep! When are we going?"

"Right after breakfast," Betsie promised. "That is, if you will do the breakfast dishes while I hitch up Judith. I've got the dishwater ready."

They heard a thump and a scrape on the side of the house. Startled, they ran to the door. A moment later, they watched Abijah drop from the tree and limp across the yard.

Sheila made a face at his retreating figure. "Sure, I can clean up on my own, Betsie. In fact, I'd do anything to see Debbie again. Anything except wash Abijah's smelly underwear." She held her nose with a wicked grin.

Betsie laughed so hard she hung on to the counter for support. Laughter quickly turned to tears; raising three *Yungi* was a heavy burden. Quickly she turned her back, took a deep breath, and dabbed away the moisture with a corner of her apron. "I'm glad you will have some time with your friend, but I will miss you."

"For real, Betsie?" Sheila's voice grew wistful.

Betsie nodded briskly. "For real. Now, let's eat."

CHAPTER 19

"For my heart was hot and restless,
And my life was full of care,
And the burden laid upon me
Seemed greater than I could bear."
—"The Bridge" by Henry Wadsworth
Longfellow, quoted in Betsie's journal

"Gosh, I wish my bee sting hadn't set us back a couple of days, Betsie." Sheila grimaced, one hand cradling her sore foot. "It helped some to soak it in vinegar and baking soda a couple of times, but it just about killed me to put off visiting Debbie. I feel bad that you're behind on your dress, too. But," she said as she bounced on the buggy seat, "I'm so glad Debbie was home when I called today."

Betsie held the reins steady as she drove away from the fabric store. "I believe you, dear heart, for it's only been an hour since you used the pay phone to call her, yet that's the fifth time you've told me you were glad."

Sheila's grin was sheepish. "It's just . . . I guess I've missed a lot of stuff while I've been here. Debbie's mom is taking us swimming all day tomorrow and later to the drive-in movie, and after that, one of our friends from school is having a slumber party Friday night and we'll listen to records and dance and then we're having Jiffy-Pop with Suicide."

Betsie started. "Suicide!"

Sheila clapped a hand over her mouth. "Gosh, Betsie, I'm sorry! I didn't mean what you think," she exclaimed. "Suicide is what you call it when you mix all different flavors of Kool-Aid together. It's so good! I bet you thought I was crazy for a minute, though. Anyway, on Saturday morning we're going shopping, but best of all I get to go to Sunday school the next day and then sit with Debbie and her family for the church service. I'm so excited!" Her chocolate brown eyes lit up with joy.

A buggy wheel rattled as Betsie surveyed Sheila curiously. "'I was glad when they said unto me, let us go into the house of the Lord.' I don't think I understood that *Biewel* verse before, but now I do. It tells exactly how you feel, ain't so?"

Sheila nodded. "Don't you feel that way when you go to your church? Or whatever you call it?"

"W-well, you see," Betsie stammered, caught off guard, "our church is—"

"Different," Sheila broke in, her expression troubled. "Now I know how different."

Betsie touched the girl's shoulder comfortingly as she watched the oncoming traffic. "It must have been difficult, being that the whole service was in another language."

"Well, yeah, that part was hard," Sheila admitted. "But even when our pastor talks about something I don't really get, I still . . . I mean . . . oh, skip it. I don't know how to explain it very well, I guess." Sheila waved her hand, suddenly intent on the passing scenery.

Betsie smiled at hearing her long-ago words of explanation on matters of faith parroted back at her. "*Jah*, I guess it's not important. The good Lord knows."

Sheila thumped the seat with her fist. "Then why did Mattie and Abijah say we, the English, can't go to heaven? I can't stop thinking about it. That's the worst thing anybody has ever said to me!"

Betsie winced. "*Ach*, dear heart, we talked about that," she soothed. "Don't pay them any mind. Mattie is Mattie, and Abijah only wanted to get your goat."

"But it hurts worse than my bee sting. I was so happy when I got saved, and Brother Burchett shared a special Bible verse that night. He said I should never forget it because it would help me." She sat up straight in an effort to remember. "'. . . for I know whom I have believed, and am persuaded that he is able to keep that which I have committed unto him against that day.' Second Timothy 1:12. And you know what? He was right. I feel better already." She snuggled up to Betsie. "You were right, too. The good Lord knows and He won't forget me. I'm sorry I was so dumb about Mattie and Abijah and I'm not going to worry about what he said because I know he's wrong. Instead, I'm going to think about good things, like Debbie and swimming and movies and . . ."

Betsie guided Judith into her driveway, listening with only half an ear. Oh, how heavy the burden, assuming spiritual guidance for her younger siblings and now this girl. For an instant, she wondered how *Dat* had managed it, but then it hit her—he read his *Biewel* often. Prayers must have been constantly in his heart and now, she guessed, on his lips, since he'd left the Amish church. *Mem* would do the same, because she trusted *Dat* implicitly.

Her heart ached. The minute Sheila was out of the house, Betsie needed to write a letter to beg, to plead with her parents to come home. I'm almost at the end of my rope and I need their help, she thought as she handed the package of dress goods to Sheila for safekeeping. The girl chattered happily on about her plans while Betsie cared for Judith.

". . . don't you think so, Betsie?"

With a guilty start, she nodded. "*Jah*. And now we are ready to turn Judith out and go inside, and none too soon, for I think I hear a car." She paused, disconcerted. "What time did you tell Mrs. Keith to come?"

"Right away," Sheila said, suddenly bashful. "Not that I don't have fun with you. You know how much I love you. It's just—"

"I know. I missed my home and friends when I lived with you in Hilliard."

Sheila's face lit up. "Yes! That's just how it is." She sped off to meet her friend.

Betsie watched Fledge greet Judith, feeling a little lost. Wearisome as caring for *Yungi* might be, she knew she would miss Sheila. It was a good thing she had her dress to sew and Fledge to train. She glanced idly at the vegetable garden and gasped. Where had those weeds sprung from? She shook her head with a rueful smile. Oh, no, she had an idea how she would pass the time while Sheila was away. Hard work was just the cure she needed, *Mem* would say.

"Yoo-hoo! It's Betsie, isn't it?"

She stopped her woolgathering and smiled at Mrs. Keith, who emerged from a silver pickup truck with a trailer hitch. "Yes, and you are the lady who once brought me a saddle to mend. I hope you are ready for the plans these girls have made!"

Mrs. Keith chuckled and patted back her dark curls. "Nothing I haven't handled before, don't you worry. Right, Debbie?"

But Debbie and Sheila only grinned at each other in delight until Sheila tugged Debbie's hand. "Come and meet Betsie's mare and then you can help me pack." She tucked Betsie's parcel under one arm and dragged her friend along.

The pair of women watched companionably as the girls admired Judith and then raced to the house, brown ponytail and blond tresses flying.

"Those two," joshed Mrs. Keith. She grew serious. "Debbie has missed Sheila something fierce. It sure was good of you folks to take her in."

"*Ach*, it was nothing. Won't you come inside?" Betsie's cheeks grew hot. How odd to be praised for the same charitable deed that had made her family and friends, except for Rachel, so angry.

As they entered the house, Betsie saw that Sheila had carelessly tossed her parcel on the couch. She snatched it up just before Amelia nosed her way into the bag, presumably to shred the blue fabric with her sharp kitten claws.

"No, you don't," Betsie scolded her kitten. "Just let me put the fabric in our sewing corner," she apologized to Mrs. Keith. "I can't abide a *Hutsch*, I mean mess."

"That's easy to see," the woman said as she peered here and there in awe. "I have never seen a more spotless home. No cat hair, even."

"You are just saying that," Betsie answered with a pleased smile. She laid the fabric on the treadle sewing machine as thumps and giggles echoed upstairs.

"Oh, no, I'm not!" insisted Mrs. Keith. "Your mother must be a very hard worker."

To Betsie's horror, she felt a tear well up and threaten to spill over. Ashamed, she turned her back and tried to brush the tear away before Mrs. Keith saw.

There was a tactful pause. Then Mrs. Keith said, "You know, Betsie, I've been running all day and I'm simply dying for a cup of tea. Would you mind terribly if I invited myself into your kitchen and put on the kettle?"

Betsie sniffed. "I will get it. I can't let you—"

"No, I insist. You finish putting your goods away while I get things started."

By the time Betsie had regained her composure and entered the kitchen, Debbie's mother was already rooting through the icebox.

"Cold, fresh water, that's what makes the best tea. This old icebox keeps everything colder than the fancy refrigerator I have at home. My grandma sure would have smiled to see your kitchen," she added as she filled the kettle and plunked it on the hob. Her hand hovered above the surface. "That fire could be a mite hotter, though, seems to me."

She opened the damper and then added a few sticks of kindling to the firebox before grinning at Betsie. "Well, don't look so surprised! My Kentucky roots go back to Daniel Boone pioneer days. I admit I was pretty frazzled that day I met you in the harness shop, but my old mammaw would be ashamed of me if I forgot how to fix a cup of tea the old-fashioned way." She cocked her head. "But I do draw the line at rummaging through another woman's cupboards, so I'll leave you to set out the teacups for us. I take sugar if you have some handy." Mrs. Keith settled herself at the harvest table with a sigh of pleasure.

Betsie busied herself with the task, aware that she was being mothered but not minding in the least. In fact, she felt more sheltered than she had since her parents and *Dat*'s sister Lovina left. How could an English woman wearing a sleeveless pink checkered top over silly white knee pants make such a difference?

When the tea was ready, Mrs. Keith patted the seat beside her. "Sit here while I pray. Dear Lord, thank You for this chance to get to know Betsie. Bless her for what's she's done for Sheila. We thank You for this refreshment that You have provided. In Jesus' name, amen." She sipped her tea and exhaled. "Oh, that hits the spot. Now, Betsie, tell me what's troubling you. No, the girls are fine. Right now is a time for the two of us and God."

Something in the woman's warm manner opened the floodgates. When Betsie finally stopped talking about all her troubles, she took a careful sip of her tea and was amazed to find it lukewarm. Dazed, she put a hand to her forehead. "*Was in der welt?* How long have I been talking?"

Mrs. Keith glanced at her wristwatch. "Oh, only about a half hour or so, but don't you worry. After all you've been through, I'm surprised you can still function." Mrs. Keith's eyes twinkled. "Can I share something with you?"

Betsie nodded.

"Early this morning, long before Sheila called, the good Lord brought you to mind. I prayed for you before I got out of bed without knowing exactly why."

"But how can that be?"

Mrs. Keith winked. "Kid, listen. The good Lord knew you needed Him and He made me aware, that's how. But *why* you need Him might surprise you." She leaned closer. "Don't you worry about your parents or your aunt, either. They made what seems to you like a terrible choice, leaving you and your family so they could follow Jesus, but they made the right one. They'll be fine. Don't look at me like that; it's no more than the truth. Sheila knows it, too. I'm so impressed that she forgave your brother after what he said about being saved. What great faith she has for someone so young."

Betsie bounded to her feet and snatched up the teacups, the teaspoons rattling on the saucers as she carried them to the sink. How dare this woman say it was good that *Mem* and *Dat* left everything and everyone they knew? Why had she trusted Mrs. Keith with her inmost thoughts?

Betsie jutted her chin. "Sheila!" she called up the stairs. "It's time to go."

Mrs. Keith rose from the table, unruffled by Betsie's rebuff. "Well, I've enjoyed talking with you, but I've intruded on your hospitality long enough. I'll get my handbag and let myself out."

Betsie's brisk steps faltered and she let the teacups clatter into the sink. She'd expected an apology, not a gracious good-bye. How unsettling Mrs. Keith was! Even Sheila's flighty mother seemed preferable right now. At least Phyllis Sullivan had never pressed Betsie for personal details of her life. After all, it was one thing to hear the religious beliefs of a young English girl like Sheila. It was quite another to hear a grown woman spout what directly contradicted Plain teachings.

Still, Mrs. Keith had listened, really listened, while Betsie unburdened her heart. Precious few people in her life had done that lately. In fact, she could think of only one, and he was far away, not to mention off-limits.

"Wait." She hurried into the front room.

Mrs. Keith slowed with an expectant look as she looped her white handbag over one arm. "Yes?"

She shrugged. "I want you to know that our churches are very different. If Charley, the young man I told you about, heard what you shared, he would be angry. He wanted me to send Sheila away after he overheard her Bible talk." Betsie lowered her voice as the girls thundered downstairs. "But I will not. Sheila is my friend and she will stay here until her parents return, just as I promised."

Mrs. Keith shook Betsie's hand warmly. "I knew you were special from the moment I met you. You do what you know in your heart is right. Don't you dare think the good Lord made a mistake when He sent that young lady to you. Talk to Him, Betsie. He's always there, ready to help. You do believe that, right?"

Betsie opened her mouth to reply, but Sheila and Debbie burst into the room, joined hands, and hopped in a boisterous circle, laughing until they were out of breath. The tip of Amelia's nose poked from under the couch and she hissed at the commotion, which made the girls laugh even harder.

Sheila caught sight of Betsie and sobered. "I'm sorry to leave you with all the work," she said. "I didn't even make up my bed today. I'll miss you."

Betsie scoffed. "You will have so much fun in Hilliard that you will forget all about me."

"That's not true!" Debbie jerked a thumb at Sheila. "She already told me about a million times how much she will miss you. When does she have to come back, Betsie?"

Betsie studied the two girls, so happy together. "Didn't you say something about church on Sunday?" she asked Sheila.

"Ye-es, but I don't want to leave you by yourself for so long. I can come home sooner if you need me." Sheila scuffed the floor with her toe.

"I do need you and don't you forget it. But I guess I can make do until Sunday night if I try very hard. Besides, Sadie and Abijah will be here with me."

"Thanks, Betsie!" Sheila hugged her neck. "I'll tell you all about it when I get back."

"You mean you will talk my ear off." Betsie smiled. "Do you have your house key? You will need to pick up your swim trunks."

Sheila giggled. "Girls wear bathing suits! Mike wears swim trunks, except that day we washed the car he wore cutoffs."

"*Ach*, that's right." Betsie perked up. "Remember how surprised Michael was when I smacked him in the face with that sponge? And then you dumped the bucket of dirty water over his head." She grinned at the memory.

"Your brother Michael?" Mrs. Keith asked Sheila.

"Yes. I was supposed to stay with him while Dad was gone, but he's in Tennessee right now." Sheila smirked at Betsie and went on, "Want to know who he likes? I'll give you a hint—"

"Sheila!" Betsie felt her cheeks grow warm. "It's not nice to keep your friends waiting when they hurried over here to pick you up. Come now, I asked you a question. Do you have your house key?"

For answer, Sheila fished the key attached to a leather thong from her pocket and flourished it practically under Betsie's nose. "You sound like Dad!"

Mrs. Keith snapped her fingers. "Now I remember! I saw Michael with you at the revival meeting, right?" She turned to Betsie with a speculative gleam in her eye. "He sat next to you during the service." Betsie's smile faded. "*Jah*. But that was a long time ago and I really wasn't supposed to be there." She roused herself. "Sheila, you mind Mrs. Keith and I'll see you Sunday."

She held the door as the trio filed out into the muggy June air, laughing and chattering. Mrs. Keith clutched her curls and made a crazy face before she ducked into the driver's seat. Betsie laughed and waved as the three of them sped off to Hilliard.

"At last, some peace." She rubbed her temple and hoped a headache wasn't coming on. "Kitty, kitty! Amelia, you can come out now. They're gone," she coaxed, but the calico kitten ignored her. "Oh, so you are lazy today. Stay under the stuffy couch then, if you've a mind to. I have better things to do than to argue with a cat."

A letter to *Mem* and *Dat* was her number one priority. Betsie scurried to the desk. Her pen flew across the paper as she refuted everything Mrs. Keith had stated to be true, walking a thin line between taking her parents to task for leaving and begging them to come home anyway. She licked the flap so fast that the sharp edge cut her tongue. Annoyed, she carefully licked the stamp and pounded it on the envelope with her fist.

As she passed through the kitchen, she snatched *Dat's* tattered straw hat from the peg and rammed it on her throbbing head. As she trotted to the mailbox, heat shimmered from the asphalt. A few English cars cleaved the stifling air and left the teasing rush of a breeze in their wake. The high-pitched buzz of a gas-powered chainsaw reached Betsie's ears as Joe Miller's machine ripped through lumber. Nothing else stirred.

The metal mailbox was hot to her touch as she pried it open. Betsie was surprised to see several letters already lay higgledy-piggledy. She scooped them out and spied Sheila's name on top of the stack. The Boise postmark told Betsie it was probably long-anticipated word from the dear girl's parents. What a shame she wasn't here to read it right away!

She sucked in her breath. A letter from *Mem*. She longed to run upstairs and rip it open, but she decided to wait until Sadie and Abijah were here to share what their parents had to say.

She glanced idly at the postmark of the final letter and was stunned to see it was from Tennessee. *Michael*. She looked up and down the road; no one. Nobody else was home, either. What harm could it do to sit in the shade and just see what Michael had to say? No harm at all, she decided. She deposited the other letters on the kitchen counter, poured herself a glass of water, and settled on the porch swing to rip open the letter.

Dear Pippa, Was I ever glad to receive your letter. I had a smile a mile wide for the rest of the day. I know I promised to tell you about my hitchhiking adventures, and I did write that letter, but it will have to wait for another day because I have something I need to get off my chest.

Where to begin? Reading about how you're taking care of my sister and your own sister and brother really made me think. Here I am hiding in the woods and feeling sorry for myself, but not you. You roll up your sleeves and get to work, do what has to be done, and you don't complain. It makes me feel pretty useless when I compare myself with you. I'm starting to think der Fuehrer was right about me.

I've been talking to a preacher man (that's what he calls himself; you'll hear more about him later) who gave me a ride the last couple of miles in to The Farm. He has a pretty colorful way of speaking, but the meat of what he told me is this: I need Jesus. See, Pippa, my life up to Kent State had been pretty good. Then it was dark and scary for quite some time. The preacher man showed me that what I needed was light, and not just light but THE Light, Jesus. I'm not real clear on all of this, even though I'm a Sunday school veteran, but I know I need help and he says that's a good place to start.

I know church is the last place you'd expect to see me, but I've spent a lot of time in the preacher man's church. I feel peace there, and not the peace rally kind, either, but real peace, so I believe there's something to what he's saying. In fact, I know there is, because I'm thinking of other people for the first time in a long time. I've been thinking about coming home to take Sheila off your hands. How would that be? I know she thinks of you like a sister, but she's not really your responsibility. She's mine.

One other thing. Learning about your dream of writing and how it will die when you marry is the saddest thing I've ever read. Putting down your thoughts in your journal has really helped your writing, I can tell. You have the soul of a writer, Pippa. God has given you a talent. You were not meant to hide on a farm so you can spend all your time popping out babies instead of writing books. Don't get me wrong, I have nothing against babies. In fact, I wouldn't mind having a couple with you. At least it would be fun trying.

Betsie gasped. Heat crept across her cheeks until she knew she was redder than a ripe tomato. She glanced over her shoulder to make sure Charley was nowhere nearby before she continued reading.

But there's plenty of time for all that. For now, I want you to know that I'm sorry I left you in the lurch. I'll be back as soon as I can because we have a lot to talk about. In the meantime, don't, I repeat DON'T give up your dream of writing. All you need to do is marry the right man and you can have it all. Although I guess Jesus fits in there somewhere, too. Strike that. I know He does. Thanks for listening, Pippa. Love, Michael

Horrified at the depth of feeling that "Love, Michael" conveyed, Betsie stuffed his letter into her pocket. She was Amish. He was English. It didn't even bear thinking about. And he was so . . . *forward*. She knew she was still blushing over his bold wish.

I need to get to work right away. A quick stop in the woodshed for her weeder and a lard pail and she was among the tender green rows of her vegetable garden.

The notched weeder flashed in the hazy sunlight as she stabbed at the earth. She filled the lard pail quickly the first time and dumped the weeds into the metal trash barrel to be burned. The sky grew overcast as she moved up and down the rows and time stretched out more pleasantly. At least it would have if she could have forgotten the crackling letter in her pocket.

Finished at last, Betsie stood up to stretch and fanned herself with the straw hat. A raindrop splashed on her nose and she could have sworn it boiled to steam. She pictured Sheila swimming with her school friends and wondered if Kevin, the classmate Sheila "despised," would be there to tease her. But this was not a good path for her thoughts, for she remembered Michael's teasing. At least she hoped he was teasing.

Feeling lonely, she latched the fence and pitched the last pail full of weeds into the trash barrel. Oh, how her grubby feet itched; so much for feeling damp earth between her toes. She filled the lard bucket halfway with cold water and sloshed first one foot and then the other. Good enough, she decided as she sluiced her dirty hands under the pump. Her stomach growled, reminding her that she'd skipped lunch in her hurry to get to town. She let her mind wander over the contents of the icebox, spirits drooping. Fixing a snack seemed like a chore too big to handle right now, especially if Abijah took a notion to show up.

Bread soup sounded good when it was so hot, she decided, although she felt lazier than Amelia at settling for such meager fare. She swiped wet hands across her sweaty face and headed for the house. As she crossed the porch, she heard a buggy roll into her driveway.

"Betsie, a moment," Charley called.

Her headache returned with a vengeance and she closed her eyes. All she needed was for Charley to catch her with Michael's racy letter and he'd walk away and never come back. Quietly, she slipped the letter into the milk bin. She braced herself and turned to face him.

CHAPTER 20

"A bachelor is a man who's too fast to be
caught or too slow to be worth catching."
—Noah Troyer, quoted in Betsie's journal

"Charley." Betsie massaged her forehead with her forefinger and thumb. "What brings you by?" As if she didn't know.

"Well, I—" He broke off and gave her a strange look. "One minute," he said.

She watched him stride to the pump. He shook out his handkerchief and wet it before returning to stand before Betsie with a gleam in his eye.

"Stand still." He gently rubbed her forehead and showed her a brown smear when he was finished. "You had some mud on you."

"*Ach!*" She inspected her fingertips. Sure enough, her quick rinse left something to be desired. "I'll go wash up. Come in?"

"That sounds good."

He sat at the table while Betsie drew water from the reservoir and washed her hands and face, very conscious of his presence and Michael's letter so near. She grabbed two tumblers.

"Would you like some iced tea and maybe some cookies?" she asked.

"Sure. You make good tea, Betsie."

She knew her clean cheeks had grown pink at his praise; it was pleasant to blush for an innocent reason. "We can drink it out on the front porch and sit on the swing while I cool off a little. It is so humid."

"Especially after you've been working in the garden," Charley chipped in gallantly. "You sure are a hard worker." He carried the aluminum tumblers and she followed him to the porch as chips of ice clinked.

When they were settled on the swing, Charley took a long swig of the tea. "*Ach*, that's good."

Betsie held the icy metal cup against her forehead. Condensation trickled and she closed her eyes, savoring the cold before taking a sip. Words seemed unnecessary; she sensed rather than saw Charley set the swing in motion. She doubled one grimy foot under her leg and pushed lazily at the wooden planks with her other foot.

"This is good," he sighed at length. "It's too bad we don't have more times like this. Where is Sheila, anyway?"

"Gone," Betsie replied drowsily.

Charley started. "What do you mean, gone?"

"Hmm?" She yawned and collected herself from the edge of a doze. "Oh. Sheila and Abijah weren't getting along so well. I suggested she visit her Hilliard friends for a few days. The Keiths are back from their vacation, so they came and got her. She will be well taken care of, don't worry."

"I am not worried," Charley assured her quickly. "For a moment, I thought . . . never mind. How long will she be gone?"

"Until late Sunday evening, why? What were you thinking?"

Charley shrugged. "What I am thinking now matters more. Your brother sends word that he is staying with Levi Yutzy to help with wedding preparations. This is with Naomi's blessing, so Abijah won't be sleeping in the barn. This time."

Tears of relief sprang into Betsie's eyes. No tense scenes this evening! It was almost too good to be true. "Please tell Naomi I'm obliged to her. Now maybe I can get some work done around here."

He thought a moment. "I am caught up pretty well. What do you say tomorrow we tackle those jobs together, just the two of us?"

As Charley smiled at her, the ever-present knot of tension between her shoulders unkinked. Oh, so generous of him. How good to have a man like Charley take charge! Her headache seemed to have disappeared and she felt equal to anything. "I'd like that. It will be good to have some help." Not to mention that hard work would help her forget Michael's words.

"*Gut*, then. We'll work tomorrow until it's time to pick up Sadie," he said, his words laced with regret.

"Oh, Sadie," Betsie repeated. "*Jah*." The one fly in the ointment. Determined to be cheerful, she went on. "I will see how much I can get done between now and then. I'm going to have a bite to eat first. I didn't stop to eat at noon," she added apologetically.

Charley laid a hand on her shoulder. "Yes, take some time. While you eat, you can start a list of all the chores that have gone by the wayside ever since your . . . I mean, that you need help with."

Who was this tactful man sitting beside her? She decided to thank the good Lord for His blessings instead of dwelling on the past. "I will. I've tried to keep up, but I could use your help with some of the jobs, like . . . like burning the trash"

He nodded, his smile pleased. She watched him out of sight before caressing the place where he'd touched her shoulder. Oh, this day made up for all gloomy days past. How romantic it would be when they were married and Charley was free to . . . well, do what Michael wanted to do. In a happy daze, she set out a bowl and spoon and whipped up bread soup, sprinkling the mushy mixture of crumbled bread and milk with sugar and cinnamon. *Ach*, it tasted good.

Early the next morning, Betsie nestled into her chair and flipped through her notebook to find the list she'd started for Charley.

As she let her mind roam over the list of chores they might tackle, she recalled the poetry book Michael had mailed for safekeeping. With all the commotion in the house, she'd scarcely had a minute to skim the table of contents, let alone to read any of the beautiful poems. Maybe since she had some help with the chores, she'd have more time to dip into the collection. She smiled and picked up the pencil to add to her list.

She tapped the pencil against her chin. *Repair squeak in stair tread. Right front buggy wheel rattles.* Why not fix a meal for Charley? A ripple of pleasure tickled her spine.

Work with Fledge. Split and stack kindling. She contemplated sitting across the table from Charley as they ate bowls of *Mem*'s homemade tomato soup, canned late last summer when the tomatoes were bursting with ripeness and tasted of sunshine. She smiled. Tomatoes were Charley's favorite.

Betsie snatched up a basket and was off to the cellar. After a couple of fruitless tries, she lifted up on the handle as she pulled the door. "Catchy drawer and sticky door, coming rain will pour and pour," she chanted under her breath. When the door finally opened, a hint of musty dampness wrinkled her nose as she descended the stairs. Quickly she picked and chose from among *Mem*'s dwindling stores of canned goods. The last jar of spiced applesauce, cool to the touch, sparked memories of the Troyer women bustling about the steamy kitchen, laughing and talking as they cleaned, peeled, and seasoned apples that bubbled on the hob. Sterilized jars and gleaming lids lined the table and counters; there hadn't been an inch of space left. How tired she'd been at the end of that day, but she was grateful for her mother's foresight now. She cradled the jars in her basket and mounted the stairs.

She poured the tomato soup into a kettle and found a spot on the hob where it would hold to a slow simmer, just enough to keep it warming until they were ready to eat. The bread and butter pickles and some thawed peanut butter cookies from the freezer would keep until just before she and Charley sat down to eat, when she would dish up the soup and applesauce.

When Betsie had set the table, she pulled her notebook open with a happy sigh. *Cellar door sticks*, she jotted. *Straighten and whitewash cellar.* Wonderful indeed to have tall Charley to help her reach the last of the jars from the top shelf. That way, Betsie could take stock of her stores and brush away cobwebs and track down the source of the mustiness, too. She imagined spiders lurking and shivered before a satisfied smile curved her lips. Charley would take care of her. She could count on him.

A clattery racket reached her ears and she dashed for the cookstove, convinced the tomato soup had somehow boiled over, but no. The racket was coming from the yard.

Curious, she pushed open the screen door. Charley's wagon stood in the driveway. The trash barrel belched smoke as the week's refuse burned. It wasn't like Charley to leave a fire unattended, though. She stood on tiptoe and caught a glimpse of him a stone's throw away from the barrel, partially hidden behind the smokehouse, an unused relic from the days when her family smoked their own hams.

"Charley?" she called. "Why didn't you tell me you were here?"

"Ouch!" He hotfooted it away from the smokehouse, shaking his thumb. "Oh, that smarts."

Betsie giggled. "What are you doing back there?"

"You will see soon enough, but don't come out here until I tell you." He grinned and waved the hammer at her.

She waved back as he ducked behind the weathered building. What could he be working on? The smokehouse might be old, but last time she had looked, it wasn't in need of repairs. There was only scrap lumber on the place, anyway, although Charley had mentioned something about lumber the other day. Of course, if he wanted to make a present for her, now . . . her heart pitter-patted. Maybe he had brought some materials with him to build something from the lumber he'd stored in the barn a while back. But what?

Betsie busied herself with indoor chores, lost in happy daydreams, until Charley entered, massaging his mashed thumb. Sweat and a hint of wood smoke clung to his clothes.

He glanced at her meal preparations and took an appreciative whiff. "I'm so hungry I could eat a bear." He rubbed his stomach.

"Then you will have to shoot one, because I didn't fix bear," Betsie teased with a twinkle in her eye.

He chuckled. "The trash is all burned up, Betsie. What other jobs have you thought up for us on this hot Thursday?"

Betsie ripped out the list and handed it over with a smile. "I wrote them down. Not too many."

She studied his handsome profile as he read her list with deliberation, lips moving slightly. Without being aware of it, Betsie leaned in for a closer look, her head very near his. *Jah*, there it was again. When Charley held his mouth a certain way, a slight dimple appeared near one corner. How had she never noticed his dimple before? No matter; she resolved to notice it plenty from now on, especially since it transformed him into a blond cherub, like the gentle and sweet schoolboy she'd known forever and had wanted to kiss for nearly as long. Why shy away from such feelings? After all, what Michael had hinted at would be a part of her married life. What would it be like, she wondered, when she and Charley . . .

He looked up from his reading a fraction of a second before she could guard her thoughts. Startled, he searched her face, obviously stirred by her closeness. Desire flickered in his eyes.

Before Betsie realized what was happening, Charley crushed her into an embrace that blotted out the light as he staked his claim with an ardent kiss, his hands straying boldly to her hips.

CHAPTER   21

"There I spyed all alone
Phyllida and Corydon
Much ado there was, God wot!
He would love and she would not."

—"Phyllida and Corydon" by Nicolas Breton,
quoted in Betsie's journal

BETSIE SHOVED HARD against Charley's chest with the heels of her hands, breaking his amorous grip. Eyes wide with surprise, he watched as she scuttled backwards. Her hip smacked the corner of the table and hot tears prickled at her eyelids. Shaken, she collected her wits and hobbled to the stove. With her back to Charley, she dabbed away tears and lifted the lid of the soup pot as a wave of shame and revulsion engulfed her. Her hand trembled and the lid clattered. She gripped a wooden spoon and stirred the tomato soup so vigorously that a tide of red slopped over the side.

She winced at her mistake and moved the soup to a clean spot on the hob, seconds stretching as she aligned the handle precisely. What Charley had done wasn't . . . fun. It was scary, but why?

A dark memory—one that she'd tried desperately to forget—of the attack in the harness shop welled up from the depths of her consciousness and she nearly gagged. She drew a raggedy breath, giving Charley a wide berth and chastising herself all the while. Charley wasn't Mr. Benner.

"You know, I'm not so hungry. Maybe we should go outside and get started on our chores, ain't so?" She pulled *Dat*'s old straw hat over her *Kapp*, her legs rubbery.

Charley nodded solemnly, red-faced. "*Jah*, that's maybe a good idea." His breathing gradually slowed and he cleared his throat as he consulted her list. "I'll take off that buggy wheel first, grease and tighten it up so it doesn't rattle. Then we'll cultivate the sweet corn patch and knock down some weeds. Maybe later, after I fetch Sadie, we can eat your good dinner and then work on the stair tread and the cellar door, and then if we have time, clear the storage shelves. Later this weekend, we might get to whitewashing the cellar walls."

He tucked the list in his pocket and led the way into the yard, running his brawny forearm across his face as he walked. "Whew! Awful good corn growin' weather. I just hope the corn doesn't pop while we're hoeing it," he joked. He darted a hopeful glance at her.

Betsie's laugh was shaky. "*Jah*. I will start on the corn," she said, and Charley waved her on.

Why had she reacted to his kiss like such a *Boppli*? One thing was certain; this kiss was nothing like the chaste, brotherly one he'd offered the night Michael left. No, pure animal need was more how she would describe it, as urgent as the lusty bull she'd once observed. At least this time she had fought back, unlike when she'd been attacked by Benner in the harness shop and Michael had come to her rescue.

Well, she knew how to avoid trouble. She would be a good Amish girl and cast no more admiring glances at Charley, not now that she knew where they could lead. After they were married, of course, she could look all she wanted, and more. Besides, it was her own fault for putting such an idea in Charley's head. Drat Michael Sullivan anyway for starting her thoughts down that path with his suggestive letter.

Oh, if only her parents were here as proper chaperones! Didn't they realize what could happen to a young lady with no protector?

A thought calmed her. Sadie would be with them at dinnertime. Suddenly Betsie was thankful for her sister in a way she never had been before. Though Sadie had been awfully crabby lately, they were nevertheless in this situation together. Betsie made up her mind to appreciate her younger sister more and encourage her for her hard work under Mattie's supervision. Maybe tomorrow she could even visit Sadie at the bakery since Sheila wasn't here to consider.

A good while later, she stopped to fan herself with her hat. "When it comes to hoeing, nobody can beat Betsie," *Mem* had always said. Betsie smiled at the memory and got back to work. Few weeds remained in the sweet corn patch by the time Charley joined her with *Dat*'s old hoe over his shoulder. She stiffened, glanced swiftly away, and concentrated on finishing.

"I fixed the rattle in that buggy wheel for you. I went ahead and did the others, too."

"*Denki*," she answered. Slash, slash. A couple of straggler weeds toppled as the silence stretched.

"Betsie."

Her stomach clenched. "What is it, Charley?"

"I wanted to say that it won't happen that way again." He slashed half-heartedly at a weed and stopped to lean on the hoe, waiting for her answer.

Carefully she scraped moist earth from the blade of her hoe with one toe, glad the battered straw hat hid her face. "I think that's *gut*." When he didn't respond right away, she met his gaze reluctantly. "Ain't so?"

"*Jah*, it is for the best . . . until we are married, that is." He winked at her. "There's no stopping me after that."

For a long moment, Betsie could not bring herself to speak. She moistened her dry lips. "You know, really I am almost done out here and I am so hot. It's nearly time for you to fetch Sadie. And I should check on the soup."

"*Ach*, the buggy work took longer than I planned." He checked the sun's progress. "You're right, I'd better be going. It might take me a little longer to get back, mind you. I have an errand to run. For your surprise," he added with a roguish grin. He pointed toward the old smokehouse.

He's making me a blanket chest, maybe, to store the quilts I've made. She managed a smile despite her agitation. "That's wonderful.

We will eat whenever you get back. Here, let me put that hoe away so you can be going."

She watched as he coaxed his horse out from under the shade trees where the animal had taken refuge with Judith and Fledge. Shade seemed like a good idea to Betsie, too. She wandered to the front porch and swept it clean with the old broom. A glance at the metal milk box reminded her of the racy letter inside it, and the fact that she hadn't yet checked the mail today. Better to do that with Charley away, although it wasn't likely there'd be another letter from Michael so soon. She leaned the broom back in the corner and watched Charley hitch up, waving when he finally drove away.

The walk to the mailbox was rewarded with another fat envelope from Michael. But after the day's activity, she wasn't in any hurry to open that can of worms. Her mind was *ferhoodled* enough already. She dropped the letter into the milk box and escaped into the house.

After hanging up the straw hat, she poured a glass of water, drained it in a couple of gulps, and filled it again. Then she made the rounds of every window in the house, propping them open with sticks to catch the least breeze.

Why had she thought hot soup would be good on such a sweltering day? Too late to make anything else now, she reflected, so she stirred the soup and arranged a dozen peanut butter cookies in a pretty pattern on a white plate, the way *Mem* always had.

When she had dust mopped every inch of the floors and polished the windows until they sparkled and Charley still hadn't returned, Betsie strolled to the porch again. Not a breath of air stirred under the brassy blue sky. She pushed the swing back and forth a few times before dragging to a stop. With a careful look down the empty road, she reached for the milk box lid, withdrew her hand, then reached again, opening it wide this time.

Clop, clop, clop. The lid clanged shut and Betsie straightened in a hurry. She crossed to the porch railing to wait, and as the buggy drew nearer, her mouth dropped open.

"*Was in der welt?*" she exclaimed. "Is this my surprise, Charley?"

C H A P T E R   2 2

"A woman is perturbed by what a man forgets,
a man by what a woman remembers."

—FANNIE TROYER, QUOTED IN BETSIE'S JOURNAL

BETSIE WATCHED CHARLEY swing the buggy wider than usual because he had a flat wagon hitched to the back. A patchwork of squawking hens in a makeshift crate protested every jolt of the buggy. Behind the crate, she spied a stack of nesting boxes and another crate that housed an indignant rooster, all glossy feathers and fuss. A large roll of tied-down chicken wire and a toolbox glinted in the hazy sunlight. Last but not least, she noticed a couple of sacks of chicken feed.

The romantic and somehow consoling notion of a blanket chest vanished. These squawking chickens were her present, commonplace yet practical. For the merest instant, she regretted his choice. Then she straightened her shoulders and skipped lightly down the front steps to meet Charley and Sadie.

"Oh, Charley! We will have our own eggs again. It is very thoughtful of you, ain't so, Sadie? Sadie?" she repeated.

"Out of my way." Sadie groaned. She held one hand over her mouth and clutched her stomach as she rushed past Betsie to the outhouse.

"What is it, Sadie? Are you sick?" Charley fretted.

He started after her but Betsie stopped him, the reason for Sadie's excessive crankiness belatedly dawning on her.

"She will be fine in a day or two, Charley."

"But what is it? What's wrong? She was not sick when we left the bakery."

Betsie sized him up, choosing her words carefully. True, he didn't have any sisters, but surely with Mattie around, he would have some understanding. "It's maybe woman troubles," she hinted delicately.

Charley turned beet red. "*Ach.*"

She nearly giggled at his consternation. Who had the upper hand now? "Don't be embarrassed, Charley. It's natural."

The outhouse door creaked and Sadie emerged, pale and beaded with perspiration as she mopped her mouth with her handkerchief. She took one look at their sympathetic expressions, burst into tears, and hurried inside.

"Poor girl," Betsie said tenderly. "Well, I don't believe she will be eating with us. In fact, she will most likely be in her room for the rest of the night, but don't worry. I will put on some water and make her a cup of something that will soothe her miseries. Also, I will fill up a hot water bottle for her. Come and wash up after you've tended to the chickens."

Feeling very womanly and knowing, Betsie headed for the house. The instant she opened the door, a patchwork blur streaked into the yard.

"Amelia! Charley, the chickens!" Betsie screeched.

In the nick of time, he snatched up the crate and lifted it above the bed of the wagon, but the frantic kitten merely hooked her claws in Charley's broadfalls and ascended his leg in an attempt to get at the birds, mewing all the while. Flustered, Charley tried to shake her off and almost lost his grip on the crate as the hens squawked and flapped for their lives.

Betsie laughed until she had to lean against the side of the house, wiping her eyes at Charley's clumsy dance to chicken music and caterwauls. Weakly she crossed the yard, knelt, and unhooked the kitten's claws from the fabric of his trousers.

"Amelia, you naughty kitten! You will have to wait for your chicken dinner." Betsie tried to cuddle the furry predator, who squirmed and licked her chops. Who would have dreamed that Sadie's miseries and Amelia's antics would even the score? She relaxed.

Charley readjusted his grip on the crate. "I see I'd better get the chickens settled in the smokehouse for safekeeping until I can finish their chicken run. I went to the Hochstetlers' moving auction the other day and picked up this flock for you. Sam says they are fine layers." He beamed at her.

"It was very good of you," Betsie smiled. "Maybe I can get some egg money coming in. *Denki.*" She carried Amelia into the house and shut the screen door firmly before she let the kitten down to feed her.

She was still smiling later as she served Charley a bowl of tomato soup, a dish of applesauce, and the bread and butter pickles. After their silent prayer, she passed the crackers. She and Charley ate quietly while the teakettle steamed.

In short order, Charley's spoon clattered into his empty bowl. He rubbed his stomach meditatively. "Oh, I like tomatoes. I believe I will have more soup, if there is some left. Also is there any bread and maybe peanut butter spread?"

"*Jah*, there is." Betsie answered, disconcerted. "Maybe this is a funny kind of supper when you're used to Mattie's cooking."

"Mmm-hmm," he said, his eyes on his bowl as she ladled it full.

Eyebrows raised, Betsie sliced some bread and put the jar of peanut butter spread and a knife beside his plate. Charley slapped together a sandwich and dipped a corner into his second steaming bowl of soup.

"Now, that's the way we always have it at home," he sighed with satisfaction as he chewed. "But don't worry, you will learn."

"I guess I will," Betsie remarked. She got up from the table abruptly and tamped tea leaves into the tea ball with unnecessary vigor. It took a minute to locate Sadie's favorite teacup, the delicate white one with the purple violets. While the peppermint tea steeped, she located the hot water bottle, ramming the stubborn drawer shut after a couple of tries. She filled the red bottle, making sure the stopper was secure. When she'd wrapped the bottle in an old towel, she dunked the tea ball in the cup a few more times for good measure and sprinkled in two heaping teaspoons of sugar, just the way Sadie liked it.

As she approached the table, she noticed that the peanut butter cookies had disappeared at an alarming rate under Charley's jurisdiction. Betsie set Sadie's teacup on the dinner plate at her place. She snagged a couple of the cookies and added them to the plate, should her sister feel better later. Charley frowned.

"Go ahead with your supper," Betsie urged. "I'll take care of Sadie and will be back down here to finish my supper in two shakes of a lamb's tail." She tucked the hot water bottle under one arm and braced the plate with the tea cup balanced on top against her chest.

"Oh, Betsie?"

"Yes?"

"Any more cookies?" He pointed at the plate where a solitary cookie remained.

Her hands full, she gestured with her chin. "Try the cookie jar on top of the icebox."

When she reached Sadie's door, she paused. "Sadie?" she called softly. "It's Betsie. Are you all right?"

"Go away," her sister moaned. "My insides are on fire."

Betsie nudged the door open with her hip. "I won't bother you for long."

The teacup clattered on the plate as Betsie walked into the room, and Sadie, who was sprawled facedown across her bed, opened one eye. "Is that peppermint I smell?" she asked weakly.

"*Jah*, I made you some tea. Can you sit up a little and take a sip?"

"No."

"Come now, it will help you feel better," Betsie coaxed.

"Oh, all right." Sadie gritted her teeth and half-raised herself to a slump before reaching for the cup. She blew to cool the tea and took a tentative sip. "*Ach*, that's good, sugared up just how I like it. And you . . . you made it in my favorite violet cup." She took another sip and sniffled, her eyes tragic. "I've been awful mean to you, Betsie, and also to the English girl. I-I think it was because she looked a bit like that terrible girl who always called me Butterball when I went to first grade at the English school. You know the girl I mean. *Ach*, I can't recall her name."

"Shh, it doesn't matter . . ."

"—and I am so sad over all the people moving away, like *Mem* and *Dat* and H-Hershbergers," Sadie hiccupped. "Oh, w-why did they have to g-go?"

Betsie raised an eyebrow and cut her sister off before she could wax maudlin. "Hush, Sadie. I said some mean things, too, and *Mem* and *Dat* are coming back, you'll see. You rest and get to feeling better," she said as Sadie guzzled the tea. "Anyway, Sheila is in Hilliard with friends for a few days, and Abijah is staying with Levi to help out, so don't worry. See here, I brought you a couple of peanut butter cookies if you feel like nibbling later." She set the plate on the washstand beside the bed.

But this was a mistake. Sadie took one look at the cookies and paled. "I think I'm going to *vommix* again," she groaned.

Betsie grabbed the speckled basin from the washstand in the nick of time. She stayed with her sister for a few minutes until her stomach settled down. Then she tucked her in with the hot water bottle pressed to her middle. "I'll check on you after a while," she promised, but there was no response from Sadie's huddled form.

Soberly Betsie carried the befouled basin down the stairs. As she turned the corner to the landing, she met Charley, toolbox at hand as he tested the treads for squeaks.

"Do you happen to have any talcum powder?" He slurred the question around a couple of nails that he held between his teeth.

Betsie nodded. "Let me get rid of this and I'll fetch it from my room." She refrained from adding that she'd sprinkled the powder under her clothing when today had dawned terrifically hot.

In the kitchen, her perpetually hungry kitten lapped tomato soup from Betsie's unfinished bowl. *Mem* had never allowed pets in the house for precisely this reason. Flooded with memories of her mother, Betsie shooed Amelia away and cleared the table, washed the nasty bowl with hot water from the reservoir, and started to put on some more water to boil for the dishes, but she decided redding up could wait for once. Instead she washed her hands and grabbed a couple of stale cookies from the blue crockery jar.

As she munched, she squeaked past Charley to fetch the powder. "Here you go," she said when she returned.

Without comment, he took the container and held the offending tread, which he'd pried from the riser and stringers with the hammer claw, in the other hand. Carefully he shook powder along the riser's edge and then lined up the tread on top before relocating a few nails to fasten the step down securely. "This will tighten it good enough for right now, but I will do it more thorough when this is our house someday soon."

He moved aside to let her pass, but Betsie almost missed the step. "What did you say?"

Charley stowed his hammer in the toolbox and smiled up at her, his teeth flashing in the shadows. "I said it will be good to fix up this house when it's ours."

Her breath caught. "This house belongs to *Mem* and *Dat!*"

"But they are not here," he reminded matter-of-factly, "and meanwhile, a good farm is going to waste. When we are married, we can work together to make something of it once again. I was thinking maybe a truck farm. Then we can sell our produce, eggs, and such at the bakery."

"I see you have it all figured out." She folded her arms to still her trembling. "You will take over my family's farm with your plans and the chickens and all, even though we pray to the good Lord every night on our knees, begging Him to send our parents back. I've kept the faith they will heed His call, but now I see you don't believe it will happen," she accused. "Maybe you hope it won't."

"I didn't say that," Charley protested. "Don't fly off the handle. Of course I hope your parents return to the church, because iffen they don't, they will burn for eternity. I wouldn't wish that end on anyone." He stood and dusted powder residue from his knees, avoiding her eye. "But I have to wonder. What kind of parents leave their two young daughters home to fend for themselves, anyway?"

Seething with anger, Betsie readied a scathing retort but suddenly cupped a hand to her ear. "Did you hear that? Listen, there it is again."

Low and far away, thunder rolled. No sooner had one faint peal died away than another sounded. The dull rumbles grew more distinct with every passing second.

Charley's face was grave. "A storm is blowing up fast. Sounds like a bad one and I wouldn't be surprised, as hot as it's been today. Better get Sadie down here. I'll check on the chickens, put the horses up, and keep an eye on the sky. I'll warn you in plenty of time if we need to take shelter. Might as well shut up the stove and put the lights out, too, just in case. We don't want a house fire if the weather turns ugly."

She swallowed and caught his sleeve as he started down the steps.

"Charley, I—"

"No time," he cut in. "Get Sadie."

CHAPTER 23

"Where had I heard this wind before
Change like this to a deeper roar?"
—"Bereft" by Robert Frost,
quoted in Betsie's journal

Betsie grabbed a couple of flashlights and stuffed them in her pockets. It was the work of a minute or two to douse the fire in the stove, dial the damper shut, and turn off the gas light. She took the stairs two at a time and burst into Sadie's room, the windowpanes rattling as the wind rose.

"Sadie!" She shook her sister's shoulder. Thunder boomed, louder now, and lightning glared. "Sadie, you have to get up. A bad storm is coming. It's maybe a tornado. Get ready to go to the cellar."

Flash after flash of lightning lit the maple tree in stark relief against the ominous sky as the branches writhed in the wind. Fascinated, Betsie tiptoed to the window as Sadie moved feebly, but she backed away as the tree was whipped nearly sideways by a big gust. Lightning illuminated the greenish-purple clouds that coiled like dirty whipped cream around a brighter central spot. The cloud base swirled, halted, and swirled again, lower now. She thought of her friends and family and chewed her lip.

"I don't think I can make it all the way to the cellar," Sadie moaned.

"No choice," Betsie grunted as she slammed the window shut. She snatched up the patchwork quilt, draped it over Sadie's shoulders, and braced her arm to support her sister as she got up. The girls inched their way to the door. An intense flash of lightning blinded Betsie temporarily and she rammed her toes into the doorjamb. Stifling an exclamation, she hobbled forward and flicked on one of the flashlights she'd stowed in her pocket.

"Wait here!" she ordered. Hastily she shut the windows in her room and Abijah's, wondering what good she hoped to accomplish if a tornado struck the house. Then she returned to Sadie, who was crouched in pain.

The beam of light bobbed as they shuffled down the stairs in lock step, Betsie nearly pitching headlong when Amelia scampered between her bare feet with an indignant yowl.

Safely in the kitchen at last, Betsie deposited Sadie in a chair and waited on word from Charley. The odor of stale food and dirty dishes wrinkled Betsie's nose as thunder cracked and boomed. Talking was useless over the nearly constant din, so Betsie raced to close the rest of the windows. In the intermittent glare of lightning, Betsie spotted the letters on the counter and snatched them up before ramming the last window shut.

She returned to Sadie's side to find her sister cocooned in the quilt. Betsie wrapped her in her arms. As the thunder cannoned, she felt the vibrations as Sadie clutched her middle and moaned.

The storm was nearly overhead now. Betsie fancied she could hear sizzles before the flashes and simultaneous booms. Then the constant peals of thunder and the roar of the wind died so suddenly that Betsie's ears rang. A new sound penetrated her consciousness— ping, ping, ping, the eager rattle of hail.

The storm was upon them, but where was Charley? She let go of Sadie.

"Betsie!" her sister protested.

But Betsie already had the screen door wide open. "Charley!" She cringed as a terrific bolt of lightning pierced the gloom. She spotted him as he stared at the sky, mesmerized. "Charley!" she screamed again.

He heard her then. With wide eyes, he barreled toward her, buffeted by a terrific gust of wind that whipped his hat from his head and winged it into the darkness. Torrential rain and icy marbles of hail pelted him just before he burst into the kitchen.

Betsie slammed the door shut. "We should go to the cellar now, ain't so?"

Charley didn't answer. His breathing was labored and Betsie played the beam of the flashlight over his face, troubled at his glassy stare. He shivered convulsively as rivulets of water puddled at his feet.

Adrenaline pumped through her veins and galvanized her into action. She grabbed Charley's arm, smacked the flashlight into his palm, and herded him and Sadie toward the cellar.

Wood shrieked against wood as she dragged the balky door over the planks. She shoved Sadie and Charley forward and the three of them plunged through the dark opening and careened down the stairs as though the very hounds of hell slavered at their heels.

Something furry brushed Betsie's bare toes as she crossed the chilly cellar floor; she hoped it was Amelia. She fumbled the second flashlight from her pocket and directed the beam over the contents of the windowless cellar, taking stock as though she'd never been there before. Glints of light reflected off the jars. She imagined shards of glass spiraling through the darkness and shuddered.

She stubbed her toe against something plastic yet yielding. The flashlight revealed several empty five gallon lard tubs. She pulled her sister and Charley over and pushed them down on the makeshift seats. Her teeth chattered as she perched on the middle one and gestured at Sadie to share the quilt. Betsie grabbed an edge and drew it over her head, her mind arguing that the fabric's protection would be minimal against projectiles of glass, and nil against splinters of wood or cement blocks. She reached to switch off Charley's flashlight to save the battery before switching off her own, making the darkness complete.

Sadie shivered next to her. Betsie could feel Charley's shivers, too. Though there were only the three of them in the cellar, the grim specter of sudden death made an almost palpable fourth. Betsie trembled at the thought of the fiery punishment that awaited three unbaptized sinners if this was indeed their time to go. This is it, she told herself. If we die right now . . .

Gradually she became aware that she was praying aloud. *Mem* and *Dat*, Abijah, Rachel and Sam, Sheila—Michael; the faces of Betsie's friends and family swirled through her thoughts as she prayed for safety, for mercy.

The reports of the thunderstorm reached a crescendo as she finished praying, but peace filled Betsie's heart. As she marveled over this, an energetic bundle of fur clawed its way onto her lap. With a glad cry, she nudged Sadie and handed over Amelia for what comfort the warm, purring kitten offered. She leaned against Charley and clasped his cold hand. Reassurance that they would be all right welled up from deep inside her. Was it her imagination, or had the storm abated somewhat?

The next instant, a mighty crash shook the house to its very foundation and Sadie screamed. Betsie peeked out from under the quilt, half expecting an unobstructed view of the stormy sky, but darkness met her eye; they were still protected from the elements.

"I don't know what that was, but I do believe the worst is past," she reassured, relieved that she no longer had to shout to be heard. She snapped on her flashlight again and the light cheered her heart. "Thank the good Lord, we are safe."

Sadie trembled as she stroked Amelia's fur, but Betsie knew her sister would be all right. She turned to Charley and strained to hear what he was saying under his breath.

"It's all my fault, all my fault," Charley muttered. "We could have been killed."

"Was in der welt?" Betsie exclaimed. She smoothed her front hair, disheveled from the quilt, and straightened her *Kapp*. "Don't be silly, Charley. Small wonder you got confused, out in a storm with hail pounding on your bare head that way. No harm done except you lost your hat, and that's easily replaced. We made it to the cellar in time and here we are yet, safe and sound."

"No, Betsie." Charley wrung his hands. "You are wrong. We may have been spared, but the good Lord has sent this storm as a warning about my . . . actions earlier this afternoon." He cast off the quilt and faced her, his wet blond hair plastered across his forehead. "I've made up my mind. I am going to speak with Jonas. I mean to join the church and be baptized just as soon as he will allow it. I can't go on risking my life this way. Where would I be right now if this storm had taken me? Why, roasting in hellfire, that's where. At least if I had been baptized already, I would have had some chance of going to heaven if I did die. I hear this preached often enough to know it perfectly well." He nodded several times. "Yes, I am joining the church, and Betsie, you and Sadie will do the same."

Suddenly drained of energy, Betsie didn't know whether to giggle or burst into tears. The storm had provided a jolt, it was true, but she didn't feel led to make such a hasty decision about joining the church. She certainly didn't care to have the choice forced on her, not even by Charley. She started to reassure Sadie, too, but her sister was too quick for her.

"Hush, Charley." Sadie hugged the quilt to her and leaned to see past Betsie. "Weren't you listening while Betsie prayed? It's true that all the wrongs I've done lately were burning my soul like a hot firebrand during the storm. But Betsie prayed for us, couldn't you hear her? She prayed that we would be safe, and here we are." She met Betsie's astonished gaze. *"Denki, Schweschder."*

Betsie was too overcome to speak for a moment. "I was scared, too," she admitted at last. "As I prayed, though, my fear lessened and I could almost hear *Dat*'s voice reassuring me that this was only the big spring storm that he used to warn us about. How many times did we hear him say it happened near Memorial Day every year, regular as clockwork? We just forgot about it, that's all, until the good Lord helped me recall, and then the fear went away. Give Amelia to me, Sadie. Let's get you out of this musty, chilly cellar and back into bed. Then maybe Charley and I can check to see what damage the storm did." She snuggled the kitten under her chin.

"A moment, Betsie," Charley said, his voice more sure now. "I believe if you will examine your own heart this evening, you will maybe find that you're harboring some rebellion of your own, deep inside. I must ask you to reconsider joining the church. Especially—" he checked himself with a glance at Sadie. Then he started upstairs, his flashlight probing the darkness.

Confused and more than a little hurt, Betsie hoped the storm had not turned Charley missionary-minded, the unkind name reserved for those who called down fire and brimstone on friends they deemed lacking in the faith. She shivered and followed slowly behind Sadie.

CHAPTER 24

"The time to relax is when you don't have time for it."

—NOAH TROYER, QUOTED IN BETSIE'S JOURNAL

SHE WAS ONLY HALFWAY up the stairs when she heard Sadie's and Charley's footsteps quicken as they navigated the kitchen.

"Betsie, come and see!" Charley's voice was tense with excitement.

"Be right there," she answered through chattering teeth. *If you are sure you want to associate with a sinner like me,* she added to herself.

She found Sadie and Charley clustered in front of the screen door. She chewed her lip and hung back. "Is it very bad?"

"See for yourself." Sadie moved over to make room and Charley directed the beam of his flashlight outside.

Frowning, Betsie peeked between them and gasped. The big maple tree, the one that she'd kept an eye on as the storm approached, now stretched across the driveway and pointed toward the barn. She directed her light to reveal a gaping hole in the green grass near the house. The grip of the tangled roots deep within the rain-soaked earth had been no match for the high winds.

"What a blessing it didn't blow the other way, toward this house." She mourned the loss of the friendly green canopy that had lately shaded the side yard. Now the treetop hid a portion of the pasture fence, crushed beneath the weight of the massive tree.

"First thing tomorrow, I'll get Sawmill Joe over here to cut that up,"

Charley promised. "I'm awful glad I parked my buggy in the barn. Good thing there's another gate, too."

The adrenaline rush that had sustained Betsie suddenly ebbed. Since when did Charley make the decisions around here? "Tell Joe he can keep half the wood for his pay," she answered shortly. She had never been more ready for a day to end. "I wonder how your mother fared, Charley? Just because the wind did no greater damage here doesn't mean it was harmless elsewhere, ain't so?"

Charley blanched. "You're right. I'd better go check on her. Also, I can tell her of my decision to be baptized. She will be awful glad to hear it."

"When you go, would you mind," she began, careful to phrase her request as a favor and not an order, "stopping by the Yutzys' place for a moment to check up on Rachel and her family, and especially Abijah? If we don't see you back here, we will know they are fine," she assured him with a bright smile as she lit the gas lamp and replaced the flashlights in the drawer.

He nodded. "If they are all right, I will see you both in the morning, then." His toolbox clanked as he stepped high to avoid broken branches and puddles.

"Ohh," Sadie groaned the minute he was out of sight. She rubbed her middle. "The pains are coming back strong."

"What are you still doing down here, then?" Betsie smiled tiredly. "Bed is the place for you. Off with you, now. I will do the dishes and I'll soon follow."

"You have done so much to take care of me today. I'd gladly do the dishes for you, Betsie, if only I felt well enough," Sadie said in a small voice.

A rush of love for her sister warmed Betsie. "*Ach*, don't worry, Sadie. Tell you what," she went on. "We got a letter from *Mem* today." She slipped the letter from her pocket and handed it over, recalling with a start the other letter. "If you're still awake when I've finished the dishes and all, I'll refill your hot water bottle and bring it up, and we'll read the letter together. What's more, I promise if you're already asleep, I won't open the letter until first thing in the morning and we'll read it together then. Word from our parents is too precious to keep to ourselves, ain't so?"

"That sounds so nice. And Betsie?" Sadie paused and timidly folded Betsie's hands in her own. "You and your prayers really did keep me from going to pieces in the storm. You were so calm and strong when I was so scared, but I would have been much worse if not for you."

Betsie adjusted the quilt around her sister's shoulders with tenderness. "That was the good Lord's doing, not mine," she said. "But I'm glad my prayers helped you, too. Go get some rest, now, and don't worry. With the good Lord's help, we can make it through anything."

CHAPTER 25

"I thought getting shot would be the worst thing that could
ever happen to me, but now I realize it's not even close."
—MICHAEL SULLIVAN, QUOTED IN BETSIE'S JOURNAL

IT WAS LATE WHEN Betsie finished cleaning the kitchen, almost nine
o'clock. She guessed Abijah and all the rest must be safe as Charley
hadn't returned to report otherwise, and for that she was thankful.
Dutifully she refilled the hot water bottle, wrapped it in a clean dish
towel, and carried it to Sadie's room, weary to the bone.

Her sister's door was ajar and a shaft of light shone on the wood
floor in the hall. "I'm ready to read the letter with you now, Sadie,"
Betsie murmured tenderly. She eased the door open and stopped.

Sadie was fast asleep, the sheet bunched around her knees and *Mem*
and *Dat*'s letter curled in her hand. Betsie took the envelope and laid
it gently on the nightstand. She tucked the water bottle against her
sister's middle and drew the sheet up to Sadie's chin before turning off
the lamp.

What an awful day. She arched her back and stretched, then plod-
ded downstairs and onto the front porch, where she was amazed at
how the storm had cooled the air. Stealthily she retrieved Michael's
letters from the milk box and darted into the kitchen to bask in the
welcome warmth of the cook stove.

She struck a match to light the candle she'd placed in the middle of the table. The flicker and glow of the flame comforted her. She sat down with an exhausted thump, opened the newest fat envelope, and drew out several sheets of paper. Was she up to reading such a long letter now? No. She decided to hide it for safekeeping until tomorrow. As she folded the sheets together, she caught sight of the salutation, "Hey, Pippa." She smiled and doubled one leg underneath her as she read on, entranced by the English world and its many bewilderments. The letter began with a couple of lines scrunched in at the top.

Hey, Pippa, This is the letter I promised you. Can't wait to see you again. Love, Michael

She had to admit that the English were extravagant with love. Probably they used the word so much it had lost all meaning. It wasn't a term she was used to hearing, except from Sheila. She glossed over it for now and read the rest.

I think I promised to tell you about how I hitched rides to get down here to The Farm. Hitchhiking is an interesting way to travel, but I wouldn't recommend it for you, Pippa, unless I'm the one who picks you up. The drivers who let me ride along were mostly decent, but you never know. Any minute you could be hacked to pieces by an ax murderer, am I right? I had this plan where, if a driver even looked at me funny, I was gonna pop the door, roll out, and hit the road, literally. Haven't had to use it yet, knock on wood.

Anyway, I'd walk along the side of the road with my backpack and stick out my thumb, the universal signal for wanting a ride, and I really didn't have to walk too far before the first driver rolled to a stop. I climbed aboard the semi and told the truck driver I was headed south.

Lefty was a heavyset guy who sported a sweat-stained feed cap with "DeKalb" imprinted on a flying ear of corn. He didn't look twice at my hair or clothes, so I mostly kept my mouth shut and listened while he talked. It didn't take long to see I'd picked a real winner right out of the box. Old Lefty was a crackpot with one big idea. He swore up and down that man had never really landed on the moon almost two summers ago. See, he'd watched the lunar landing on TV and all, but he was convinced that it was a trick by the U.S. government. Hey, I'm no big government fan, but come on! Even the Amish know man really landed on the moon. I mean, I guess you do.

Anyway, he had this wild idea about a television studio made up to look like the moon's surface, and he said that the lunar module, *The Eagle*, was really only a model spaceship. According to Lefty, there was "no way under the sun that three men could have flown that contraption to the moon and back, let alone land it there and leave an American flag behind. Heck, the flag's waving in the breeze in them pictures, and even a redneck like me knows there ain't no air in space!"

The closer we got to the Ohio River, the more Looney Tunes Lefty got, flailing his arms around as he ranted instead of keeping both hands on the wheel at ten and two. A couple of times I thought he was going to roll us off the highway and I'd be a goner, which would pretty much defeat my goal of staying alive. I finally lied and told him I was only going as far as Cincinnati. He seemed real disappointed; I don't think anyone had listened to him in quite a while. Hey, can you blame them? When he let me out downtown, I walked away fast like I knew where I was headed, but I'd learned something from Lefty: Without faith, it's possible to miss out on something wonderful, even when it's right in front of you.

My next ride was with a lady and her two kids, a boy and a girl. I couldn't believe my eyes when she stopped, because she drove one of those long convertibles. I think the car was an old Cadillac, fire engine red, a real time capsule. She had the radio tuned to an Elvis song, "Return to Sender," and you can't get much more uncool than Elvis.

I hopped over the door and slid into the front seat. I said hi to the kiddies in the back, but they were too busy to talk. The boy had a green twin pop and the girl had a red one and they were licking them like crazy. Between the action of the wind and the sun, those popsicles melted for all they were worth, dripping syrupy green and red trails down the kids' arms. Together they looked like Christmas. I'm pretty sure the kids stuck to the car seat when it was time to get out, Pippa. It reminded me of the time we went to the Milky Way Ice Cream Shoppe and ran into the Little Leaguers. You didn't say so, but I know you wanted to hose the place down. Don't try to tell me you didn't.

Anyway, the mom said her name was Jolene. She would have been pretty ten years ago, but here she was in 1971 with her hair tied up in a bright blue scarf to keep it from blowing in the wind and wearing these cat-eyed sunglasses. Her husband was overseas in Vietnam, she said. I glanced at those kids again and felt kinda sick. What if they waited on their daddy to come home from the war but he never made it?

We had no more crossed the Ohio River into Kentucky than Jolene pushed her sunglasses on top of her head and mentioned that she had all sorts of handyman chores to do at home but no one to help her. She said her house was close by. I was kind of confused because she'd told me I could ride with her as far as Lexington, but I decided a couple of hours one way or another wouldn't make much difference, so I made up my mind to help her out if I could.

I opened up my mouth to say okay, but right about then I caught her looking me over and I had a revelation. It was pretty plain that what Jolene really wanted was me.

THE BACHELOR

Thank the good Lord Abijah hitchhiked with Zeke and not the first driver who came along. Heart pounding, Betsie flipped over the sheet of notebook paper and continued reading Michael's letter.

When I noticed her ogling me that way, the first thing that popped into my mind was how you must have felt when that scumbag attacked you in the harness shop, Pippa. Like a zebra haunch in a cage full of hungry tigers, right?

We barreled down the highway toward her house, and I knew there was no way I could utilize my emergency plan, you know, the one where I opened the door and rolled out. I was trapped and the old feeling of full-blown panic took over.

I wish now that I'd just told Jolene the truth—that I wasn't interested—but at the time I didn't see any way out but to tell another lie. What I said was that I didn't like to talk about it too much because it made me sad, but I was on my way to visit my grandma who was at death's door in a nursing home in Covington, Kentucky, and I didn't have a minute to spare if I wanted to tell her good-bye.

It took some fast talking to convince Jolene to drop me off at the first gas station we saw, but I told her the nursing home was a short walk away, so she did it. When I got out of the car, I took out my wallet, peeled off a buck for each kid, and told them to help their mother. Then I ducked inside the building and stayed put until she drove off, which leads me to lesson number two: When you love somebody, you want to be faithful to them even though you're not sure how they feel about you.

Maybe I just needed to get out of Ohio, because the next few drivers were pretty normal. Sometimes we stopped at a truck stop or a diner for a bite to eat and sometimes we made do with snacks from wherever we gassed up. You know me; give me an apple and I'm happy. Some of your delicious banana cream pie would have gone down mighty easy, though.

I did a lot of thinking while I watched Kentucky roll by outside my window. Like, I hoped my old man would have some success with talking Phyllis—strike that, Sunshine Sullivan, star of stage and screen—into coming home. And I wished I'd been nicer to Sheila. She's great. Kinda golly, gee whiz and all that, but a better sister than I deserve. I hope I can make it up to her. And I thought about you.

Anyway, a few hours and drivers later, we crossed into Tennessee and climbed Jellico Mountain. I thought I'd feel the weight of the world drop off my shoulders since I was in the same state as The Farm at long last, the place where I'd begin my new simple life. But as I tallied up how far from home I was, I realized something else instead, Pippa—a truth that smacked me right between the eyes and knocked me down so low that I didn't see how I'd ever make it back up again.

Suffice it to say, it wasn't a very merry homecoming when I rolled into Summertown a couple of hours later and headed for The Farm. Well, except for this. The last couple of miles in, I hitched a ride with a guy who drove a green (where it wasn't rusted out completely) Ford pickup with a missing tailgate. A red hound dog growled at me from his seat of honor beside the driver, so I hopped in the truck bed.

You'll never guess what was strapped to the back of the cab above the window. Would you believe a shotgun in a gun-rack? Yeah, my worst nightmare, a gun. Funny thing was, seeing it didn't bother me that much, not after my big revelation. See, I thought getting shot was the worst thing that could ever happen to me, but now I realize it's not even close.

I braced myself cross-wise, my back against one side and my feet against the other, and leaned on a couple of musty bales of hay as we climbed hills, rounded curves, and bottomed out in a couple of creek beds that knocked off so much rust that I was scared my foot would pop through the corroded metal. Every once in a while, Ol' Faithful the Red Hound Dog let out a howl that must have petrified all the small game for miles around.

But all good things must come to an end. The driver hollered out the window that this was as far as he could take me because the road wasn't too good from here on in (!). I grabbed my pack and he told me to follow the dirt road that went off to the left. I walked to his window to thank him, but Ol' Faithful lunged across him, going for my throat, so I jumped back and just waved. The driver seemed like a good guy and I was sorry to see him go, but he hit the accelerator, the tires spun up a rooster tail of dust, and he was off. I'd barely turned around when I heard the engine scream in protest as he backed up the truck, Ol' Faithful howling to beat the band.

The truck stopped opposite me. "Shut up, Red," the man said, and Red (I guess that's Ol' Faithful's real name) did. Then the man started talking to me, glasses glinting through the cloud of dust.

"Son, I live not far yonder, just over that next hill in the prettiest little holler in Tennessee." He nodded to where it loomed ahead. "I've dropped a lot of fellas and more'n a few gals off here at The Farm in the last few weeks, and in a short time I feel like I've seen it all. But I want you to listen to me," he said, pointing to emphasize every word. "You don't belong with the likes of these-here folks."

The air was so humid that I was sweating buckets, but a chill ran through my veins. I tried not to show how much he'd rattled me, but he seemed to know anyway.

"What do you mean by that?" I asked at last.

"I'm a preacher man, son. The name's Lonnie Pratt and talking with Jesus is what I do. But you know what? It ain't a one-way conversation like a lotta folks think." He frowned and mopped his ear with a turkey-red bandana where Red kept licking it. "I'm not trying to convince you one way or t'other. I just want you to know that if you ever need a friend to talk to, walk on over that hill to my house. Better yet, come this Sunday morning and go to church with me. I'd be mighty proud to see you there."

I stammered something that must have made him happy, because he smiled real big and drove off like he'd accomplished what he set out to. His truck disappeared over the hill and I was alone. But I'd learned Lesson Three: God knows me better than I know myself.

I'm not going to waste your time describing the kind of people who live at The Farm or the kind of stuff they're into. There's a precious few who really do want to take care of Mother Earth and all, but most of them have their heads in some pretty weird places.

Anyway, I wrote you that I picked out this decrepit old bus for my very own. I fixed the window that was stuck, so I'm not mosquito bait anymore and I'm all set next time it rains. I have a lantern strung up now, and as I'm writing this, I can hear every summer cicada and whip-poor-will for miles around. The sky is so black out here in the middle of nowhere that I can see thousands upon thousands of stars, maybe even millions, more than I ever realized existed. It's a humbling experience. I wish you were here beside me in the starlight, Pippa.

This letter is really long and I didn't even get to tell you about the farm animals and all the kids. Some of them run around stark naked—the kids, I mean. Maybe I'll tell you about them next time.

I don't really want to stop writing, but I guess I should. Please, if you can find it in your heart, write back and let me know how you're doing. I wish you the best and hope to hear from you soon. Your friend, Michael

Betsie's back ached from bending over the letter to make out the tiny handwriting. She rubbed her neck and held the paper closer to the light; it looked like Michael had written something else above his signature, but he'd erased and written over it. She squinted and shook her head. Whatever it had been, it was too faint to decipher by candlelight.

What a letter! She felt like she'd been along for the ride through Ohio, Kentucky, and then the back roads of Tennessee. She reread snatches here and there, amazed at the subtle changes in Michael. One thing was certain. It had been a long, long day, one where she'd experienced nearly every emotion possible. Tomorrow's chore list was already crammed full with work that needed to be done, but as long as she got a good night's sleep in between, she welcomed the chance to keep busy.

She padded to her room, Michael's letters safely tucked in her pocket. As she climbed the stairs, she thought of Michael, alone among strangers, fast asleep on the floor of an old school bus. How different his life was from hers.

After her eyes adjusted to the faint light, Betsie raised her window, hoping for a breath of air now that the storm had passed. Before lowering the shade, she squinted into the darkness, searching for the shape of the fallen maple tree.

The rising full moon was partially obscured by fast-moving clouds so it didn't offer much light yet. As Betsie shifted for a better look, a glimmer caught her eye. She glanced upward and her mouth dropped open. So much more of the sky was visible now that the maple tree was gone. For a moment, the clouds overhead parted and bright stars sparkled in the gap. Lost in wonder, Betsie watched as the wispy clouds sailed among the endless stars. It was a long time before she climbed into bed.

C H A P T E R   2 6

"The way some people look for faults,
you'd think there's a reward."

—Noah Troyer, quoted in Betsie's journal.

Betsie jumped when the new rooster crowed the next morning. She stretched, patted back a yawn, and swung her feet out of bed. As she did up her hair, she frowned. What a nightmare. A lingering image of menacing dust bunnies made her shiver as she finished dressing. She had a dim memory of waking up abruptly in the night, shaking and crying out for Michael to save her. Her cheeks grew hot. She hoped Sadie hadn't heard.

Now that she was awake, she realized how silly the dream was. She smiled at the thought of Michael waging war against random puffs of dirt, his unruly auburn hair caught up in a bandana, wielding a broom. Now that would be a sight to see.

As she dashed out of the room, she saw Michael's forbidden letters where she'd carelessly left them on her nightstand. So that's why he'd been on her mind. She scooped them up and tucked them in the book of poems, then shoved it far under her bed. No dust bunnies under there, she was happy to note. She shrugged and hurried to awaken her sister.

"Sadie! Are you up yet?" She hurried into the hall, pushed her sister's door open, and gasped. Pretty Sadie looked awful.

"Betsie," she whimpered. "I'm so glad to see you. I don't think I can work in the bakery today. I feel awful tired and achy, and I'm still sick to my stomach. I can't bear the thought of Mattie's sour face."

"*Jah*, you are pale and no mistake. Do you want me to tell Charley for you?"

Sadie nodded miserably. She seemed much younger than seventeen and very vulnerable. "How Mattie will scold next time I see her. She's been talking about hiring someone else to help out, but today she won't even have me there."

Betsie cracked a smile. "It's no secret why she has such trouble getting help. It's that tongue of hers. I don't know how you stand it."

But Sadie wasn't biting. "Do you think maybe . . . you can take my place today?"

"Me?" Betsie laughed and drew the curtains to block the glaring sunlight that streamed over Sadie's bed now that the maple tree was gone. "I'm not that good of a baker, not a fancy one, anyway."

"But you can do it, Betsie, I know you can. It's not so hard, and maybe this way, Mattie will not mind so much that I'm not there." Sadie watched her hopefully. "I know Mattie's awful, but I put up with her because she's Charley's mother. I figure she must have some good in her. I just haven't put my finger on it yet. Anyway, the bakery is just a place to pass the time until I get married and have *Bopplin* of my own someday. That's all I really want." A tear rolled down her cheek. "You'll probably be a great-grandma by the time I marry."

"Don't say such things, Sadie. You could wind up married before I am." Betsie chewed her lip. Work all day with Mattie Yoder? Perish the thought. Still, the woman was Charley's mother, as Sadie had pointed out. Maybe the good Lord was providing this chance to get to know her better and perhaps even show Mattie what a hard worker she was.

Before answering, she fished the hot water bottle out from under the bedclothes.

"All right. Charley promised to help me with that tree and other jobs today, but he'll have to work on his own so his mother can have the help she needs." She smoothed Sadie's hair. "You rest, now. I'll take care of Mattie."

Sadie curled up on her side and hugged her pillow to her stomach.

Dark circles under her eyes emphasized her frailty. "*Denki*, Betsie," she whispered.

When Charley arrived to pick up Sadie, Betsie fed Amelia one last morsel and watched the calico kitten tidy her face with a dainty paw. "Take good care of my sister," she whispered before she hurried outside.

"*Ach*, almost chilly this morning after the storm," she commented as she climbed in beside Charley.

He looked at her askance. "I am glad to see you, but where is Sadie?"

"Woman troubles still," she answered briefly. "I am going to help your mother today so she won't be on her own. I'm sorry I won't be here when Joe Miller and his sons chop up the tree, but I know I can count on you. Do you think you can find time to take care of the horses and the chickens, too?"

"So Sadie will be alone today," Charley said as he looked both ways and carefully urged his horse onto the road. "Of course. I am glad to help." He ruminated for a moment. "And I guess my mother can use you somehow."

Betsie struggled to keep her expression neutral. "Oh, don't worry about me. I can fetch the heavy bags of flour and scrub out dirty baking pans just fine. I can make myself useful, all right." She folded her arms and concentrated on a point between the horse's ears.

"I didn't mean it that way." Charley shifted uncomfortably. "It's only everybody knows Sadie is the best baker in Plain City and maybe that's why Yoder's Bakery does such good business. You've said so yourself."

"Yes. It's true no one can beat Sadie when it comes to cakes, cookies, doughnuts, and the like." She smiled, a warm glow filling her heart. "But there are some who believe my banana cream pie beats them all. So maybe that's what I will do today—fix some pies."

Charley steadied his horse. "Well, we'll see if that will be all right with *Mem*."

Betsie laughed. "Of course it will be all right. Everyone likes my pies. Don't worry."

For the rest of the drive, they confined themselves to neutral observations about the weather and the scenery, exclaiming over the size of the trees brought down by the storm. Here and there, a rickety outbuilding had toppled over in the high winds. A few houses in town sported aluminum siding that had twisted and peeled back.

"We just missed having a much worse outcome, that's what I think." Charley pointed out a broken window on the English school. "Did you happen to notice this morning whether your roof leaked? Hail can do as much mischief as high winds."

"I don't think it leaked," Betsie mused. "But I'll check better when I get home. That is, if I'm not too tired."

"No, don't bother," Charley said. He parked in front of the bakery, reached for her hand and squeezed it. "I will take care of everything, Betsie."

"That's nice to hear," she said. "But where are you off to, Charley? Aren't you coming in with me?"

"*Ach*, no. After all the damage we saw, I want to talk to Sawmill Joe before anyone else does. We need him to take care of that maple today. Maybe we even can get enough good wood out of that big tree to finish off the chicken run. That would be quite a savings for me." He looked very pleased with himself.

Betsie fumed silently. Can he think of nothing else but the day he takes over our farm? Why doesn't he realize that would only happen if my parents never rejoin the church and our community? And what follows is, I will never see them again.

Immediately she was ashamed. He is only trying to help me because he cares for me. She hoped gratitude showed in her eyes as she waved good-bye.

No time like the present. She squared her shoulders and marched into the bakery, the delectable smells wafting out to greet her. The bell that dinged above the door was nearly a twin of the one in the harness shop. In all the times she'd been here with *Mem* over the years, she'd never noticed it, but now its chime reminded her of mostly happy hours. She smiled, remembering Michael's antics and the quiet as she neatly stitched the leather for harnesses, belts, and saddles. She adjusted her *Kapp* and straightened her shoulders.

"There you are at last, Sadie, but you are late. I will keep a bit back from your pay," Mattie snapped, her thin back to Betsie as she drew a pan of cookies out of the oven. "Lock the door behind you and get to work."

"Sadie is ill, Mattie," Betsie stated as she wound her way among the wooden display stands and shelves to the glass-fronted display case. "But she is a good girl and she didn't want to leave you without help, so I am here to take her place today. I hope that is satisfactory."

Mattie straightened, a scowl at the ready. "Doesn't look like I have much choice, I suppose. Sadie is a pretty good baker and folks come in expecting to buy her baked goods. Not *yourn*."

Betsie silently counted to ten. "You're right about Sadie. I was talking to Charley on the way here, though, and we thought maybe I could make some banana cream pies today. I fix good ones and I believe your customers will like them," she replied. "I don't mean to boast, of course." Even though I do make the best pies in Plain City, she added to herself.

"You leave the running of this here bakery to me," Mattie sniped. "It's mine and Charley's name out there on the sign, not *yourn*. What I need help with this morning is the checking out once we open. Are you any good with an adding machine?" She pruned up her lips like she doubted it.

"*Jah*," Betsie said, not trusting herself to say more.

"All right. Until we open, I'll tend to the baking and you can take in the dairy deliveries when they arrive and restock the big icebox. After that, you can sweep and dust shelves, straightening as you go. Any time I tell you I have a tray of goods ready, that means the items need to be arranged in the display case or boxed up and displayed on the shelves. After we open at nine, you will check out our customers. But before all that, walk to the bank and get change." Mattie fished a twenty-dollar bill from the cash box and thrust it at her.

Betsie swallowed. "All right," she said as she took the bill, but Mattie had already turned back to her baking before Betsie unlocked the front door.

"And don't go out that way. Folks will think we're open. Lock up and use the back door," Mattie scolded.

Slowly Betsie complied. As she picked her way amid the stacks of broken pallets behind the bakery, she was of half a mind to walk all the way home. But no. If Sadie could stand it—and Betsie had to admit she didn't know how her sister did it—then she could too. It was just one day. She decided to relax and enjoy the short walk to and from the bank.

Despite Mattie's qualms, Betsie easily kept up with all she was asked to do after the bakery opened. She enjoyed seeing her friends and neighbors as they made their purchases. Everyone, it seemed, was bursting with news of last night's storm, each tale spinner topping the last with melodramatic details.

The best story came from Enoch Gingerich, Ada's husband and Betsie's neighbor from down the road. He related a long account of the storm as he tapped the counter with a gnarled forefinger, eyes so wide and voice so earnest and excited that Betsie found it difficult to wrench her attention away so she could total his order.

"Oh, were we glad when that bad storm finally passed! I hear you lost a maple tree, but would you believe it, Betsie? The wind was so strong over our way that it plowed up all my new potatoes clean out of the ground!" He hooked a thumb between his work shirt and braces and rocked on his heels.

She stopped her tally and the chatter of the adding machine ceased. "Dug up your potatoes?" With a doubtful shrug, she added, "Well, I've heard a windstorm can drive a wheat straw into a tree, so I guess—"

"*Jah*, but what do you think?" He stroked his beard gravely. "Those potatoes fell back to earth so hard they was mashed!"

Betsie wagged her head and pulled a wry mouth, one hand on her hip. Enoch grinned and broke into a rusty chuckle.

"That's a good one on me!" She laughed along with him and handed over the paper sack that contained his purchases. "Don't you eat all those cinnamon rolls at once, now. Tell Ada I said hello."

Enoch pushed open the door and the shop bell dinged. Betsie frowned, her nerves suddenly on edge. She shook her head, pivoted on her heel, and ran smack into Mattie Yoder.

CHAPTER 27

"Give some people an inch and they want to be rulers."

—FANNIE TROYER, QUOTED IN BETSIE'S JOURNAL

BETSIE BACKED UP a couple of steps and smoothed a stray hair from her forehead. "How you startled me, Mattie!"

"*Jah*, I see that." She pointed out the window at Enoch's buggy, her scrawny fingers putting Betsie in mind of a chicken's claw. "What was that Enoch said?"

"About his potatoes? *Ach*, he was only pulling my leg—"

"Before that," Mattie interrupted. "Something about your maple tree falling over. Did it do any damage to the house?"

"No, Mattie," Betsie began slowly, her guilty conscience pricking because of her harsh judgment of Charley's mother. Maybe Mattie did care. "*Denki* for your concern. No, the damage was to the pasture fence, and some to the yard, of course. Charley managed to put the horses in the barn and he even gathered my new chickens in the old smokehouse before the storm broke." She neatened the stack of newspapers beside the adding machine, lining up the edges precisely.

A sly smile split Mattie's dark face. "Any girl would be lucky to have him. Charley is a *gut* boy, the way he takes care of everything. Once those hens start laying, we will have fresh eggs to sell."

Betsie tipped her head quizzically. "I will have fresh eggs to sell, you mean."

Mattie ignored her. "And you are sure there was no damage to the house?" she probed.

"I don't think so," Betsie frowned, "but then, I didn't have time to check. Maybe Charley should inspect the attic to make sure the roof didn't leak. But tell me, Mattie, did your house sustain any damage from the wind?"

Mattie picked up a curled adding machine receipt from the floor in front of the checkout and pitched it in the wastepaper basket under the counter before answering. "The house didn't come through the storm as good as I'd like, but I imagine we'll be in our new place in a few months, so it don't differ much."

New place? Fear made Betsie's voice weak. "Don't tell me you and Charley are moving to Missouri, Mattie!"

She scoffed. "Move out west and leave Yoder's Bakery behind after all these years, just when it's starting to pay? Don't be foolish. No, I expect to own a fine place around here, one of these days. But I don't pay you to stand around and jaw." She glanced out the window. "Fewer customers come at this time of day. I'll tend to what few we have and you can bet I won't do so much talking as you. You go in the back and make some of those banana cream pies. I picked up some fresh bananas at the IGA earlier, so you can get right to work." Mattie opened the cash box and busily counted the contents.

Betsie stared after her before heading for the kitchen. Not for the first time, she wondered what Charley's father had seen in sharp-tongued Mattie. Maybe it was a mercy for him that he'd passed away when Charley was only a baby.

Yes, and what about Charley? She thumped ingredients on the counter, fuming all the while. How did a contentious woman like Mattie raise a son as pleasant as Charley? Oh, he can be a mite rule-bound and he is somewhat spoiled by his mother, she admitted to herself, but it's not his fault he was an only child. And soon he'll have his own big family.

As she blended the ingredients and rolled out the pie crust, a measure of peace returned. She stirred the bubbling pudding and whipped up the cream in turn, all her motions practiced and sure. Why should she care so much what Mattie said? Betsie knew better.

She pricked the crust with a fork and popped it into the oven to brown, content once more. Charley would most likely stay for dinner after he picked her up. He'd be hungry, maybe covered with sawdust after a long day of work on the tree and the fence. She decided to forgive his presumptuous behavior of yesterday. She'd often heard that an approaching storm could affect a person's mood, so maybe it had knocked matters between them out of whack, but now . . . she smiled as she tidied up her work space. Perhaps Mattie would send one of the pies home so Betsie could surprise Charley with it.

"Betsie!" Mattie's shrill voice broke in on her happy thoughts.

"Coming!" She pulled the golden brown crust out and set it on the counter to cool. She rubbed her hands with her apron, tiny balls of dough peeling away from her fingers as she hurried to the front, where she stopped short. Bishop Jonas Gingerich and Rachel Yutzy's father Silas confronted her, both of them frowning.

"You wanted to see me, Mattie? What's the matter?"

The look on Mattie's face was smug. "These men want to talk to you." She stayed put, like she'd paid admission for a show.

"*Was in der welt?*" Betsie clapped her hand over her mouth, her knees wobbly. "Is it the chainsaw? Has Charley been hurt?"

"No, no," Jonas spoke up quickly, "It's another matter. Silas, here, tells me your brother Abijah has been helping out at his house, getting ready for the wedding and all."

"It's Abijah who's been injured, then?" Her heart thumped wildly and skipped a beat.

"No one has been injured, Betsie, thank the good Lord." Silas's eyes were kindly, but his tone was firm. "Abijah and Levi were loafing out behind our barn a little while ago when they should have been working. I worked a full day in the fields when I was their age, but I know it's different at your house, what with your *Mem* and *Dat* gone. For the time being," he added.

Betsie wanted to shake Silas's hand. It seemed there were still some who believed her parents would return. "I'm sorry they weren't working, Silas."

His eyes were grave. "I'm afraid there's more to the tale, Betsie. You see, Abijah was teaching Levi how to smoke, and the boys very nearly caught the barn on fire."

Betsie closed her eyes, sick to her stomach. A barn fire! She knew it was only the mercy of the good Lord that spared the house and the boys, too. She cast about for the proper response, but she couldn't speak.

Silas seemed to understand. "Abijah said he'd taken some dried rabbit tobacco from his brother's place and brought it home with him. That's what the boys were trying to smoke, but they got to coughing and threw down the pipe in the weeds. Thank the good Lord it was so wet. I smelled smoke and put out the little bit of a fire before any real damage was done. Some scorched grass is all, except the pipe is burnt up and good riddance."

Betsie released her breath in a long sigh. "I am so thankful there was no damage, Silas."

Jonas spoke now. "Damage or no, this is a serious matter in the eyes of the People, Betsie. Word is spreading that Abijah is in rebellion."

Humbly she addressed Jonas. "What should I do?"

"You could leave Abijah with me for a couple more days," Silas spoke up. "I believe good, hard work will cure him, and we sure could use an extra pair of hands while we prepare for Rachel and Sam's wedding. What do you say, Betsie?"

The temptation to wash her hands of the matter, to let somebody else handle the discipline, was strong. "Are you sure Abijah won't be too much trouble?" Betsie asked, her voice barely above a whisper.

Silas removed his hat and scratched his head. "No, I'm not sure, but I know you've got your hands full enough without a runaway brother adding to your problems. Now that I know he must be watched, that's exactly what I'll do. Where I go, Abijah goes, and I have an awful lot of hard, needful work planned for the next few days. Come this visiting Sunday, I'll drop Abijah up at your house."

"You are a good servant of the Lord, Silas." Jonas Gingerich turned to Betsie. "We will hope a man's firm guidance is all Abijah needs, but if he gets into such monkey business again, Betsie, we'll have to try stronger measures. We can't let a young man bent on destruction run loose in our community."

CHAPTER 28

"But the wisdom that is from above is first pure, then
peaceable, gentle, and easy to be intreated, full of mercy
and good fruits, without partiality, and without hypocrisy."
—JAMES 3:17, QUOTED IN BETSIE'S JOURNAL

BETSIE GULPED. A young man bent on destruction, Jonas had called her brother. Suddenly the feeling was strong in her heart that *Dat* wouldn't have handled his son's transgressions this way. Although her father was firm, he was always gentle in manner, too. Silas's heart was certainly in the right place, but surely punishment alone wouldn't solve the problem. Wouldn't it be better to find out what was causing Abijah to act in this wild way? There was no guarantee he would tell her, or whether he even knew himself, but she felt she had to try.

But oh, what a tussle she'd had when she tried to convince Jonas to let her work for the Sullivan family in their harness shop. That victory had been hard-won. She wasn't sure she had another such battle in her.

She raised her head and faced the men, ignoring Mattie the best she could. "I am grateful to you for telling me of this matter, Silas. I would like for you to do as you have offered, but I would like a chance to talk with my brother first," she finished in a rush.

Mattie scoffed. "Talk? What good will talking do? A whipping is what that boy needs."

Jonas drew himself up. "Though we are talking in your bakery, this is none of your concern, Mattie." He turned his back on her. "Betsie, you are very young yet. Better leave a matter like this to Silas," he cautioned.

Surprised and grateful that Jonas defended her, Betsie said, "I have barely seen Abijah since he returned. My brother is always running off, but I don't yet know what he's running from or why he's acting up this way."

"Well, maybe he's like his *Dat*."

Shocked silence met Mattie's accusation. Every nerve in Betsie's body felt exposed, rasped raw. How could this woman be so cruel?

The bell above the door dinged and Betsie nearly jumped out of her skin. Her heartbeat slowed as she watched Miriam Bontrager, Mattie's neighbor and Lovina's convalescent friend, limp into the bakery. She clung to Ellie Beiler's arm as Ellie soothed her fussy son Jakob. Miriam's laughter pealed while Ellie related some amusing story from her repertoire.

As the women inched their way to the bakery display case at the back of the store, they spotted Jonas and smiled a welcome. The warmth in his answering smile did not match the angry glint in his eyes when he spoke. "Better go see to your customers, Mattie. And another time, watch your tongue."

Mattie's lips thinned into a hard line as though she was biting back a spiteful reply, but she did as Jonas said.

"Come, let us go outside, Betsie," Jonas invited.

"But I can't do that while I'm working!"

"Mattie will be fine on her own for a bit. She's been on her own for nigh on twenty years, anyhow." Jonas held the door open, waiting.

Betsie drew a shuddery breath and followed the two men outside to just beyond the buggy rail. To her surprise, they did not resume talking right away, and that suited her trembly insides just fine. After a few moments in the fresh air, she felt better.

At length, Jonas spoke. "I have been talking with the good Lord about your request, Betsie, and I feel that maybe you are right," he told her. "You should talk with your brother first. After that, if need be and if you are agreeable, Silas will lend a hand as he has offered." Jonas appealed to his friend for assent and Silas agreed.

She was so overwhelmed with Jonas's gentle wisdom that a lump rose up in her throat. Talking with the good Lord was the first thing *Dat* would have done, Betsie knew, and maybe if she'd done more praying herself, she wouldn't be in such a fix now.

What a change had come over the bishop since the last time he and Betsie had spoken. How had it come to pass that the man who had banned her wayward parents from the community was now taking Betsie's part against Mattie's wagging tongue and sharing about praying?

It was more than she could figure out at the moment, so she said, "I'd be beholden to you, Silas, if my brother could stay at your house until Charley picks me up after work later. We can stop off for him on our way home, if that's all right with you."

Silas smoothed his beard. "*Jah*, Betsie. I hope tonight he don't come sneaking back to my house, though. What do you think? Levi told me that Abijah bragged about climbing down the tree by his window when he wants to get out of the house in a hurry."

Betsie broke into a broad smile and oh, did smiling feel good for a change! "The good Lord made sure that wouldn't happen anymore, Silas. Last night's storm blew down Abijah's escape route."

She left the men talking quietly beside the buggy, feeling strangely at peace. Who could have imagined an outcome like this after such a horrible beginning? With wonderful men like Jonas and Silas on her side, she could conquer anything—even spiteful Mattie Yoder. *Jah*, after a long rough patch, it seemed to Betsie like Plain City, Ohio, was once again a pretty good place to be.

CHAPTER 29

"Moreover if thy brother shall trespass against thee,
go and tell him his fault between thee and him alone:
if he shall hear thee, thou hast gained thy brother."
— MATTHEW 18:15, QUOTED IN BETSIE'S JOURNAL

A FEW HOURS LATER, Betsie and Abijah sat together in the pasture, their backs resting against a fence post. Abijah's straw hat hid his eyes as he pulled a tuft of grass that had gone to seed. He chewed the end of a blade as Fledge cropped contentedly beside him.

Betsie put her hands behind her head and stretched, almost grateful that spiteful Mattie had kicked her out of the bakery as soon as she got back inside. Lucky for her that Silas hadn't driven away yet. After she told him what happened, he'd offered to drive her to pick up Abijah and take them both home. What did her dignity matter when she got to leave such unpleasant company early?

She turned to her brother and sighed. "Here I thought I was disciplining you when I asked you to work with Fledge while we finished taking care of the maple tree, Bije. That *loppich* pony has a mind of his own and it seemed like you'd have your hands full. Instead, you've got him following you around like your faithful dog, practically begging to be harnessed up and driven. He's like a different animal! What all did you make him do?"

"Nothin'." His tone was surly.

"Oh, I know better than that," she cajoled. "You must have worked him hard to get him so docile. If we are to make a living by breaking ponies to drive and selling them, I must hear how it's done, especially from an expert like you."

Abijah squeaked the blade of grass from between his teeth and pitched it before leveling a gaze at Betsie. "Maybe when I was a little boy you could fool me into doing what you wanted by talking pretty, but it won't work anymore. Besides, I already told you the truth. I didn't ask him to do one thing."

Pray. The command came from somewhere deep inside.

I should have left it all up to Silas. I can't do this, dear Lord. It's too hard to be both a mother and a father when I am only a sister. My brother's always one step ahead of me and nearly grown. Help me.

She moistened her lips. "I'm making a mess of things, Bije. It seems as though you were still my baby brother when you went off to Eli's, but now you're almost a man." She sighed and picked a daisy, twirling the stem between her fingers. One by one she plucked the petals and dropped them into her lap. "I don't know how to talk to you anymore. I end up making you angry, and that's not what I want to do. Let me try again." She took a deep breath. "How did you gentle Fledge?"

"I let him be, that's all." Abijah shrugged as she fidgeted with the daisy. "I figured if I get tired of being told what to do, a pony might, too, so I didn't ask him to do nothin'. I let him be, and he likes being left alone, don't you, boy?" He stretched a browned hand to rub Fledge's muzzle.

Betsie sat very still. "He sure does," she said, her words stretching out as she decided what to say next. "But a pony like Fledge can't just loaf and eat. On a farm like this, he must work and be useful to earn his keep, ain't so?"

"*Jah*, I guess so, but maybe he's been doing the wrong kind of work, right? You said his back is too ticklish for him to be ridden." He grinned suddenly. "I wish I could have seen you riding him."

"You would have had to look quick, for he got rid of me pretty fast. Served me right, I guess. I shouldn't have been riding horseback," she said with a prim set to her mouth. "But back to Fledge. He didn't like being ridden because it was wrong for him. But how will he earn his keep if he doesn't take to a pony cart?"

Abijah hooked one arm under Fledge's jaw and patted the other side of his head. He leaned away from Betsie, his face plastered against the pony's neck. When he spoke, his words were muffled. "He'll take to it. All we need is the cart so I can try." There was a long pause. "But if he doesn't, why can't we let him try something else? What if he's good at other things?"

"I don't think we are talking about a pony anymore, are we, Abijah?" Betsie said very gently. "What is it you want to do instead of working on a farm?"

He stared into the distance, his eyes dull and hopeless. "It doesn't matter. I would never be allowed to do it."

"So you do have a dream," she prodded. "Tell me about it."

"You won't tell Levi or his *dat*, will you?"

Betsie shook her head, afraid to say anything lest she lose his fragile trust.

He took a deep breath and plunged ahead. "I want to go back to school, even though I already finished the eighth grade. I want to get my high school diploma and then go on to college. I want to study biology or maybe even be a doctor, one for animals or maybe for people, I don't know which. The one thing I'm sure of is that I want to keep learning. And I can't do that here on the farm."

"But why not?" Betsie burst out. "You could study here at home, get books from the library in town and read them. I've even heard you can get what's called a GED—"

"Study when?" Abijah cut in, a desperate gleam in his eye. "After I've mucked out the stalls? Or cleaned the outhouse? Maybe I could read some after I plow up the garden for ten hours, or maybe in the winter there would be more time once I've chopped and split up the whole wood lot to keep us in stove lengths. There is little time for studying and reading, especially now that there's only three of us. The choice is work hard or go without eating. You should know that better than anyone," he finished bitterly.

Betsie stared at the flower petals in her lap and thought of the poetry book, committed to her for safekeeping and unread so far. Maybe Abijah was right.

"I can see why you are angry. It hurts to want something you can't have. I want *Mem* and *Dat* here at home once again. It's hard to wait, especially when some people don't think they're ever coming home," she said darkly. "But I haven't given up hope yet, and neither should you. Wanting to learn isn't a bad thing, Abijah." She looked him straight in the eye. "But teaching your best friend to smoke and nearly setting a barn on fire is very bad, and you know it. Why did you do it?"

"That's not how it happened," he said through clenched teeth. "Silas thinks Levi is a perfect angel. I can tell you he's not, but no one would listen to me."

"Well, I am listening now," Betsie reminded him mildly.

Abijah rubbed his face with both hands. "Susan keeps herbs and such for cures when the family is ill. I heard her talking one day about rabbit tobacco; such a funny name! Well, you know how much I love animals, so my ears perked up and I listened. Eli had come in from the field on a windy day and he was coughing a lot from the dust. Susan said a cup of rabbit tobacco tea would fix him right up, but Eli said the cure worked better for him when he smoked it. I watched him push it into a corncob pipe and draw in the smoke. Well, he got to coughing and hacking so much that he had to lean over the sink until everything came up. He said he was as right as rain after that. Later, after Susan and Eli went to bed, I got into her herbals where they were hung up in the attic and found the dried rabbit tobacco—I could tell by the smell. I pulled off a good hank of it and stuffed it into an envelope. I kept it in my pocket in case I ever got to coughing and couldn't stop." He hung his head. "Also I took Eli's pipe."

"So you stole these things from Susan and Eli. And do you mean to tell me that you were trying to cure yourself by smoking this rabbit tobacco?"

"No, not myself," Abijah said. "Levi got a tickle in his throat and I was trying to cure him by letting him smoke, but he got sick and pitched the pipe away before he *vommixed*. I tried to find the pipe in the long grass, but I got so scared when I saw the smoke that I couldn't move. Levi was too sick to care by that time, so I managed to get him away from there and hoped that the good Lord wouldn't let the barn burn down, and the house with it. And that's the honest truth, Betsie! I never meant for things to turn out this way. I know I've been mean, especially to . . . to the English girl." His expression changed to one of jealousy. "It was awful hard, though, to see her sitting on the bed without a care in the world, reading a book. I wished I had that kind of time. That's why I said what I did."

Betsie couldn't help herself. She hugged Abijah. He tensed for a moment, then returned brief pressure before backing off.

"I don't think you will need to go back to Silas's place for discipline. I believe you learned your lesson. Next time I see Silas, I will set him straight about what really happened and why," she vowed. "But before that, I am making two new rules for you."

"What are they?" Abijah closed his eyes, shoulders slumped.

She suppressed a smile. "The first is, if you ever again want to give somebody your rabbit tobacco cure, you must steep it in a tea."

Abijah's eyes popped open, gratitude written all over his face. "I will remember."

"*Gut*. And the second rule is this: since learning means so much to you, if we can get all our chores done early, we will go to the library. You could start with a book about herbs and one about animals, too, or maybe training horses."

"Do you mean it, Betsie?" Her younger brother's face shone.

She nodded, near to bursting with happiness.

CHAPTER 30

Lately, the trip to the mailbox is the highlight of my day.

—BETSIE'S JOURNAL

LATER THAT AFTERNOON, Betsie drove the buggy into the barn after she and Abijah spent a pleasant half hour in the Plain City library.

"Whoa, Judith," she said. The thought of all the work she'd put off made her weary, but one look at her brother's face as he held the thick book told her the sacrifice was worth it. "You go on into the house, Bije. I'll be in after I unhitch."

To her surprise, Abijah put the book on the seat and stopped at Judith's side. He caught the mare's bridle. "*Ne.* I'll unhitch and tend to Judith, and then I'm going to wash the buggy. It's awful muddy. After that, I'll fill the wood box, bring in some corn cobs for kindling, and start on whatever else you need done around here." He grinned at her shock. "Eli did say I could be pretty handy when I had a mind to be."

She frowned. "*Denki* for the help, but that reminds me. Are you sure you let Eli know where you were going, or did you run off without a word?" The unwritten letter to her older brother still weighed heavily on her conscience, but if she wrote that letter, she would have to include news of the shunning. Wouldn't it be better, she reasoned, to write news of *Mem* and *Dat* after they returned home for good? Otherwise Eli would fret needlessly, she comforted herself.

"*Ach*, they knew I wanted to come home from the first day I got out there. If you think we work some here, you should watch Susan once she starts in." He pretended to wipe sweat from his brow. "It's hard to believe that she's Rachel and Levi Yutzy's big sister, as much fun as they are. Susan acted like she was the bishop or something, the way she ordered me around. I never had a minute of peace for thinking and wondering. Anyway, like I told you before, Eli's broken leg was nearly healed by the time I made it to their house. He didn't really need my help anymore, but he sure wasn't going to turn it down. I left him a note when I left, and I wrote to him when I got home safe. Don't look at me that-a-way, it's the truth. I sent the letter from the Yutzy place before Levi made me come home."

"I guess that's why I haven't heard from him," Betsie mused, secretly happy that she could put off a letter a while longer. "Well, I will carry your book into the house. I have a good idea—you can read while you eat. You're already sitting then, anyway. And since you're helping me, I'm going to help you by fixing an extra good meal. An extra good, big meal," she corrected herself. "But before I do that, I will finally take some time to piece and cut out my *nayva hokkah* dress for Rachel's wedding."

Abijah finished his unbuckling and lowered the buggy shafts before carefully leading Judith forward. "Doesn't the bride usually sew all the dresses?"

"Rachel doesn't have time since they're getting married so soon. I'll tell you what, I didn't know how I was going to get my dress done," she confided, "since Sadie's gone all day and too tired and cranky to help with much of anything once she gets home. Now that I've worked a few hours with Mattie, Sadie's crankiness is not such a wonder any-more." She shifted the book to her other arm. "Anyway, with your help, I think I can finish my dress in plenty of time."

"That's *gut*." Abijah slipped the crown-piece up and over Judith's ears. She shook her head with a rumbly snort and switched her tail. Fledge answered her with a shrill whinny and Betsie and Abijah laughed. He scratched behind the mare's ears, a dreamy expression on his face, and Betsie left him to his work.

She walked toward the smokehouse, careful to avoid the deep hollow where the maple tree had lain after it thudded to the ground in the storm. Sawdust and wood chips were all that remained of the pretty tree, aside from the knobby posts that made up the new section of fence and the chicken run.

Betsie smiled; Charley must have gotten the men to mend the fence and help him knock together the run, shiny with new chicken wire and attached to the side of the old smokehouse. She pumped a bucket of water and felt a deep sense of contentment as she refilled the water pans. Her laying hens clucked contentedly as they scratched for grubs. They'd be doubly safe from predators once she shut them up in the newly fitted hen house for the night. How pleased and surprised *Dat* and *Mem* would be to see this progress. She would tell them about it in her next letter.

It would be really nice, she mused, to extend the fence around her vegetable garden so the chickens could scratch there of a sunny afternoon. Chickens and gardens just naturally went together. She'd have to talk to Charley about it. Or maybe, she corrected herself, Abijah could build the fence. With a grateful heart, she headed for the house to tackle her sewing.

As she swept up odd scraps of blue fabric, Betsie considered how she had misjudged her brother. All he'd needed was a little understanding. Talking things over had their place. She'd once thought talking was useless, but Michael had convinced her otherwise—how else but by talking? She grinned. *Ach*, how he could jabber, but what he had to say was usually very good to hear.

Thoughts of Michael brought to mind all the things she'd like to tell him. She carefully stowed her pinned dress pattern pieces out of Amelia's reach so she could work on them tomorrow, then she stepped to the desk, dug out paper and pen from the stationery drawer, and strode purposefully into the kitchen. The only evidence that remained from their hearty dinner was half of a shoofly pie on the counter.

Once Betsie was seated at the table, her thoughts spilled onto paper with an ease that surprised her. It was almost like Michael was seated across from her and they were having a conversation.

When she finished writing, she ran the letter out to the mailbox and put up the flag. Things had certainly taken a turn for the better around here! She had the good feeling she got when everything was crossed off her to-do list. Only . . . something was not quite right.

Then Betsie remembered the letter from her parents. Yes, that was it. She'd saved it to read with Sadie, but then the storm came and drove all thought of it clean out of her mind.

She'd missed her chance today, with working in the bakery for Sadie and then all the fuss over Abijah. Both of them were already asleep now. Never mind. She dashed up the stairs and retrieved the precious letter. Back in the kitchen, she ripped it open and began reading.

Dear Sadie and Betsie, Well we are glad to hear from you once more, although we wish you saw things different than you do. Your *dat* says to tell you we are fine where we are, better than fine. The good Lord loves you more than you can possibly know, even more than we do. We want to say now what we never did say too much, although maybe we showed it. We love you girls so much, Abijah, and all the rest, too. Can't you find it in your heart to come up for a visit again? And maybe sit and read the *Biewel* together, as we used to do? Oh, yes! Me and your *dat* and Lovina have such good times of fellowship, such peace. We so want that for you girls, too.

It's hard, so very hard, to be away from you girls. Sometimes I feel it is more than I can bear. We left everything and everyone behind except for Lovina, and what a blessing it is to have her here! She has reminded us that maybe living in Plain City is not such a hardship as it might be, for your bishop Jonas is much more lenient and kind than the one she knew in Holmes County. But she adds that following Jesus is better, for "His yoke is easy, His burden is light." Oh, so *gut* to have her here, but then I think of how much I miss you girls and oh, my heart hurts something awful.

Betsie pressed a hand to her own heart. How well she knew the feeling *Mem* meant. She went on reading.

> When that happens, I get out my new *Biewel* and read Mark 10, verses 28 to 30: "Then Peter began to say unto him, Lo, we have left all, and have followed thee. And Jesus answered and said, Verily I say unto you, There is no man that hath left house, or brethren, or sisters, or father, or mother, or wife, or children, or lands, for my sake, and the gospel's, but he shall receive an hundredfold now in this time, houses, and brethren, and sisters, and mothers, and children, and lands, with persecutions; and in the world to come eternal life." And of course this is true, for we have so many new friends young and old at the church here in Belle Center. When we walk about the town, as we often do of an evening, we see many who we know, and oh, so wonderful to stop and chat about the good Lord's many blessings.
>
> Oh, my dear girls! If only you could understand what sweet assurance we have now. Please do your best to come and visit us, and if it should be that your heart whispers and tells you to join us in following the good Lord, our happiness will be complete. I will close now, but Noah wants to add a line or two, so I will hand this letter over to him.

Betsie turned over the page and resumed reading. *Dat*'s crabbed handwriting brought to mind his hands, roughened and gnarled from years of hard work, yet full of tenderness and so dear to her heart.

> My sweet girls, I take up the pen to add a few lines to what your mother has written. Yet it is not I, but the author of Hebrews who says: "Today if ye will hear his voice, harden not your hearts." Take these words to heart and come away from Plain City, to us and to Jesus Christ. Noah

Betsie traced her father's signature with a reverent finger. How she longed to lay her head on *Mem*'s shoulder to find rest for her weary soul, longed to see *Dat*'s kind blue eyes shine with joy as he read aloud a passage from his beloved *Biewel* in his rumbly bear voice.

She chewed her lip until she tasted blood. She could never leave Plain City for good, as *Dat* urged. Her path was certain; she meant to join the Amish church and marry Charley, in that order.

If only a short visit were possible, though! She sliced a crusty loaf of bread and slathered the thick slices with peanut butter spread. If Michael were around, he would take her to Belle Center to see her parents, as he'd done once before. The way he loved to drive that Super Bee of his, she felt sure all she had to do was ask.

It wouldn't be fair to ask him, though, not when he was so far away. He'd been so excited about starting his new life at The Farm. Although . . . Betsie pondered as she shook *Mem*'s canned green beans into a pot and laid a few thick slices of bacon over top before peppering them well and putting on the lid. In his letter, Michael had not seemed so sure of himself once he arrived in Tennessee.

Well, she would wait and see what his next letter said about it. If he still sounded uncertain of his decision, what harm could there be in asking him to come home? For a while, anyway. She would just have to be sure Charley didn't find out. It was something she would have to ponder. Ah well, she had all the time in the world for a visit to Belle Center. Rachel and Sam's wedding fast approached. She would be very busy for the next week—less than a week, she realized, with a glance at the calendar. *Mem* and *Dat* certainly weren't going anywhere. She tucked the idea of a visit away for safekeeping, feeling happier and more hopeful than she had in a long time . . . maybe ever.

CHAPTER 31

One more care piled on my shoulders and everything
will topple like a child's tower of blocks.

—BETSIE'S JOURNAL

BETSIE HAD JUST put the finishing touches on her morning journal entry when a buggy rolled into the drive. It was too bad Mattie had insisted that Sadie work on Saturday to make up for her absence when she was ill. How convenient it would have been for Sadie to prepare today's meals while Betsie worked on their dresses!

"Sadie, Charley's here!"

She smoothed her front hair and adjusted her apron before walking sedately to the door to greet Charley with a pleased smile.

"*Guder mariye*. Sadie should be down soon. Come in and wait, why don't you?" She opened the door wide and pressed a warm paper sack into his hand as he passed. "You can take these along with you. I baked oatmeal chocolate chip muffins this morning and I managed to hide a couple from my brother," she joked. "Right, Bije?"

Abijah took a huge bite of scrambled eggs and bacon and nodded absently. As he chewed, he groped for the muffin on his plate while turning a page in his book, his expression rapt. *Stalking the Wild Asparagus*, by Euell Gibbons. Betsie shook her head. Such a funny title.

"Abijah, it is good to see you again. I have a favor to ask of you this morning." He waited until Abijah glanced up at him. "I hear you are becoming quite the horseman. Could you drive Sadie to the bakery for me this one time? You can drive my horse if you are careful. I trust you will drive him straight back here after you drop Sadie off. I need to talk with Betsie. Can you help me out?"

"*Jah*, sure! I'll be right back." The younger boy's voice teemed with excitement. He shoveled the rest of the eggs into his mouth and crammed the muffin into his pocket. With the precious book carefully tucked under one arm, he dashed up the stairs.

Betsie scraped muffin crumbs and egg bits into Amelia's bowl before stacking Abijah's breakfast dishes on the counter. "You made him so happy, Charley. We've had a rough start, but he's improving fast."

"*Jah*, I talked to Silas last night and he seemed to feel that you had done your best with your brother on your own. I told him that you asked for my help with Abijah a while back, but he kept running off. Now that he's home, I told Silas that I will step in. It takes a man's input to discipline *Yungi* properly." Charley opened the paper sack and sniffed appreciatively at the muffins. "From now on, you can do your part with your good cooking to help him grow big and strong like me. By the way, looked to me like his trousers are a mite too short, as well, but you are a good seamstress. It will be nothing for you to let out the hem, ain't so?"

Flabbergasted, Betsie opened her mouth to answer just as Abijah thumped down the stairs and ran outside, the hems of his trousers hitting him well above the ankles. Well, maybe Charley was right, but when had her brother been home for her to work on his everyday clothes? Not to mention where she could squeeze in the time to let out his good church trousers. Out of sight, out of mind, that's what *Mem* always said. She started to speak a second time, but the screen hinge squeaked again. Abijah sheepishly grabbed his straw hat and clapped it on his head before running off to Charley's buggy.

Though the interruption was slight, it presented Betsie with a chance to think before a smart retort could pass her lips. "What all did Silas say when you told him your plan about stepping in?" she asked.

Charley scratched his head. "Not too much, come to think of it. He is so busy with the wedding and all that he probably didn't have any time for jawing."

Betsie caught her breath as Sadie made the turn at the landing and joined them in the kitchen. The dark blue dress her younger sister wore brought out the blue in her eyes and her cheeks were rosy once again, a welcome sight after her spell of feminine miseries.

"Abijah will drive you today, Sadie," she said. "Charley wants to talk to me."

"Yes, Bije told me," she answered, breathless with hurry as she jammed her feet into her shoes. "I'm late. I don't have time to wait for breakfast."

"Here, take my muffins." Charley thrust the paper sack into her hands. "I have plenty of time, so Betsie can cook me another breakfast."

"Maybe I will take them, as long as it's all right with you, Betsie." There was an unspoken question in her sister's eyes.

Betsie suspected Sadie was worried about their dresses for Rachel's wedding, so she put extra assurance into her nod. "Sure, take them. I hope you have a good day at the bakery," she added, though privately she doubted that was possible. "Don't worry, I will take care of everything here."

But after Sadie left, Charley sat at the table like a bump on a log, in no hurry to talk about anything, as far as Betsie could see. She rustled up a breakfast for him, along with plenty of anxious thoughts of the sewing she'd planned to get done this morning. She'd gotten up extra special early to tend to the chickens and horses, too, and she'd planned to start on her stitching right after breakfast. She tried not to let her anxiety show as she served Charley eggs fried over easy, the way she knew he liked them, along with bacon fried almost—but not quite—to a crisp, another favorite.

He looked up from his plate and smiled at her. "Some toast would go mighty good with these eggs. I like to sop it in the yellow."

Betsie pressed her lips together and cut a couple of slices from the loaf of bread. "I suppose that's how Mattie fixes breakfast for you?"

Charley nodded happily and rested his chin on one elbow while munching on the bacon. Quickly Betsie buttered the bread and stuck it in the oven to brown. "What was it you wanted to talk to me about, Charley?"

"Oh, don't worry about that right now. We have plenty of time," he said, suddenly magnanimous. "In fact, you are working awful hard. Why don't you sit down with me and have a cup of coffee? Is there some made?"

She frowned and shook her head. "Only *Dat* drinks coffee so I have not bought more. I could make you some tea, though. I already had mine."

"That's all right, don't bother." He drained his glass and held it out to her. "I'll have another glass of milk instead."

She filled his glass and snatched the toast from the hot oven in the nick of time. "Here you are. If there is nothing else you want, I am going to get a start on these dishes."

He waved a hand in assent. As Betsie worked through the dishpan, her hands soapy and warm, she felt her tension ebb and disappear like soap bubbles down the drain. By the time she put the last fork in the dish drainer, she was able to smile at Charley when he told her he was finished with his breakfast.

She scraped his dish and washed it. Surely now was the time. "What was it you wanted, Charley?"

He stretched and slapped his belly. "You sure are a good cook."

Awful free with his compliments this morning, she huffed to herself. If she didn't know better, she'd think he was trying to butter her up. Nonetheless, her stomach fluttered at his praise. "Is that what you wanted to talk about?" she teased.

His chair scraped and Betsie heard his heavy footsteps as he crossed the floor to stand behind her, one hand on each of her shoulders.

"No. But I meant what I said. Your cooking is one of the things I like so much about you, Betsie," he whispered. She felt him lightly stroke the back of her neck.

Flustered, she gripped the edge of the counter, her back rigid. Soapy water plopped from her hands to the floor. She watched her pulse race in her wrist. The anxious feeling swelled like a creek in flood until it was all Betsie could do to keep from bolting. Her vision narrowed to bursts of light while darkness fluttered all around.

"Charley." Her mouth was dry. "C-can we go outside? I need a breath of fresh air."

He squeezed her shoulders, his hands lingering for a moment. "All right," he answered without much enthusiasm.

Betsie's hands shook as she plied the dish towel. What was the matter with her? She followed Charley, wobbly as a newborn foal.

Once outside, she sat on the concrete step and rested her forehead on her knees. After several deep breaths, her vision cleared enough that she could make out the interwoven threads in her apron. The high sweet song of a goldfinch in flight penetrated her consciousness, too, and a measure of peace returned.

"Are you all right, Betsie?" Charley's voice was anxious now.

She moistened her lips, halfway raising her head. "If you could fetch me a cold glass of water, I think I'll be fine in a minute or two. You'll find the pitcher in the icebox." She rested her head on her knees again, not waiting for his reply.

When he returned with the water, she felt restored enough to sit up and take a sip. "I don't know what came over me," she said apologetically. "Between the fire in the stove, the hot dishwater, and the running around, I guess I got overheated. I feel some better now."

"You're still awful white," he said, peering at her face. "Sit still a while and take another drink."

Betsie obeyed. "*Denki* for taking care of me, Charley," she said at last. "I believe I will be able to start my sewing in a little while, but first, what was it you wanted to ask me?"

He broke into a smile. "*Ach*, that's funny. You hit the nail on the head."

She creased her brows. "How do you mean?"

"Last Sunday when I was driving my mother home from church, my horse acted up. It was all I could do to rein him in, but, well, my good white shirt . . ." He trailed off.

"What about your shirt?" she asked, confused.

Somehow Charley managed to look pleased and embarrassed at the same time. "I guess my shirt had been washed so many times that it split straight down the back when I braced to tighten up on the reins. Now I can't wear it to Sam and Rachel's wedding. So I was wondering, since you're so good with the sewing machine and all, if you could sew me a new white shirt before next Thursday," he finished in a rush.

Betsie's heart pounded. "Me? Why not your mother?"

Charley avoided her eyes. "She said maybe I should ask you, since she's so busy at the bakery all the time. But think, Betsie. Does a bachelor like me want his mother mending his shirts? Or does he want the woman he is going to marry to sew for him?"

The steady rhythm of trotting hooves echoed as a buggy passed the house. Betsie turned to watch it and pulled a wry mouth. Mattie had done it again. Reprimanded by Jonas for Betsie's sake, she'd retaliated with a surefire way to monopolize Betsie's time. She doubted she could finish everything before the wedding, but she couldn't say no. Before too long, she'd be making all Charley's clothes anyway. Why this strange reluctance about sewing for him, then? And why had the harness shop come to mind?

She suppressed her uneasiness. "*Jah*, I guess I can cut out and sew a shirt for you, in between working on my dress and Sadie's, and letting out Abijah's hems. Maybe Sadie'll get to feeling good enough to help out some once she's home from work. What am I to make it from?"

"*Mem* has the fabric already. I'll bring it over and then I will help you with your work around here as I have been doing, don't worry. Abijah and I should be able to keep everything going while you sew. But we'd better get started."

He offered his hand to help her up from the step and Betsie stood soberly beside him. We will talk like this all the time, she reflected, when Charley and I are married. "I wonder if *Mem* ever felt like she needed another pair of hands to finish a day's work?" she asked without thinking.

"Likely she did," Charley answered. "But that's what a houseful of children is for, ain't so? Now let's go inside." He flexed his biceps and held the door. "I don't know too much about sewing, but I do know that you will need to take my measurements before you can get started on my shirt."

CHAPTER 32

"For where two or three are gathered together in
my name, there am I in the midst of them."

— Matthew 18:20, quoted in Betsie's journal

ON SATURDAY EVENING, Betsie hunched over the sewing machine in
the corner of the front room, one foot forward and one behind as
she pumped the treadle. She guided the blue fabric smoothly along
the throat plate, taking care to keep up a steady feed as the thread
whirled off the bobbin and down through the needle. The last thing
she wanted at this point was a snarl.

When she finished the final seam, she collapsed against the seat
back and wiped a droplet of sweat from the end of her nose. A muscle
in her neck had worked itself into a kink at least an hour ago, but she
hadn't had time to stop and tend to it. She massaged the kink now,
rolling her head back and forth blissfully as she rubbed. Oh, so *gut* to
finish the machine work! All that remained on both dresses was the
hand stitching of the hem and such.

She snipped the thread and held up her handiwork for approval.
"How does it look, Sadie?"

Sadie gave the windowsill a final swipe with her dust rag before
examining the piece with a critical eye. "Wonderful, Betsie," she said
finally. "I can't believe you ran up both dresses in one day. I never
heard of such fast work."

"I had no choice," Betsie answered with a wan smile. "I won't finish all my sewing before Thursday otherwise. I'll go hang these up for now and maybe you can start hemming them tomorrow while I cut out Charley's shirt."

"Watch this!" Abijah breezed into the room with Amelia perched on his shoulder. He stretched out his right arm and snapped his fingers. The calico kitten minced along his arm toward his hand, scrambling once on a loose fold of shirtsleeve to regain her balance. When she reached Abijah's hand safely, her reward was a morsel of something Betsie couldn't quite see. Amelia latched onto it with her paws and curved it into her mouth with an excited mew, chewing with obvious relish. Then she extended her claws and licked the flavor from between each toe, her eyes closed in sheer delight.

"How long did it take you to teach her that?" Sadie came over to stroke between Amelia's furry ears.

"Not long. A few minutes, maybe." Abijah's eyes glowed. "It wasn't so hard."

Betsie squinted. "What's that you're feeding her?"

"Hot dog." Her brother fished in his pocket and fed the kitten another piece.

"Abijah!" she scolded. "Those hot dogs are for us, not the cat! I was so happy when I found a pound of them in the freezer, too. Hot dogs are all I'll have time to cook, what with sewing and everything else we have to do. But, really, it is an awful *gut* trick you taught Amelia. And maybe," she relented, "one hot dog won't hurt. Likely I won't have time to eat, anyway. Just don't feed her any more," Betsie finished.

But Abijah's attention was fixed on something else she'd said. He frowned. "Did I hear you say you have more sewing to do tomorrow? It's Sunday. I thought we would go a-visiting."

Sadie paused by the front window, sadness in her eyes. "There's no one left to visit. All our friends have moved away."

"Oh, Sadie. It's not that bad." Betsie sighed. "I wish we had time for visiting, but we have too much to do. Anyway, we will see everyone on Rachel's wedding day, ain't so? And that reminds me, Bije, go up and bring your church trousers down here. I already washed them this week, but I'm going to let out the hems and press them so they are long enough for Thursday."

He stared at his grimy feet before meeting her eye. "Are you sure you have time?"

"*Jah*, of course. Run get them, now. Well, what's the matter?" Betsie prodded when he didn't move.

Sadie said gently, "Betsie, probably he feels the same as me. You have done so much for us lately. We are only now realizing that we couldn't have made it through these days without you. Isn't that it?" she appealed to her brother.

"Well, partly." Abijah winced as Amelia caught his thumb between her claws and licked it with her rough tongue. He rubbed behind her ears with one finger. "But also I've been awful mean—"

Betsie stood with both dresses draped over one arm. "Don't speak of that. I'm happy that we are a family again, but do you know what would make me ever happier? Having *Mem* and *Dat* back home. And that reminds me. Wait here."

She hurried up to her room and arranged the dresses on hangers. She thought again of the furious pace she'd set as she pieced and sewed the dresses and hoped a sleeve wouldn't fall off in the middle of the wedding, but she shrugged and put the worry out of her mind. With the latest letter from her parents in hand, she rejoined her brother and sister in the front room.

"Rest a minute and I'll read *Mem* and *Dat*'s letter aloud. It's not very long and they have nothing new to say, but I think you should hear it. Then let us pray together that they come to their senses and return to us and the church."

She settled on the couch with a sibling on either side. Abijah deposited Amelia on a blue cushion and her rumbly purr of contentment added to the cozy family feeling as Betsie began reading.

No one said anything when she finished. She passed the letter to Sadie and then to Abijah. Each read it over again as though they wanted to savor the words their parents wrote.

"It's awful good to hear from them," Sadie ventured at last. "But it would be even better if we could see them again." She wiped her eyes on a corner of her apron.

"Then we must pray that we will," Betsie said. She bowed her head and reached for her sister's hand, surprising even herself, but she noticed with gratitude that Sadie didn't pull away. Then wonder of wonders, Abijah awkwardly fumbled for Betsie's other hand and she held on tight. The three of them sat for a long time and talked silently with the good Lord about *Mem* and *Dat*. What was more, Betsie felt absolutely certain that He was listening.

CHAPTER 33

"And high overhead and all moving about,
There were thousands of millions of stars."

—"Escape at Bedtime" by Robert Louis
Stevenson, quoted in Betsie's journal

Betsie yawned. Why, oh why had she stayed up so late? When she'd finally climbed into bed, her body, especially her calves, had ached so badly from the marathon sewing session that sleep was impossible, so she'd dug out the poetry book that Michael had sent to her for safekeeping.

At first, it had been so restful to let her head sink deep into her feather pillow while she leafed idly through the pages. But then she'd gotten caught up in the words, each one chosen with exquisite care and melded carefully to express profound thoughts. She devoured works by King David, Henry Wadsworth Longfellow, Carl Sandburg, Percy Bysshe Shelley, Charlotte Mew, and especially Robert Frost. A couple of times she gasped with delight as she read thoughts the poets had shared straight from their hearts.

That Michael had been here before her was plain to see. He'd marked many of the poems, noting in his tiny, precise handwriting why this poem or that one was especially memorable. Betsie read one of them, "The Death of the Ball Turret Gunner," and shivered to discover that such stark images of war and death could be contained in a poem of only five lines.

She shut her eyes tight and shuffled the book to another page, hoping to read a work that would not cause more of those awful nightmares she'd been suffering. But how appropriate! "Escape at Bedtime" was the first poem she saw. As she read and reread the words of Robert Louis Stevenson, she sighed with pleasure. "But the glory kept shining and bright in my eyes, and the stars going round in my head," she murmured drowsily.

When she awoke, a long time before daylight, the poem book was still in her hands. Although she was groggy from reading so late, she'd slept soundly, the beauty of the words remaining with her.

She decided to dive right in and finish Charley's shirt early, if she could, and then move on to hemming the dresses for her and Sadie, and then Abijah's trousers. She chewed her lip; should she sew on the Sabbath? She decided to risk it. As she pinned and snipped the white pattern pieces, snatches of poetry came back to her and lightened her heart. Even the poems she didn't like so much had taught her something: words carried power.

When the knock sounded on the kitchen door, she jumped. Her next thought was that even though the Troyers had not stopped for visiting Sunday, it had kindly stopped for them. She grinned at her parody of a poem contained in the Emily Dickinson book Michael had given her to keep, back when she stayed in Hilliard with the Sullivans. Strange that so many poets wrote about death, she mused as she left the sewing machine and trotted to the kitchen.

She saw who it was and hurried to push open the door. "Jonas, I didn't expect to see you here. It's early." She craned to see the rest of the bishop's family, but he was alone.

"I hoped I'd catch you before you started out to visit this morning." Jonas said by way of greeting. "Is it all right if I come inside for a bit?"

Betsie whisked a white thread from her sleeve and guilt smote her. "Of course. I've just been working on a shirt. For Charley. For the wedding, I mean. I had to sew my dress and Sadie's, and there just hasn't been enough time to get it done unless I worked on it today." Should she admit as much to the bishop? "I shouldn't be sewing or doing any kind of work on the Sabbath. Is that why you've come?"

He shook his head as he sat down at the table. "*Ne*, don't trouble yourself over it. Things are changing fast here in Plain City, Betsie, what with people moving and Rachel and Sam marrying in a rush before they leave. You wouldn't have to be working on those wedding clothes for a few months yet if that were not the case."

"That's true." Betsie bit her lip. What exactly had Jonas stopped by for, then? But then she knew: Sheila. Mattie had finally done her work. Betsie steeled herself and hoped she didn't look as haggard as he did; there were deep hollows under his bleary eyes.

"Have you heard from your folks, Betsie?" he finally asked.

So that was it. He was checking on the shunned. "We got a letter this week. They say they won't change their minds for anything, and that includes Lovina." Betsie hung her head.

Jonas stroked the smooth wood of the table thoughtfully. "That means they're not coming back."

"They say they are not. But Sadie, Abijah, and I still pray that they will."

"You sound just like your *dat*, you know." Jonas smiled slightly. "He and I had many talks before he left, and I counted him as one of my closest friends. Noah is an awful smart man, one who has great faith."

Tears of shame sprang unbidden to Betsie's eyes. "How can you say that? He and *Mem* left, and you are the one who made the decision to shun my parents."

He winced. "As the bishop, it was necessary for the church's sake that I follow the *Ordnung*. You know that, Betsie."

She thought she detected a pleading tone in Jonas's voice. Was it possible he regretted his decision? She'd never given a thought to what a burden being the bishop must be. As she pondered this new idea, Jonas drew a small book from his pocket.

"Noah and Fannie gave me this English New Testament right before they left, although I didn't know of their plan at the time. How I enjoyed talking with Noah. Lots of people are afraid to talk with their bishop, but not your *dat!* He asked me to read this Bible. I want you to know that I have, although mostly after he left, because I hoped to prove him wrong." He hesitated a moment, then leaned forward in his chair, his words coming out in a tumble. "Betsie, I want to visit your parents. Can you write down for me the address where they are staying?"

For a moment she said nothing, speechless with delight. Finally she clasped her hands and nodded, her smile so big it hurt her cheeks. "It is the answer to our prayers! You are going to help us and bring *Mem* and *Dat* home!"

"Well . . ." Jonas faltered, "I will talk with them, anyway. It is up to the good Lord what happens afterwards, ain't so?"

"*Jah, jah*, I know," she said, irked at his reluctance. For how could he fail? In her mind's eye, she was already watching herself, Sadie, and Abijah as they leapt from the front porch to welcome their wayward parents home. How wonderful to lead *Mem* and *Dat* around the farm, to return the full measure of responsibility for the family's upbringing, the house, and the land over to them once again. She thought of the flock of chickens and the repaired stair tread. Yes, and to present it all in even better shape than when they left.

She retrieved her notebook from the drawer where she kept it and from memory jotted down the address of the house in Belle Center where her parents were staying. What a blessing that she would never have to see her parents in those despised English clothes again. How odd *Dat*'s kind face had looked without his familiar beard. Never mind, she consoled herself. It will soon grow out once he is at home again.

"Here you are." She ripped out the sheet of notebook paper and pressed it into Jonas's hand. "Oh, so happy you have made me, Jonas! Only wait until I share the news with my brother and sister! You are so *gut*, so *gut* to help us in our trouble. Wait, don't go yet," she urged.

She opened a cabinet door and reached for the old cookie jar, the one with the broken lid. Dollars rustled as she counted out train fare from the money Mr. Sullivan had paid her for Fledge's keep. "This should cover your ticket and *Mem* and *Dat*'s, too. And don't forget Lovina, *Dat*'s sister! Bring them all home and may the good Lord go with you, Jonas! But what is the matter now? Here, take the money, I insist."

"No, Betsie," he began in a strangled voice. He cleared his throat before continuing. "Keep it. I believe I can get a ride with somebody from town when I go."

"All right." Soberly she replaced the money in the cookie jar. If only she had time to visit Belle Center again, but the fifty-mile trip would take Judith six hours. With all Betsie had to do, she couldn't spare even one hour to ride in a car, let alone the time spent visiting with her parents and driving back. "Tell me, when will you go up there? Tomorrow?"

He shook his head and pushed back his chair to stand. "I won't go until Friday, maybe. The day after Sam and Rachel are married."

"Ohh." She stretched the word until it dwindled to nothing. "How could I have forgotten about the wedding? Friday seems very far away. My parents have been gone over a month now, but surely I can wait five more days if it means they will come home soon. Yes, it will be a good way for me to learn patience," she concluded as she walked him to the door.

Jonas donned his hat and lifted his hand in a half-hearted wave before pausing on the doorstep. "Betsie," he said gently, "I must tell you something. In the last few days, I have seen you work to help your sister keep her job at the bakery, even though it was not so pleasant. I've seen you win your brother back when he was on the brink of rebellion. You've shouldered responsibilities far beyond your years, yet your character has grown ever sweeter. When I talk with Noah and Fannie, I will tell them they did a good job raising you. Continue to heed them, Betsie, in everything that you do. They are the wisest people that I've ever known." With a sad smile, he took his leave.

Betsie watched the bishop, his shoulders bent as though under a great weight, as he crossed the yard to his buggy. Her cheeks burned at the unaccustomed praise and she covered them with her hands. The fresh-scrubbed linoleum cooled her callused feet as she wandered to the front room to take her seat at the sewing machine once again.

What a strange mood Jonas was in. She chalked it up to the necessity of going out into the world to snatch her parents back from the flames, but that didn't explain his introspective mood, his reluctance to join in with her excitement over her parents' homecoming.

No time to worry about it, she scolded herself. Should she tell Sadie and Abijah the good news right away? She could hear them stirring upstairs. They'd be down to start their day in a moment or two. How wonderful it would be to share that *Mem* and *Dat* were coming home!

Although . . . what if Jonas failed in his mission? But no, the good Lord was on their side. The idea of failure was not to be borne. Besides, Jonas was the bishop and he upheld the *Ordnung*. He couldn't lose.

Still, she decided to wait a bit before telling her brother and sister. No use to get their hopes up too soon.

"One thing is certain, Betsie Troyer," she admonished herself aloud. "If you don't get to sewing on this shirt and finish it, Charley will have nothing to wear to the wedding. And what will Mattie have to say about that? I don't want to find out, that's for sure." She worked the treadle and the machine whirred. Dimly she was aware of her brother and sister as they ate breakfast and started on the chores. The sewing machine gobbled the white shirt pieces like a hungry animal as the morning stretched into afternoon.

A persistent meow finally summoned her to the kitchen, where Amelia politely pawed at the door. Betsie arched her aching back muscles as she complied with her kitten's request. Tired to the bone, she put a pot of water on to boil and decided to cook up the whole pound of hot dogs for lunch. Why not? It would save time if they had hot dogs for dinner, too.

Dinner. Betsie's heart gave a leap as she made the connection. Sheila was coming home tonight! Betsie could hardly wait to share the good news of her *Mem* and *Dat*'s return with Sheila—Mrs. Keith and Debbie, too. Yes, and Betsie could finally deliver the letter postmarked Idaho and even share what Michael had to say. Privately, of course.

Since she was away from the sewing machine for a few minutes, Betsie decided to raid the cellar for some more of her mother's precious canned goods, climbing to the topmost shelves as she scavenged. Her bare toes curled around the shelf's edge as she groped among the jars that were left. How often as a child she had watched *Mem* climb the shelves this way, even when her middle was bulky with Abijah. Oh, how wonderful to think of *Mem* arriving home in time to replenish the dusty shelves with this year's harvest.

Glass jars clinked in her basket as she felt for the next shelf with her big toe. Out of the corner of her eye, she noticed a dingy scrap of cloth barely within her reach. She paused to snatch at it, mindful of the pot of water she'd left on the stove, but to her surprise it didn't yield. She squinted in the dim light, barely able to make out that the white cloth was snagged on a nail head. Gently she tugged it loose and tucked it into the basket to pitch when she got back upstairs.

Fortunately the water on the stove was just coming to a boil and Betsie slid the hot dogs into the pot. As she unloaded the jars from the basket, she noticed the scrap again and took a closer look at what she was about to throw away.

"Why, it's one of *Mem*'s old handkerchiefs," she whispered, her voice full of love. She clasped the worn cotton against her cheek. "Soon she will be right here among us, where she belongs." She tucked the handkerchief into her pocket and resolved to do whatever it took to bring her parents home.

CHAPTER 34

I suppose the good Lord has a reason for delaying
answers to prayer, but oh, how I hate to wait.

—BETSIE'S JOURNAL

IT WAS DUSK BEFORE Betsie had an opportunity to share the good news with Sadie and Abijah over a late supper. First she thanked them for taking up the slack with the chores so she could focus on sewing. Then she told them of her hopes for Jonas's visit to Belle Center. When they'd finished eating, Abijah sauntered off to tend to the animals with a smile on his face and Betsie hummed as she washed the dishes. Sadie swept up with good energy at first, but gradually the scrape of the broom straws slowed. Betsie glanced up to catch her sister, chin propped on hands folded atop the broomstick, staring out the window.

"You've been mooning about all day, Sadie, ain't so?" she probed. "Is something troubling you?"

The broom scraped half-heartedly again. "No."

Betsie took in her sister's lowered gaze. She set the last glass in the dish drainer and dried her hands. "Come now, share with me. Maybe I can help. I know what it's like to have troubles, after all."

A contemptuous smile curved Sadie's pink lips. "My sister, who has the strongest, most comely man in Plain City on a string, has troubles, all right." Her voice caught. *"Ach,* Betsie! I'm sorry. *Mem* and *Dat* may be coming back, but Atlee Hershberger never will. All I ever wanted was to work in the bakery, marry Atlee, and have a big family." Sadie jabbed at the floor.

"Ah Sadie, dear heart." Betsie brushed a tear from her sister's cheek. "You are a beautiful young woman and the best baker for miles. The boys will be lining up to drive you home from the singings."

Sadie took a step back and leaned the broom in the corner. "Well, one of my dreams will never come true now, but don't you worry about me. I will catch me someone to marry before long. Maybe someone even better." She looked around at the spotless kitchen. "If we are done in here, I think I will go out on the porch where it's cooler."

Betsie watched as her pretty sister sashayed through the front room. Still waters run deep, she thought ruefully. Sadie and Atlee really were interested in each other. No wonder Sadie was even crabbier than usual . . . especially with all these wedding preparations. But, Betsie reflected, Sadie was right. It wouldn't take her long to find somebody new. Likely the boys her age were already conniving to take Atlee's place.

By the time Betsie stepped out on the front porch, the moon was rising, nearly full as nighthawks swooped and soared overhead to chase insects in the mellow light. She flexed shoulders stiff from being hunched over the sewing machine all day and stretched out on the swing. The murmur of Sadie's and Abijah's low voices as they rocked in their chairs lulled Betsie until a tardy robin sounded a jarring alarm from the lilac bush. She knew she should check to see if Amelia had slipped out to threaten the nest hidden there, but she remained flat on her back on the porch swing, too exhausted to open an eye. She would just rest a bit until Sheila returned from visiting her friend.

The crunch of tires on gravel snapped Betsie to alertness; she must have dozed off. The moon had risen higher and the night air felt cool to her cheek, although her limbs didn't feel cold. Confused, she tried to sit up, but her arms were entangled in softness. It took a few seconds to realize that her siblings had thoughtfully covered her with an afghan before heading inside to bed.

A truck idled in the driveway, the beam of the headlights cutting through the darkness to reveal a swarm of flying insects. Betsie shuddered and brushed her hand before her face as she walked to welcome Sheila.

The passenger door flew open before the engine died and the girl launched herself into Betsie's arms. Still disoriented from her impromptu nap, Betsie returned the hug awkwardly before holding Sheila at arm's length as she yawned. "It's good to see you, *Schnickelfritz!* I believe you have grown an inch since Wednesday."

"Oh, I missed you so much, Betsie, but I had such a good time! Wait until you hear about all the stuff we did, especially—"

"Sheila, honey." An agitated Mrs. Keith stepped down from the cab and patted Sheila on the back as Betsie yawned hugely. "Poor Betsie looks like she's asleep on her feet. Why don't you and Debbie fetch your bag out of the truck and carry it inside?"

"I did fall asleep, waiting," she admitted. "Sadie and Abijah are probably asleep already. We all worked very hard today, so be quiet as you go in."

"Okay, we'll be as quiet as mice," Sheila promised earnestly, her suitcase in hand. She caught Debbie's eye and both girls dissolved into giggles.

"You'll have to do better than that." Mrs. Keith crossed her arms and glared with mock severity, but she couldn't hide a grin as the girls tiptoed across the porch with exaggerated care.

"Those two have been giggling their heads off ever since we left here Wednesday," she told Betsie fondly, "but I wouldn't have it any other way. Sheila has blossomed into a special young lady, which is incredible considering what she's been through lately. I chalk it up to her newfound faith, but you've had a hand in shaping her, too, Betsie. The whole time she was at our house, she never stopped talking about you and what you've done for her. You'll be a fine mother one of these days."

"Sheila is a sweet girl, that's for sure." Betsie rubbed her forearm self-consciously. "Oh! I have had the most wonderful news since I saw you last. Bishop Jonas is going to visit *Mem* and *Dat* this Friday. My parents are coming home!"

"Coming home?" Mrs. Keith repeated, clearly shocked. "What makes you think so, Betsie?"

Puzzled that Debbie's mom didn't seem more enthusiastic, Betsie tried to make her good news plainer. "Why, Jonas said he was going up there to speak with them, and I know once he tells them they need to come back home and make a kneeling confession in front of the church, they will do so and everything will be back to normal. But what's the matter? You don't seem very happy for me."

"Oh, Betsie." Mrs. Keith sighed with a shake of her head. "I don't know what to say."

Betsie's eyebrows rose. "You could say you're happy they're coming home," she said stiffly. "It is awful when your parents leave. Ask Sheila; she knows." Why did she need to point it out to this English woman?

"Oh, I know, honey. You poured your heart out to me the other day so I know you've been through the wringer since your parents left. Yes, there are similarities between you and Sheila," Mrs. Keith admitted with great reluctance. "It's just . . . have you prayed about this?"

Betsie stared. "Why, of course I have prayed, every night on my knees, no less! Every night, no, all the time we pray for them to come home to us!"

"But that's just it, don't you see? It sounds like you've prayed for what's better for you and your brother and sister instead of thinking about what's better for your parents . . ."

Mrs. Keith's words stung worse than the time Peggy, the Hilliard cashier with a crush on Michael, had slapped Betsie's face. Her anger sparked. "What's better for my parents? If *Mem* and *Dat* don't come home and rejoin the church, they have no chance of going to heaven when they die. If they rejoin the church and strive to live a good life, doing all they can to follow the *Ordnung*, they have a chance. It's as simple as that. Bishop Jonas knows it is best if my parents come home to rejoin the church, and I know it. And now I think it is time you should be going."

Mrs. Keith shook her head with regret and raised her palms. "I can see that I've offended you again. Sometimes God gives us hard tasks. What I had to say may not have come out right, but I did my best. If you'll fetch Debbie, I'll wait in the truck."

Mrs. Keith took a couple of tentative steps and turned to face Betsie once more, her jaw firm. "No, by golly, I didn't do my best. Betsie, I'm the one who needs to make a confession. You see, Sheila was afraid that you believe a person can't know whether he is saved before he dies. She was very upset about it, so I promised her I'd try and straighten it out. I thought maybe she'd gotten her facts jumbled up somehow and your parents really left over some other issue, a minor disagreement between them and the Amish church, perhaps.

"But then I got to thinking, would your parents have left their home and church—not to mention a precious daughter like you—over a triviality? Well, that was a horse of a different color, so I set out to find some answers, and I have good news. Your parents know beyond the shadow of a doubt that they've been forgiven. They know they've been saved."

"You have no right to say that!" Betsie burst out. "You've never met my parents."

"Oh, yes I have." Mrs. Keith shrugged. "I may not be a private eye, but this old-fashioned mom still has a few tricks up her sleeve. Instead of swimming at the pool one day as we'd planned, the girls decided that we should drive up to Belle Center, sort of as an adventure. Sheila remembered your parents live in Belle Center now, so after we dropped Mr. Keith off at work, we got a map at the gas station. It only took an hour one way, not counting when we got a little lost. Once we drove into town, we found the post office and asked where the Troyers from Plain City were staying. The postmistress was happy to help. She said she often chats with your parents when they're out walking."

The woman's account tallied with what her parents had written in their last letter. Betsie took an involuntary step toward her. "You really have seen *Mem* and *Dat*?"

Mrs. Keith caught her hands and nodded eagerly. "And your Aunt Lovina, too. The six of us talked for a quite a while, and also that nice man they're staying with, Mr. Shock. Your parents told us exactly why they decided to leave and all that's happened as a result, but it doesn't matter to them, except they miss their family and friends pretty badly. The long and short of it is, I know for a fact that Fannie and Noah have the sweet assurance of being in the presence of our Lord Jesus Christ the very instant they pass from this earth. The same goes for Debbie, Sheila, and Mr. Keith and me, for that matter. I pray every night that you will accept that assurance, too, Betsie." Her smile trembled.

Tears welled up in Betsie's eyes and her throat tightened. What would it feel like to be sure of salvation? Such sinful talk, yet Jonas had reminded her of how wise her parents were. How could they be so smart and yet be deceived?

"Did *Mem* and *Dat* seem well?" she couldn't help asking.

"Fit as a fiddle," Mrs. Keith said with a catch in her voice. "They send their love to you and your brother and sister. Th-they also asked me to drive the three of you up so you can be together again," she added rapidly, pressing her advantage. "It's nighttime. No one will see you leaving and don't you worry about Sheila. We'll bring her home with us, though she'll miss you like crazy. One word from you and we'll be off. You can be reunited with your parents in about one hour. What do you say, Betsie?"

CHAPTER 35

"You can choose your friends, but you
can't choose your relatives."
—FANNIE TROYER, QUOTED IN BETSIE'S JOURNAL

BETSIE FELT DIZZY. Here, dropped in her lap, was the very opportunity she'd been hoping for. With all her heart, she wanted to flee to Belle Center, to be free of all her burdens, to see her parents again. The pull of spending time with her parents to persuade them to come home was unbearably strong.

As she was on the point of agreeing, a breeze stirred and something fluttered from Betsie's sleeve in the moonlight. She bent to pick up a snippet of white fabric—from the shirt she'd made for Charley. To wear to Rachel's wedding.

She closed her eyes. "I can't go." Denial nearly strangled her. She forced herself to turn away and stumbled toward the house, blinded by tears, until the sound of sneakers pounding on the porch startled her to a halt.

"Did you tell her, Mom?"

"No fair, Deb! I wanted to ask first. Betsie, are you going with us to visit your parents? Are you going to stay with them?" Sheila chimed in, her voice anxious.

Betsie fumbled in her pocket for her handkerchief and turned to blow her nose, unable to reply.

Sheila patted her back. "Gosh, I'm sorry, Betsie. I didn't mean to make you cry."

"I am not crying, *Schnickelfritz*. I only have some dust in my eye. But, remember? I am going to help Rachel with her wedding on Thursday and also I have a lot of extra baking and things to do between now and then, so I mustn't go." She didn't trust herself to say where.

"Well," Mrs. Keith said, smoothing her daughter's hair, "my offer still stands. Anytime, Betsie. You name the day."

Betsie ignored Mrs. Keith. "Good-bye, Debbie," she said instead. "I'm glad you and Sheila had a nice time together. Say your farewells and come inside, Sheila. It's late."

She noticed Sheila watching her carefully. "Are you okay, Betsie?"

"*Jah*, just awful tired, so I'm going in. Hurry, now." She held the door for Amelia and slipped inside.

By the time Sheila joined her, Betsie had mastered her emotions. At first, she objected when Sheila begged to stay up late and tell about her visit.

"There will be plenty of time for that tomorrow," she insisted. "I have been working since the crack of dawn. Your stories will keep," she said as she opened the drawer in the desk, "but this won't. You received a letter from Idaho while you were gone."

She handed the envelope to Sheila, whose eyes were huge as she touched the envelope gingerly. "What does it say?" she whispered.

"It is not my mail. It's yours, ain't so? Run along now, and take it with you. You can read it tonight and we'll talk about it tomorrow morning. Don't forget to turn off the gas lamp when you're finished reading," she said through a wide yawn. She dabbed her watery eyes. "And now, if I can make it, I'm going to shut the house up for the night and go to bed before I fall asleep on my feet like Judith."

Weary to the bone, Betsie chose a peppermint from the dish of hard candy *Dat* always kept under the hot water bottle in the drawer in the kitchen. She unwrapped the crackly cellophane and popped the peppermint into her mouth, savoring the burst of flavor as she lowered the gas lamp, checked to see that she'd closed the damper on the cook stove, and locked up. When she was finally ready to go upstairs, she was surprised to see Sheila still rooted to the spot, a miserable expression on her face. The letter dangled from her fingers.

"I'm scared to see what it says, Betsie," she quavered.

"*Ach.*" She relinquished the welcome of her bed with a regretful sigh. "I know just how you feel. Wait a minute and I will read it with you."

She returned from the kitchen with the candy dish and offered some to Sheila. The girl's smile of gratitude went straight to Betsie's heart. She was patient as the girl picked and chose among the few remaining pieces, mostly the sharp horehound kind that no one liked except *Dat. I must buy more candy and also coffee the next time I go to town. That is, if Dat doesn't come home first and beat me to it,* she reminded herself sternly.

When they were settled on the couch, Sheila with a root beer barrel tucked in her cheek, Betsie took the letter.

"You're sure you want me to read it?" she pressed. At Sheila's anxious nod, she ripped open the envelope and held it so Sheila could read along.

"'Dear Squirt,'" Betsie began with a fond smile.

"That's Mom's handwriting! Dad must have found her!" Sheila exclaimed. She snatched the letter from Betsie and read the rest rapidly. Twin stars danced in her eyes when she looked up. "She says she and Dad are working through some things and she loves me bunches. She'll write more soon," she summarized, and then she burst into tears.

Betsie wrapped her arm around Sheila's shoulders and rocked back and forth as the girl wept. "There, it's all right. Go ahead and cry, I don't blame you one bit," she said as tears formed in her own eyes. She offered her handkerchief to Sheila. "You've been through a hard time and no mistake."

Sheila blew her nose and tried to speak, her words still jerky with sobs. "I'm just s-so happy there's a chance we can be a family again, Betsie! Thank you for s-staying with me. I know you're tired and I feel bad about keeping you up, but I want to tell you something." She sat up straight, her brown eyes red-rimmed. "I used to wish that I had a sister. I wished it really bad when Mike was being so weird and mean to me, but things got a little better when school started last fall.

Debbie and I grew a lot closer, and it was great. For a while, I played like she was my sister, but I didn't tell her because I thought she'd think I was dumb."

Betsie chuckled. "I think you are worrying over nothing. I can tell she likes you very much."

"I guess you're right," Sheila said with a shy grin, "but anyway, I don't play like she's my sister anymore. Do you know why?"

"Because Debbie is your best friend instead?" Betsie asked softly.

"No. I mean, yes, she is, but that's not why." Sheila moved closer, her heart-shaped face serious. "It's because I'd rather have you for my sister."

"Oh," Betsie said. She tried to say more, but the words caught in her throat. "You are very sweet," she finally managed to get out.

"I'm not just saying it, though! I mean it with all my heart," Sheila assured her.

"I know you do, *Schnickelfritz*. I would like that, too. But since we are both already born into different families, we will have to play like we are sisters, the way you used to with Debbie," she joked.

Sheila shook her head vehemently, her ponytail bouncing from side to side. "No, don't you get it, Betsie? All you have to do is marry Mike, and bingo! We would be sisters! So what do you say?" She leaned forward, on fire with excitement as she waited for Betsie's answer.

Betsie stared at the girl, *ferhoodled*. "Sheila! We have talked about this before—"

"Nuh-uh. I've talked about it before, but you haven't. Come on, I know Mike likes you, and I think you like him, too. Right, sister?" Sheila grinned and doubled her legs beneath her, Indian style, her hands tightly clasped.

Talk about a one-track mind! Betsie clutched her forehead. "Sheila, Michael is my good friend. That's the way I think of him, or I did when he was here. Now that he's gone—"

"But you like to write letters to him, right? Even though Charley"— she wrinkled her nose with distaste—"told you not to. Or at least I bet he did."

The conversation was spinning rapidly out of control. Betsie tried again. "I do like Michael, but not the way you say. Think about it, Sheila," she added, deliberately choosing her words so as to soften the blow, "you know I was raised Amish. I haven't joined the Amish church yet, but I will one day in the future. And when I do, that means I cannot marry someone unless he is Amish, like me. But I don't have to marry your brother"—she hastened to assure the girl as her face fell—"to be your sister. As far as I'm concerned, you and I are sisters right now, and we always will be. Now then," she said, changing the subject in desperation, "I know you saw my parents. I-I miss them so much. Tell me, how did they seem?"

Sheila faltered for a moment at the abrupt change of topics before her eyes lit up and she regained her usual poise. "Gosh, I'm sorry, Betsie!" she said at last. "I should have known you'd want to hear all about our visit. I mean, in my last letter to Dad, I begged him to tell me how Mom was, every last detail. But he didn't, so I-I need to write to him again." She nodded her head. "Yeah, that's it. After I get in bed, I'm going to write to Dad again and tell him off for not doing what I asked. I'll be right back and then I'll tell you all about your parents."

Relieved that she'd diverted the awkward questions about Michael, at least for the time being, Betsie watched with amusement as Sheila scampered to the desk. She certainly acted like a sister, in every sense of the word.

When the girls walked upstairs together, Sheila waved paper and pen as she related bits and pieces of her visit to Belle Center. The bandage on *Dat*'s chin where he'd cut himself shaving, the way *Mem* had done up Debbie's long blond hair Amish style while she talked, just as she'd always done Betsie's and Sadie's hair—no detail was too small to share. They sat on Sheila's bed as Betsie listened eagerly, tucking the comforting details away in her memory to treasure . . . at least until the end of the week, she reassured herself, when she would see her parents for herself. For now, Sheila's account gave Betsie a warm glow of closeness.

But when she finally lay down to rest, Betsie found that thoughts of *Mem* and *Dat*, as dear as they were, weren't at the forefront of her mind. Instead, she mused about the day Rachel and Sam had been baptized into the church after the long service. One day in the not-too-distant future, Betsie herself would be the one kneeling and affirming her faith. She wondered who among her friends would be up there with her when she took her kneeling vows in front of everyone.

She had almost nodded off when she came to with a start. Of course, Charley would be up there with the other men, affirming his faith at the same time she affirmed hers. In due course would come the Sunday when the names of all the couples who intended to marry were published. Her name would be read out along with Charley's, and soon afterwards, they would become man and wife.

Guess I need to speak with Jonas about joining the church, as Charley suggested. Then we can get married. Thoughts of her wedding day made Betsie's heart race. She tossed and turned for a long time before finally falling into a restless sleep.

She awoke to find Sadie shaking her shoulder. "Betsie! *Was in der welt?* Why are you screaming for Michael?"

Betsie gulped and sat up. "Did I wake you?" she muttered. "I-I'm worried about Sheila, I guess. She's all alone." She held her breath.

"Stop worrying about everyone else and go to sleep," Sadie groused, but she patted Betsie's shoulder before she staggered back to her bed.

Betsie waited until she heard Sadie's bedsprings creak before she flopped back onto her pillow, rubbing her forehead as if to erase the most vivid nightmare yet. The harness shop bell had dinged and Benner, blond and broad-shouldered, asked her to mend his riding jacket before grabbing her and forcing her to the floor. As Betsie struggled to escape, Benner's face changed. It was really Charley whose body crushed her, who leered at her from inches away. She panicked and screamed for Michael to save her, but he didn't appear. She shuddered. Thank the good Lord she'd awakened when Sadie shook her.

These nightmares must not continue, she told herself sternly. *Officer Schwartz told me Benner is dead. He fell off his horse and broke his neck. He can't harm me ever again; I'm safe. Safe.* Exhausted, she pulled her quilt over her head and fell asleep.

CHAPTER 36

"We don't realize how wonderful today is until tomorrow."

—NOAH TROYER, QUOTED IN BETSIE'S JOURNAL

"ARE YOU SURE you're all right, Betsie?"

"*Jah*, fine," Betsie assured her, and she meant it. What a pleasure it was to see everyone together at the breakfast table; that is, after Sheila sheepishly came in the side door and took her seat. Betsie supposed she'd been to the outhouse.

She'd tried without much success to forget the tantalizing carrot Mrs. Keith had dangled in front of her nose, a visit to her parents any time she pleased, but at least she'd pledged Sheila to secrecy about that. Sheila never lacked for subjects to talk about, however.

". . . so that's what we ate at the slumber party. Cool, huh? Ugh, are my legs sore from riding Debbie's horse yesterday. Sky King's barrel is so much bigger than Fledge's! Not that Fledge would let me ride him anywhere near as long as I rode Sky, though." Sheila brightened as she took a bite of a slightly stale cinnamon roll. "Yum, these are so good, Sadie!"

Sadie's cheeks pinkened at Sheila's praise. "I am glad you like them," she answered mildly before turning to Betsie. "I didn't get all the wash sorted, but I made a good start. Dishcloths, towels, sheets, and pillowcases, that's where I'll begin. Unless Abijah has some smelly socks wadded up somewhere," she said in an effort to tease her brother.

211

"Um." Abijah, with chin in hand and Amelia ensconced on his lap, turned a page in his asparagus book. One of the cinnamon rolls lay on a plate at his elbow, untouched.

Sadie grinned and gulped the last of her milk. "Sounds like Charley's here. Want me to tell him to come in, Betsie?"

"I don't think that sounds like him," Betsie glanced out the screen door. "It's a trailer like the one Fledge arrived in."

"Oops." Sheila gulped her milk and jerked a thumb at Abijah. "It's for him, sort of. Debbie's dad is bringing the old pony cart Debbie used when she competed in driving events at horse shows. Since she does all riding events now, I asked Mr. Keith if we could borrow the cart. He said we could use it for as long as we liked. He works at the Franklin County Fairgrounds in Hilliard and he had some business out this way. He told me he'd probably stop by this morning. Sorry I forgot to warn you." She took a deep breath and another bite of her cinnamon roll, in that order.

Abijah listened with growing interest. "A pony cart? For me to use with Fledge?"

Sheila bobbed her head. "It's a pretty nice one, too."

"That was a very kind thing to do, Sheila. Let's go out and take a look," Betsie urged.

As they approached him, Mr. Keith walked behind his silver pick-up truck to let down the trailer ramp. He waved. "Hey there, Squirt, good to see you again," he greeted Sheila. He acknowledged Abijah with a nod. "Want to help me unload this contraption?"

Abijah nodded eagerly. "*Jah*, I can do that."

Betsie heart ached as she watched her brother. If only *Dat* was here to work with Abijah. She put the ungrateful thought out of her mind and pinned her hopes firmly to Jonas's Belle Center visit, rapidly approaching. Once the bishop, full of Godly authority, talked with them, it was only a matter of time before *Mem* and *Dat* would reclaim their rightful places in their children's lives.

"It is a big help for you to loan us this cart," she told Mr. Keith. "This pony won't let anyone ride him, so I wondered if we could make him useful by training him to drive. Abijah has done a *gut* job of ground-driving Fledge to get him used to a harness. In fact, he learned so quick that maybe he was a driving horse before."

"How does it happen that you don't know his background?" Mr. Keith asked, puzzled.

Sheila hurried to open the gate for Mr. Keith. "I'd always wanted a pony, so my dad bought him for me pretty cheap at an auction after the owner passed away. All I know about Fledge is that he loves to eat and no one can ride him for long."

Mr. Keith eased the cart through the gate and pushed back his hat. "Well, we'll soon see what he can do. I'll help you hitch up. Why don't you bring his harness out and then fetch him over here, son?" he said to Abijah with a friendly smile.

Abijah hesitated and pointed at Sheila. "He's really her pony. Maybe she should do it." He tried to sound nonchalant, but Betsie could see how much it cost to deny himself the pleasure.

Sheila shook her head. "Oh, no, you don't. Fledge doesn't listen to me, so you do it. But I'll come and help, if that's okay with you."

Happy with this arrangement, Abijah brought out the harness and slung it over the fence. Betsie watched with the others as he whistled for Fledge. The brown and white pony left Judith's side and moseyed over to see what the fuss was about, craftily keeping just out of the boy's reach, but Abijah was patient. When he sidled up to the fence, Abijah grasped his halter. Fledge snapped at him, but Betsie knew it was all an act.

With an ease born of years of practice, Mr. Keith hitched Fledge up to the two-wheeled pony cart. "You can see how much lighter it is than a buggy."

Fledge tossed his head uneasily at the sound of the strange man's voice. "It won't take you too long to get the hang of it," Abijah reassured him softly, scratching the fidgety pony's chin while Fledge in turn nibbled the boy's suspenders. Abijah's laugh rumbled out and Betsie caught her breath. When did her brother get to sounding so much like *Dat*?

At last, Mr. Keith unhitched Fledge and said it was Abijah's turn. Betsie's heart warmed as she watched her brother working quickly but surely, concentrating to get every buckle right.

When he finished, Mr. Keith checked over the fastenings, taking his time. Abijah gave Fledge a hearty slap on the neck and took his seat in the cart. He looked calm, but Betsie noticed that his eyes glowed. "Are you ready? Drive him once around the pasture here," Mr. Keith suggested. "The ground's pretty uneven, but those rubber tires will help. Better keep a good hold on him, though. Stand back, Sheila, in case Fledge acts up."

"What if he gets so excited he upsets the cart? I can't have my brother hurt," Betsie said nervously. "Maybe you should drive him first instead," she told Debbie's dad.

"Betsie, I can do this. Let me drive him," Abijah pleaded. "Fledge trusts me and he wants to do this for me. And see, here comes Charley. Ask him. He will say to let me do it, I know. After all, I'm almost a man."

"Not yet, you aren't," Betsie muttered under her breath. She hurried to meet Charley. "Abijah wants to drive this cart that our friend is lending to us. What do you think? Shouldn't someone else try Fledge out first? Maybe you?"

"Don't be silly. Abijah should drive," Charley scoffed. "I drove our own buggy everywhere when I was much younger than he is, eight or so. He'll be fine." He leaned on a fencepost, propped his foot on the wire fence, and settled in for the show like he had all the time in the world.

"So that settles it. Easy does it now," Mr. Keith cautioned Abijah, backing away slowly.

Betsie held her breath as Abijah tightened the reins and chirruped. Fledge stood still for a moment. Slowly he bent his neck double as if to check out the unfamiliar object he was hitched to. Then he tossed his head and walked forward at a sedate pace while Abijah grinned from ear to ear.

"He's doing it," Sheila breathed.

"*Jah*, he is." Betsie felt a little foolish for doubting. What an amazing way her brother had with animals. It must be as Lovina had said, that when it came to animals, Abijah was Noah Troyer all over again.

They watched Abijah circle the cart around the far end of the pasture. Fledge arched his neck and picked up his hooves in a smart trot as he drew the cart toward them, his pride showing as he served the boy he'd accepted as his master.

Mr. Keith let out an appreciative whistle. "How long has he been working with that pony?"

"Less than two weeks," Betsie replied.

"That's pretty good, even if Fledge was broken to drive at some point. If your brother ever needs a job, we always have room for an expert animal handler at the fairgrounds, especially with this year's fair coming up in July," Mr. Keith informed her.

Betsie nodded, pleased at the idea. She knew Abijah would love it, and the pay would be welcome, too. Maybe he could even save a little for those college classes he wanted to take someday. "All right, I will tell h—"

"Abijah will need to talk with Bishop Jonas," Charley cut in sharply, "to secure permission before he takes a job away from home. Isn't that right, Betsie?"

Startled, Betsie nodded again. "Y-yes. Of course, that's what I meant."

"I see," Mr. Keith said. "Well, don't delay too long. I need to figure out how many hands I'll need, but I can only hold a spot open for so long. I might make an exception in his case, though." He nodded toward Abijah, who had pulled Fledge up a short way from where Sheila stood. "I'd better be going. Glad you folks can put that old cart to good use. Be seeing you, now." He fastened the trailer doors. "So long, Squirt!"

Betsie and Sheila waved as Mr. Keith backed the truck down the driveway, careful to avoid exciting Charley's horse. Betsie put her hands on her hips, satisfied with the events of the morning, but eager to get on with her own work.

"Ready to go, Sadie? You really shouldn't keep Mattie waiting any longer," she hinted.

Her sister nodded and climbed into the buggy, but Charley made no move to join her. "Maybe since Abijah is such a good driver, he can drive Sadie again," he told Betsie. "I must talk with you."

Irritation shot through her. She barely managed to quell it before she answered. "Can what you want to discuss wait? I've already spent far too much time watching Fledge. Now I must press your shirt and wedding clothes for Sadie and me to get ahead enough on tomorrow's work, and that's in addition to finishing the wash today. Also I must find time to bake some extra loaves of bread and such to help out with the meal."

Out of the corner of her eye, Betsie noticed that Sheila and Abijah had stopped fussing over Fledge and were both looking her way. She glanced at Sadie and intercepted a frown, presumably over the sharp tone she had taken with Charley. Betsie grimaced. Even though she'd been getting along much better with her sister, Sadie was still Sadie.

Unaware of Sadie's disapproval, Charley only shrugged. "I will tell you now and save some time," he said. "I plan to talk with Jonas today. I will tell him that I want to start classes to join the church, like you must have." He smiled, very confident.

Betsie realized that everyone in the yard, Sheila especially, was waiting to see what she would say. "What do you mean, like I must have?"

"Why, my mother and I drove by here yesterday. On our way to visit someone, down the road." He fumbled for words. "We saw Jonas stop in, and we figured that was why."

"Jonas stopped by on another matter entirely. We didn't talk about joining the church. Yet." *Rejoining is more like it,* she added to herself.

Charley's glance was inquiring, but Betsie was nettled now and she had no intention of clarifying. Instead she went on, "Go ahead and talk to Jonas. You might have a long wait, what with Rachel's wedding on Thursday. I imagine he's pretty busy."

"Maybe you're right," he agreed at length. "I'll wait until Friday to talk with him. Anyway, Abijah can drive Sadie tomorrow morning because Sam needs me early. I will be by later to help you take your bread and whatnot to Rachel, though."

"*Jah,* that's good. See you then."

Abijah watched Charley drive away, a funny look on his face. "Who could he and Mattie have been visiting at that hour of the morning? You said Jonas came awful early."

"Oh, maybe he was just talking in a general way," Betsie made an excuse to hide her own suspicions.

She smiled grimly as she strolled to the mailbox. If Mattie Yoder was expecting to catch her out in some misbehavior, she would have a *gut* long wait, for Betsie had been so busy lately that she all but met herself coming and going. She barely had time to finish a day's work, let alone to misbehave.

The mailbox yawned empty at this hour, of course, so Betsie went inside, glad that Sheila and Abijah were getting along so much better. She wished she could say the same for herself and Charley.

What was wrong with her lately? It seemed as though whenever she and Charley were together, Betsie panicked and threw off sparks worse than Amelia when her fur was rubbed the wrong way. I should be grateful for all Charley's help around here. I couldn't have done it without him.

But I could have, she reminded herself with vigor. I was managing fine until he stepped in. Yes, I've been exhausted. Yes, it's emotionally taxing to do the jobs of both a mother and a father, but with the help of the good Lord, I've been keeping this family fed and together, and I've been doing a fine job of it, too. I just wish Charley could see past the fact that I'm a woman.

And then she had to laugh. Who did she sound like? Why, like 'Sunshine' Sullivan, or at least the way Michael described his mother's quest for equality. Phyllis had left Ohio to find herself, but Betsie didn't have that luxury. If only she could make Charley understand how much she longed to have her family together again.

Well, that's easy enough, she decided. I'll tell him. But as she drabbled her feet through the cool dewy grass, a thought struck her. What did *Charley* want? She'd never thought to ask him. The more she thought about it, the more ashamed she grew. Poor Charley, she thought. I'll ask him first thing when I see him tomorrow. Then we can work together for what we both want.

CHAPTER 37

"If you can dream—and not make dreams your master . . ."
—"If" by Rudyard Kipling, quoted in Betsie's journal

"This book is too hard!"

Abijah slammed the asparagus book down on the table, a fierce scowl on his face. Betsie and the two other girls looked at each other and then at Abijah in mild surprise.

"I've been looking at the drawings of plants because there are too many big words. I'll never finish reading it," he went on, his voice strident. "I'm taking it back to the library after I drop Sadie off. And I'm never taking out another book again. I'm done with reading."

Betsie's head pounded. Just when everything had been going so well, too. She opened her mouth dutifully to reprimand her brother and to urge him to persevere when Sheila cut in.

"Yeah, it looks like a pretty hard book. Can I see it for a sec?" She held out her hand.

He made a face and tossed it across the table at Sheila, nearly upsetting her glass of milk.

"Abijah!" Sadie cried.

"I don't care!" He scraped his chair back from the table with a defiant glare.

Betsie shot him a warning glance, but she was relieved when he missed it. He looked like he'd lost his last friend.

Sheila broke the awkward silence as she flipped the pages. "Whew, that's a tough one, all right." She marked the page she'd been looking at with one finger. "This is exactly the kind of book that Miss Yoho— she was my teacher last year—had in mind when she told us to read with a pencil and paper handy."

Abijah didn't respond, but Betsie saw him sneak a sulky peek at Sheila from beneath lowered brows.

Encouraged, the girl continued. "She said make a guess at what a word means, write it down, and look it up in the dictionary later. Don't get frustrated. Keep reading."

"That would be a great idea if we had a dictionary, but we don't," he sneered, his tone superior.

Betsie quailed. The whole situation was getting out of hand. In another minute, Abijah would have Sheila in tears, just like the last time they clashed.

To her surprise, Sheila was calm. "Then make a list and show me the words you don't know. If I know the definition, I'll tell you and you can write it down. But there are probably ones I don't know either." Sheila's eyebrows scrunched together. "Maybe next time you go to the library, you can borrow a dictionary to look up the words neither one of us knows."

Perhaps it was the matter-of-fact way Sheila offered to help, or perhaps it was the way she admitted there were limits to her knowledge; Betsie wasn't sure which. Either way, the fire in Abijah's eyes was doused by sheer gratitude. He walked around the table to retrieve his book.

"I will start a list. And . . . *denki*," he added humbly as he left the room. In a moment, they heard him rustling for paper in the desk.

Sadie stared at Betsie. "Who is that boy?" she whispered in a loud aside.

"Abijah's not the only one around here who can tame a stubborn beast, ain't so?" Betsie laughed softly and flashed a pleased smile at Sheila.

Sheila grinned. "Nah. I needed some extra help with reading a couple of years ago and I learned good word attack skills, that's all. But you know what? Maybe I could be a teacher one day." Her eyes grew misty.

Betsie tapped her cheek with a forefinger. "You can be a teacher this very day."

"What do you mean?" Sheila asked, startled.

"Well, you know I will be very busy today as I help Rachel prepare for her wedding. It would be a help if you visit with Katie Miller. Seems to me I remember she was having some trouble with her reading, too, and now I see you're just the person to help her."

"Aw, Betsie, I'm not a teacher! I'd have to go to school for years and years to learn how to do it right," Sheila protested.

"Oh, yes, you are a teacher. I saw you teach Abijah just now. Besides, I have something I need to talk over with Charley, and I . . ."

It was Sheila's turn to scowl. "Oh, Charley, the Big Boss Man. Why does he hang around here so much, anyway?"

Sadie smirked and propped her chin on her interlocked fingers. "Yes, answer that, Betsie." She batted her eyes rapidly.

Betsie kept her face straight with difficulty. "Shame on the both of you. You know perfectly well that Charley has helped us out in a hundred different ways."

Sheila cocked her hip, arms akimbo. "Oh, Charley's the Boy Wonder, all right. Skip it. I don't mind going to Katie's for a while if it means I don't have to see Dutch Boy. He's definitely cute, but he's way too bossy for me, always wanting his own way and ordering everyone around like he owns the place. Okay, okay, I'm going," she told Betsie. She hustled to the stair landing. "But nothing you say will make me change my mind about Charley . . . or anybody else." She arched her eyebrows at Betsie and scuttled upstairs.

Sadie stared after Sheila, her forehead lined with confusion as Betsie blushed furiously. "*Was in der welt* has that English girl got against Charley? The girls I know all think he hung the moon. Why, they say you and I are lucky because he spends most of his time—"

"Sadie!" Betsie interrupted sharply. "Abijah will be down any moment, ready to take you to work. We can't spend the morning jawing when I have so much to do. Hurry, now." Betsie hunched over the dishpan to hide her hot cheeks and scrubbed at a plate so vigorously that her fingernail doubled backwards. *"Ach*, that smarts! My nail ripped, right down by my fingertip," she exclaimed. "Would you fetch me the clippers from the hairpin dish on my dresser and bring them when you come back down?"

Betsie didn't know which was more uncomfortable, her broken nail or Sadie's long pause. Sweat trickled down her back. Sadie was smart as a whip. Had she guessed that Charley and Betsie planned to marry?

"Jaaah." Her sister drew the word out. "I'll fetch them for you."

"Denki." Betsie tried to quell her rising panic. "Tell Abijah to hurry, too. Silas Yutzy needs his help, as well."

Ach, she needed some breathing room or she would never make it through this long day.

Betsie felt better by the time Charley arrived. She'd already walked Sheila over to Katie's house with a reminder to help Katie's mother with chores if she possibly could and a promise to pick her up before supper. The solitary walk home, free of questions and explanations, felt good as she stretched her legs and breathed deep.

Charley delivered a note from Naomi Yutzy listing the crockery and cutlery she wanted to borrow, at least so far, and Betsie and Charley spent a good hour polishing and shining, wrapping the pieces in old newspapers, and packing the lot of it away in boxes. Charley loaded them in his wagon and Betsie tucked an old sheet around the boxes to keep the road dust out. Then Charley and Betsie loaded up what few loaves of bread she'd scrounged time to bake so far.

"So much in our house we no longer have use for," she finally sighed when they were well underway. She shook out her handkerchief and blotted sweat from the back of her neck and under her chin.

"Don't worry," Charley made bold to say. "You will put it all to good use when you feed our family one day."

"I hope to see my own parents reunited with us and sitting at the table long before the day comes that we have a family," she retorted without thinking. Too late, she remembered her resolve to discover what he wanted out of life. Ashamed of her sharp words, she watched his capable hands, steady and strong on the lines as he guided his horse. "Charley, I've told you over and over what I want. What about your dreams?" she asked in a small voice.

"Dreams?" He glanced sidewise, wary. "You mean like at night?"

"No, not that kind of dreams." She ran her thumb over her broken nail and tried to be mindful of his practical way of thinking. "Maybe I should have asked, what do you want most in life?"

He braced his foot more firmly against the buckboard and guided his horse around a turn. *"Ach*, that's easy. I want my own farm."

"And what else?" she prompted.

"Nothing else."

Betsie stared at him in consternation. Indeed, he appeared perfectly satisfied. "But what about—"

"No. You asked what I want, and that's it, Betsie. It's all I've ever wanted," he said. He guided the horse to a stop on the grassy verge near the covered bridge on Axe Handle Road. Earnestly he faced her while his horse stomped and took a breather. "You don't know what it's like to be a farmer with no farm. Maybe it's foolish of me, but I've often been angry with my *dat* for dying when I was a baby." He clenched his fists. "If he hadn't died, we might have had a big farm of our own, with many horses, cattle, hogs, chickens, and everything else I've ever wanted to raise. Put a field in corn or wheat? No trouble at all! Build a windmill to power a pump that waters the livestock? Sure!" He stared at his hands. "So many things I could have done differently, if only he had lived."

Betsie's tongue stuck to the roof of her mouth. Of all the dreams in the world, acres of earth and herds of livestock were practical, but held no imagination. Of course, with the *Ordnung* as a conscience, there was no need to daydream or think for oneself; in fact it was discouraged. But what about a family? How did Betsie figure into Charley's future, for that matter? She tried to tell herself that he was thinking like an Amish man, a provider, but she still wondered how someone she knew so well could be such a stranger. She attempted to console him, but Charley waved her off, his expression stern.

"You can't know what it's like to have your mother work to support you when you're a man like me. Do you know what it's like to farm shares for other people? To sweat under the blazing sun, but to know when the day is done that you'll only profit from half of your labor? Do you know what it cost me to beg for draft horses when I needed them to plow your fields after your *dat* left?" His voice filled with despair. "Do you know how I felt when the windstorm approached that night, before you called to me to come inside? All I could think was, 'I am going to lose this farm, too, after all the plans I've made.' No, believe me, Betsie, there is no room for pride when you farm for others." He stared at his hands, disgusted. "And now we must be going."

He urged his horse forward, but then he yanked the reins, checking the horse so quickly that the buggy wheels skidded to a stop in the loose gravel. He turned on Betsie and addressed her forcefully. "What I want is what rightfully belongs to every Amish man: my own farm, my own children, my own wife. All doing what they are supposed to do. That's what I want."

She could almost hear his teeth grinding in anger. As the horse trotted briskly down the road, Betsie peeled herself from the corner of the buggy. She had nothing to fear. After all, this was the kind man who had helped her around the farm and said he cared about her and, despite her unwise choices, remained faithful. Remembering her promise to make things better between the two of them, she reached across the space and touched Charley's elbow, at a loss for words.

My own wife, he had said. A lump formed in Betsie's throat. That's me. That's what he wants. "Charley. I-I'm ready to talk with Jonas about joining the church."

CHAPTER 38

"Parting is all we know of heaven,
And all we need of hell."
—"XCVI" BY EMILY DICKINSON,
QUOTED IN BETSIE'S JOURNAL

"DON'T TARRY, BETSIE. Come now."

A work-worn hand smoothed Betsie's hair. Try as she might, she couldn't open her eyes to see who tenderly stroked her brow, but she thought she dimly recognized the voice.

"Betsie? Betsie, dear heart, how I love you."

And then she knew. *Mem's* come home. *Mem* and *Dat* are back, without any help from Jonas.

Betsie sat straight up, suddenly wide awake. She put a hand to her chest, panting as though she'd run a mile. Early morning light honeyed the oaken dresser but revealed no one in the room with her.

Unwilling to discount the sensation, she flipped back the covers and dashed into the hallway—empty. Intense longing welled into tears.

"Oh, how I miss you, *Mem*," she whispered as the tears spilled down her cheeks. "Please come home soon. I need you."

Enough of that. She gritted her teeth and marched to brush her hair until it crackled with static electricity. Of course *Mem* would return, with *Dat* and Lovina, too. Hadn't she prayed for that on her knees every night since they left?

Patience, patience, patience—surely the good Lord would send *Mem* home in time for her own wedding day in the not-too-distant future. Today's happiness belonged to Rachel and Sam on their wedding day.

"Betsie? Did you call me?" Sheila, her hair tousled every which way, squinted from the doorway to her room.

Betsie blew her nose. "Yes, high time you woke up—we overslept, so get dressed. You will find clean clothes hanging." How surprised Sheila would be to see Mem's Plain dress that Betsie had stayed up late to hem so the girl could wear it to Rachel and Sam's wedding without tripping. She'd even rinsed out an old pair of stockings for her to wear. Privately, Betsie decided she didn't want to do any more sewing for a month of Sundays. "Hurry, Rachel's counting on my . . . our help."

"Okay, okay." Sheila rubbed her eyes and headed back to her room.

Betsie crossed to the peg rail and fingered her *nayva hokkah* dress one last time before arranging it neatly in her satchel, her crisp new apron and *Kapp* layered on top. She couldn't wait to see Charley dressed in his special clothes, especially the new white shirt she'd worked so hard to finish. She hurried downstairs.

"Today I made breakfast for you, sleepyhead." Sadie smiled and forked over two doughnuts. She poured a cup of steaming tea. "Abijah is hitching up Judith for us, but he said he is driving the pony cart over."

Betsie said a quick prayer that Fledge would behave himself. "Oh, doughnuts sound like just the thing!" She looked at her hands and blinked. "I thought I brought my satchel down with me."

"I'll run up and get it. You eat while you have the chance," Sadie insisted. "We'll be awful busy the rest of the morning."

Sadie soon reappeared with the satchel as she shepherded a radiant Sheila.

"I can't believe you hemmed up this dress for me after I went to bed. And an apron, too, and a *Kapp!* Now I know how much longer it takes to sew when you're Amish and you don't have an electric sewing machine." She picked up the hem and twirled to display it. "But I know it would have taken me even longer to hem it up by hand, because once in Vacation Bible School, I hemmed a pillowcase for a doll's bed for the Two's and Three's room and it took me all week. The teacher had to double up the thread for me and tie a knot because I couldn't keep a single thread in the needle. The pillowcase didn't look so hot when I finished, either. So thank you, Betsie! Sadie helped me with the pins. I look pretty Plain, *jah?*"

"*Jah!*" Betsie nodded, slightly dazed. "Now eat these doughnuts up quickly. We're running a bit behind."

Soon Sheila brushed crumbs from her apron and spoke around the last bite of doughnut. "You know, Betsie, I'm really glad that this time Charley's mother can't scold . . . oh, right, we need to hurry, don't we? Do I have time to . . . you know," the girl said, jerking her head in the direction of the outhouse.

Betsie nodded and strolled out to the driveway where Sadie waited as Sheila ran over the rise. She stood by the buggy, pleasant thoughts of wedding ceremonies and serving feasts mingling with memories of Rachel. How she would miss her dear friend. She sighed. Why did she have to lose everyone she loved?

Except Charley. She grinned as she watched Sheila sprint towards her in her Plain dress. Her eyes fell on the repaired fence. Yes, marrying Charley was definitely something to be thankful for.

Sheila skidded to a stop beside the buggy, caught the hem of her dress, and twirled again.

Betsie smiled and stuck out her hand to help Sheila take her place beside Sadie. "At last we are ready." The girl's cheeks were red like they got whenever she was excited. "What a day this will be, Sheila. I feel sure you'll never forget it." She took the reins from her sister and clucked to her horse as she leaned forward. "Let's go, Judith!"

By the time they pulled into the Yutzys' driveway, buggies already lined the lane. Abijah hurried up importantly to direct them.

"Where's your friend Levi?" Betsie asked him as she removed their satchels.

Abijah grimaced. "His *dat* caught him fooling around with Fledge. Something to do with burrs."

"*Was in der welt?*" A prickly burr, wedged under a snug piece of harness, could dig viciously into a horse's tender skin and drive him mad with rage. Had all Fledge's training been undone in an instant? "Did he do any harm?"

Her brother swung himself into the driver's seat. "*Ne.* Silas caught him just in time and took him on a trip to the woodshed. I can tell you one thing—Levi won't be messing with any more horses for a while. Nor sittin' down, neither." He cracked a smile and drove the buggy in a masterful and completely unnecessary arc before parking it beside the others and tending to Judith.

Betsie glanced toward the house and intercepted a guileless grin and wave from Silas Yutzy, apparently none the worse for the punishment he'd meted out to his Tom Sawyer of a son. She waved back with a smile, very glad that Abijah was vindicated.

"Never mind about Levi," Sadie urged. "We have so much to do! Come, Betsie."

Sadie's words were so uncannily like *Mem*'s that Betsie shivered.

"Are you kidding? You're cold? I'm sticky hot in these stockings," Sheila moaned. "Plus they're rubbing the hair on my legs the wrong way. And the bobby pins in my *Kapp* are digging into my scalp like crazy. But I'm not complaining."

"*Ach,* it's nothing. A goose walked over my grave and gave me the chills, maybe," she joked as she elbowed Sheila's ribs. "If you think you're hot now, wait until we lug these tables around some more. Come, follow me."

A couple of hours later Betsie finally straightened and surveyed their work with a critical eye. Yes, she'd seen it countless times before, but a wedding reception was a beautiful feast, from the *eck* where the bride and groom would sit to the careful place settings to the delectable smells wafting from the kitchen. Later the benches used by the guests during the service would be moved for more tables and seating.

She caught Sheila's eye and smiled. "What do you think?"

"It sure is different from the weddings I've been to, but it's pretty!"

"Sadie," Betsie called. When her sister looked up, she continued, "We're going to the porch to cool off for a bit. I'll be back shortly to get dressed."

At Sadie's distracted nod, Betsie caught Sheila's elbow and wove in and out of the crowd until they reached the front porch. Betsie eased herself onto the swing, grateful that it was vacant when there were so many people around.

"Hey, Betsie, a police car stopped here!"

"Mm-hmm." She watched lazily as a miraculously revived Sheila leaned over the porch rail, words erupting in a flood. The girl kept up a lively commentary as she observed Betsie's friends and neighbors gathering on the lawn by the road. Unable to translate what the bystanders said to a couple of English in a police car, Sheila glossed over the *Deitsh* words with bored quack-quack hand motions. Girls in bonnets and boys in straw hats joined the throng, fascinated by the revolving red light atop the police car, and Sheila didn't miss a beat as she described the scene in vivid detail. Pleased that a hurry-up English driver must be getting a ticket, Betsie rested her head and let her mind go blank. The early morning dream of her parents' return must have taken more of a toll than she thought.

"Yes, I know where Betsie Troyer is. She's my friend and she's sitting right over there, on the porch." Katie Miller's voice piped importantly and penetrated the haze of Betsie's thoughts.

She squinted at the solemn faces of the crowd by the road, surprised that they were all staring back. Sheila tugged at her sleeve and pointed, her voice shrill with excitement. "Betsie, look! It's Mike! He came!"

Betsie's heart raced. Could it be?

It was. Michael Sullivan, more stringbean skinny than ever, emerged from the police car. Though slight, he towered above most of the men, and for once he wasn't wearing gaudy hippie clothes. Instead, he was simply dressed in a rumpled white t-shirt and raggedy-hem blue jeans . . . bell-bottoms, Betsie remembered they were called. Still, he looked out of place among the sober dress of the Amish men. Michael's tousled auburn locks concealed his face until he ran a hand through his *stroobly haar*. Immediately from across the yard he locked eyes with Betsie, but instead of greeting her with that sardonic grin she knew so well, his expression was gentle—sad.

Perplexed, Betsie watched as Sheila skimmed the steps to fly into her brother's arms. She pulled away from his embrace and looked up at him before casting an anxious glance at Betsie. "Mike, what are you doing here? Are Mom and Dad back together? Did you come to take me home?"

The girl's face was bright red. Must be she's overcome with surprise, Betsie thought. Likely Michael was just as shocked at seeing Sheila in an Amish dress, for he looked at his sister funny for a second.

"Hello, Squirt," she heard him say at last, his voice low. He hugged her again, but once more he had eyes only for Betsie.

A second figure emerged from the police car. He removed his cap to reveal close-cropped, grizzled hair and Betsie recognized Sergeant Deacon, the kinder of the two police officers she'd met in Hilliard. He spotted Betsie but stared at the ground for a moment before squaring his shoulders and heading for the porch.

Michael rested a hand on the officer's arm. "No. Let me tell her, please," she heard him say. "Sheila, stay here with the sergeant."

And then she knew. Michael was in trouble, trouble far worse than any misbehavior Abijah had ever cooked up. Only . . . how had he gotten here from Tennessee? And why had the policeman fetched him to Plain City on Rachel's wedding day, of all days?

Unless . . . she bit her lip, her thoughts skipping rapidly ahead as Michael walked gravely toward her. She didn't know the ways of English law very well, but she dimly remembered something in the newspaper about prisoners being allowed to make one phone call to a friend or family member. How ironic that she, Michael's friend, lived where direct phone contact was impossible.

Yes, that had to be it. Michael needed help, so he'd come to her. Why so sad, though?

Come to think of it, wasn't that the easiest question of all? Clearly he was embarrassed to see her, to own up to what he'd done, but at last she had a reason to smile. He needn't worry on her account. After all, there were few transgressions that Michael hadn't already exposed her to during her brief stay with the Sullivan family. If he thought she would be shocked at whatever infraction he'd committed, he was very much mistaken.

"Hello, Michael," she greeted as he trudged up the steps. "How did you find me here?"

He shrugged one shoulder listlessly. "We stopped by your house but no one was home, so we asked in town. They told us at the gas station that most of the Amish would be at the Yutzy place today and we got directions."

"*Jah*, here I am." She gestured at her smudged work clothes. "My friend Rachel is marrying today and I must change very soon. But first, it looks like you're in trouble of some kind," she chided with an arch smile. "It is time to come clean, Michael. What have you done?"

Instead of answering, he folded her hands oh, so gently between his own. "Oh, Pippa."

She blushed and slipped her hands out of his grasp with a sidewise glance at the crowd in the yard.

"Sorry," he mumbled. "Look, you'd better sit down. I have news, and it's . . . it's not good."

Betsie watched his face as she felt behind her for the swing, filled with misgivings. She sought reassurance from her neighbors, who'd gathered into a tight cluster in the yard, but their lowered hat brims and bonnets concealed their faces. As she sat down, she saw Sergeant Deacon lean to whisper in Sheila's ear. She watched the girl burst into tears, sobbing as though her heart would break.

Stricken, she looked up at Michael, her insides hollow. "I'm scared. Whatever your news is, tell me and get it over with."

"I'm trying, but this is the hardest thing I've ever had to do." He swallowed and sat down next to her. "When I got Sheila's letter ordering me to come home right away, it struck a chord. I was sick of that Farm place and I started immediately. I made it home late last night and I was planning to head over to Plain City later today, but then Sergeant Deacon stopped by the house early this morning and asked for you."

Betsie crinkled her forehead. "Me? But why? I have done nothing wrong."

"Betsie, please stop with the questions. If I don't say this now, I'll never get it out." He clasped his hands tight together to stop their shaking, his face pale. "The Logan County Sheriff's Office contacted Sergeant Deacon this morning. There's been an accident. Your parents—"

"An accident? *Mem* and *Dat* have been in an accident?" Betsie shrilled. She leapt to her feet. "Why didn't you say so right away? We are wasting time. Drive me to Belle Center, Michael!"

He caught her wrist as she rushed past and gently pulled her to face him again, his eyes filled with tears as he shook his head. "Betsie, your parents . . . they didn't make it."

Dread shot through her. "You're lying!" She tried to pull her hand away. "Didn't you hear?" she beseeched her friends and neighbors as they stood motionless. "I have to go to *Mem* and *Dat* immediately. Michael, turn me loose! Let go!"

She tried to shove him away, but as panic ebbed, her knees buckled. If not for Michael's strong arms, she would have fallen. He held her against his heart as she sobbed.

"Betsie, I'm so sorry. I would give anything to change this," he murmured into her hair.

"What is going on here?" an angry voice demanded in *Deitsh*.

"Charley," Betsie gasped. She felt like she was choking. "Oh, Charley—"

As she spoke, she felt Michael lower her to the swing, where she slumped with her face buried in her hands, numb with shock.

"Hey, I know this doesn't look good, but we've had some trouble here and I could use your help," she heard Michael say.

"Did the English hurt you, Betsie?"

She heard a scuffle, and then, "Whoa, you've got it all wrong," Michael said evenly.

Somehow Betsie managed to raise her head. Charley's fists were clenched as he glowered at Michael, who stood his ground.

"No," she said, her voice thin. "Charley, you mustn't. He didn't hurt me the way you think—"

Michael took over. "Look, I just gave Betsie some terrible news and she's hurting. Let me get her some help and then we'll talk."

She watched dully as Charley barely nodded and Michael scanned the yard.

"Sheila, can you come up here?" he called at last. "We need you."

Betsie closed her eyes and a moment later yielded with a sigh to Sheila's tearful embrace. She heard Michael and Charley shuffle to the far corner of the porch, Michael talking all the while. The sound of Charley's shocked tones and Michael's steady responses reached her ears, but the words held no meaning.

I have to find Sadie and Abijah, she told herself. I must notify everyone and make arrangements.

But what she did was sit, chilled to the bone, bereft. *Mem* and *Dat* . . . dead. For so long she'd clung to the hope that her parents would come home, but now it was too late. Since they had not returned to the Amish church before they died, Betsie knew she would never see her *mem* and *dat* again. Not even in eternity.

CHAPTER 39

"Word I was in the house alone
Somehow must have gotten abroad . . ."
—"Bereft" by Robert Frost,
quoted in Betsie's journal

"Charley," Betsie called weakly.

"Here I am."

As he crossed the porch, Betsie tried to gather her wits. "Will you find my sister and brother and bring them here so I can tell them? But you tell Rachel and Sam . . . what happened." She swallowed painfully. "Let Rachel know my satchel with my dress and Sadie's is on her bed. Maybe . . . maybe someone else can wear them and take our places at her wedding."

"You can depend on me to do these things for you," Charley said with a nod. "And, Betsie, I am sorry to hear about your parents." He dragged his sweaty palms across his trousers and caught her eye for a moment before his attention shifted to the grazing horses.

She nodded too. "I know."

He nodded again and dashed away on his errands. After he left, Betsie turned to Sheila, who'd faithfully remained by her side. Betsie tried to speak, but she was overcome by the mingled love and sorrow in the girl's face.

Sheila caught Betsie's hand to show that she understood what she wanted to say. "Mike, can you take me home for a couple of days?" She twisted to catch her brother's wordless nod. "Don't worry, Betsie. I can stay with him as long as you need me to."

"It's not that I want you to go," Betsie choked out. "It's just that I have so much to do . . ." Her voice dwindled and she twisted her handkerchief.

Sheila patted her hand again. "I understand. And, Betsie?" She leaned close to Betsie's ear and whispered, "Don't forget. Your mom and dad are safe with Jesus in heaven now." As she rose to go, tears trickled down her cheeks, but she managed a tremulous smile.

Michael rested a hand on his sister's shoulder. "Thank you, Sheila. Can you go tell Officer Deacon I'll be there in a minute? I need to talk with Betsie."

"Sure, Mike. Bye, Betsie."

Betsie raised her hand briefly and let it flop to her lap. Her very bones had melted like wax.

Michael sat down. "Do you want to hear how it happened, or is that too much to handle right now?" He peered at her. "Your lips are white. Maybe I should get you some water first."

"No," she said. "Please, I want to hear so I can tell Sadie and Abijah. Charley will be back with them very soon, so there isn't much time."

He sighed. "This won't take long. Your aunt—Lovina, is that her name?"

"Yes, yes. She is all right?" Betsie's hands trembled.

"She's in good shape, at least physically. She told the sheriff that she and your parents had gone for a walk toward evening yesterday. They headed out of Belle Center because they missed your farm. The country road they ended up on is all hills and dips. Lovina said when they got to the top of a certain hill, they saw something floundering in the middle of the road, way down below in the shadows. When they got closer, they saw it was a fawn, so young it still had its spots." Michael paused and stared at his feet. "It had been hit by a car. One leg was broken, snapped clear out of alignment, and every time the fawn tried to hobble to its feet, the pain caused it to keel over." He shifted uncomfortably. "Look, are you sure you're up to this? You're shivering."

"I'm all right," she lied through numb lips. "Just a bit cold." Her teeth chattered.

"Probably shock." He scooted closer and put an arm around her shoulder. "Better?"

Past caring what her neighbors thought, Betsie nodded. Michael's closeness and warmth stopped the uncontrollable shaking that had set in. "Go on," she said through clenched teeth, though she could guess what was coming.

"I'm almost done. Lovina said once your dad knew the fawn was injured, that was it. He practically ran to kneel beside the injured animal, crooning the whole time to try to calm its fear and pain. Your mom was right beside him, one hand on the fawn and one arm around your dad. He called over his shoulder for Lovina to hurry back to the house they'd just passed and try to find some materials to make a splint, so she did." He took a deep breath. "Your aunt said the moving van barreled over the hill from behind them and they never had a chance. She's sure your parents didn't know what happened, that they suffered no pain. That's what the sheriff said, too, if it's any comfort to you. Also, Lovina declined to press charges. She said it was no use." His smile was bleak. "From what I hear, your aunt is one gutsy lady. She flagged down a couple of cars and had the drivers help her guard . . . the scene until the police came." He paused, overcome. "The minute I heard, I knew I had to tell you myself. I didn't want you to face the news alone. I'm so sorry, Betsie."

"*Denki*, Michael," Betsie whispered. "Knowing helps some, and I'm glad I heard it from you."

"Mike?" Sheila climbed the steps with something clutched in her arms. "Sergeant Deacon said to give this to Betsie." She handed it to him.

He cleared his throat and swiped at his eyes. "Thanks, Squirt," he said, his voice husky. He handed it to Betsie. "Deacon said your aunt sent this. It's your dad's Bible. She wanted you to have it."

Betsie was still stroking the cover of the beloved *Biewel* when Charley returned at last with a tearful Sadie and Abijah in tow. Betsie bristled. Charley had told them? That was her job.

"It's true, then?" Sadie choked out, her lips trembling.

Abijah stood gripping the porch rail, white-faced and gangly as he waited for Betsie to confirm the rumor that must have spread like wildfire among the wedding guests.

Betsie's anger crumbled at the sight of Sadie's glistening eyes. She nodded through her tears. "They're gone."

Michael stood up and offered Sadie his seat. "One more thing before we go. Lovina said she wants to remember Noah and Fannie in her own way, so she won't come to the funeral. She reminded us she's shunned. We'll be leaving now, Betsie. I'm so sorry. I know how much they meant to you. We'll talk more when I bring Sheila back. Good-bye," he said gently. He searched her face, taking in every detail as though he wanted to commit it to memory before he walked away.

She watched as he shook hands with Charley. "Take care of her, man, and if she needs anything at all . . ." Michael trailed off, at a loss for words. Charley pulled his hand out of Michael's and rubbed it on his trousers.

"Our phone number is in my book bag," Sheila told Abijah, who listened with red-rimmed eyes. "I keep it under my bed. Call from town if Betsie needs us for any reason at all."

Betsie watched Michael and Sheila walk away, their arms around one another's waists. How kind and sympathetic they had been. They had known what she needed even though they belonged to a very different world. Truly they were her good friends, ready to help in an instant. Sergeant Deacon let them in the police car and she followed his progress until he drove out of sight on their way back to Hilliard.

Charley coughed. "I told Rachel and Sam. They want to see you," he told her.

Betsie put a hand to her forehead in an effort to concentrate. She sighed, already overwhelmed by the list of duties spinning in her head. "I guess we should tell Jonas, ain't so?" She glanced at her stricken brother and sister, their heads bowed with grief. "And after that, Charley, could you please take us home?"

"There's Jonas now, just pulling into the yard. I'll get him for you and then I'll hitch up my horse," he volunteered, plainly glad to be of practical use and out of the way. "We'll go when you say."

Betsie nodded, her eyes following Charley as he pushed through the people that thronged Jonas in their haste to be first to share the sorrowful news. As luck would have it, Charley's mother reached the bishop first; Betsie saw Jonas's face go ashen as Mattie talked. Charley sidled up to Jonas next and ushered him toward the porch. She saw Charley point her out before he excused himself and headed for the barn.

Wearily Betsie turned her attention to Jonas as he approached. He looked about a hundred years old.

"Jonas, you're as white as a sheet. Do you need to sit down? Here, Katie," Betsie called to the girl who loitered in the corner of the porch, watching with big eyes. "Run and fetch a glass of water for the bishop, and say I said to send out some cookies with it. Scoot, now." She nodded encouragement and Katie flew to do her bidding.

"Come and sit down," Betsie urged Jonas as she stood. "You don't look well at all."

"*Ach*, Betsie. I'm the one who should be comforting you. Is it true what Mattie said? Are Fannie and Noah . . . *ach*, I can't bear to think of it." He collapsed onto the swing and buried his head in his hands.

Katie Miller returned and handed over a glass of lemonade. "I thought it would taste better," she shrugged.

Betsie managed a smile. "You did a good job. Hand me that plate of sugar cookies, but take one for yourself first," she urged. "Now, Jonas, drink up."

As the bishop sipped the lemonade and a nibbled at a cookie, his color gradually returned to normal, but his state of mind did not.

"I can't believe it," he moaned. "I was so close, so close."

Betsie took pity on him. "You couldn't know this would happen. You would have visited them in time if you had known." She refused to think about the difference one day made.

"You don't understand," Jonas said. "I should have gone sooner. Now . . ." He trailed off.

I wish I didn't understand, but I do, thought Betsie to herself, but she said only, "Don't torment yourself, Jonas. I have but one concern." She lowered her voice so Sadie and Abijah couldn't hear. "Where can we bury *Mem* and *Dat*? Since they left the church, I mean." She wrung her hands at the thought of putting her parents into wooden coffins and put the picture out of her mind.

"Betsie, don't you worry. They will be buried in the Amish cemetery," Jonas said with great determination, "where they will be an example, a good example, of two godly lives. Would that I had realized this sooner than I did," he said, his distress evident. "I've made so many mistakes. I pray it's not too late. But here is something else I want you to remember in the coming days." He lowered his voice. "You may see your parents again in heaven one day, but let me stress that they are not the reason I'm unsure. I know they are in the presence of the good Lord this very minute. Remember that. And now I must get ready to perform the wedding ceremony."

Betsie let him leave, weak in the knees. Had Jonas overheard Sheila as she reassured Betsie? But that was impossible. He hadn't yet arrived when the girl left. And what about all the sermons she'd heard him preach about former Amish going to hell? He was the one who had ordered the shunning of her parents. Her mind in turmoil, she waited for Charley.

The ride home was a blur of tears. She'd watched Charley as he drove right up into the yard. Unwilling to wait another minute, not even to see Rachel, Betsie had led Sadie and Abijah to the buggy where they collapsed onto the seats and held each other as they cried quietly.

Poor Charley. Though he tried to hide it, Betsie knew their bereavement had unnerved him. Gamely he helped them into the house, anxious to discover anything he could do to help, anything at all, he said, but Betsie knew he meant a physical task of some sort. Spiritual and emotional comfort escaped him. For now, she let him off the hook and sent him home. She had her own comforting to do, she reflected, and she climbed the stairs to tell Sadie and Abijah about *Mem* and *Dat*'s last moments on earth.

CHAPTER 40

" . . . word I was in my life alone,
Word I had no one left but God."
—"BEREFT" BY ROBERT FROST,
QUOTED IN BETSIE'S JOURNAL

AT TIMES, BETSIE hadn't been sure she would live through her parents'
funeral. The somber black clothing, the eerie quiet, the airless wooden
coffins with the frail human husks trapped inside—it was all a nightmare
with no waking up at the end, only a long succession of pain and sorrow.

When the last guest had been fed and consoled—for strangely
enough, Betsie had learned that the bereaved were the ones who did
most of the consoling—the Troyer family sat on the couch, completely
drained. It was a relief to watch Amelia as she daintily cleaned her face,
her tummy tight with filched treats.

Mattie Yoder rocked in the chair that Charley had brought in from
the porch for extra seating. She looked strangely content to be here,
knitting a pair of socks for Charley as she looked about the house in a
satisfied way.

Charley had been helpful in a thousand practical ways today, Betsie
realized, and she had been grateful. Now that everyone was gone,
though, he wandered aimlessly through the front room, spacious once
more without the guests who had filed through to pay obsequious
respects to Noah and Fannie.

She watched as Charley wound the mantel clock, carefully replacing the key and flicking away dust with his handkerchief before he stooped to pick up a section of *The Budget* from the floor, stacking it neatly in the reading basket. He shoved his hands in his pockets and paced until his attention fixed on the front door. Frowning, he removed his handkerchief again and polished a spot where a greasy nose print showed. He backed up to examine the glass and polished the smear again. Betsie's eyelids drooped from weariness.

The sound of cloth squeaking on glass roused her and she saw Benner. He stood there with his blond hair glinting in the twilight, his broad-shouldered form in silhouette against the door. Betsie sprang from her seat with fists clenched. The man turned slowly toward her and Betsie took a shallow breath. It was only Charley. It was like her nightmare—Benner changing into Charley. But that was ridiculous. Charley was a good man, dependable to a fault. He would never force himself on her, as Benner had.

And yet . . . she cast her mind back to that evening when she'd been attacked. Hadn't she thought at first that Charley had come to visit her at the harness shop when it was really Benner who waited at the door? The two men looked nothing alike in the face, but there were certainly physical similarities. She shrank back into the couch and wrapped her arms around her stomach. The man who attacked her was dead, she reminded herself. She need never fear him again.

Her mind told her she was safe, but her heart was beating wildly in her chest. She stared at a knot in the wooden floor, following the pattern into the silent kitchen and the field beyond. As she stared at Judith and Fledge peacefully munching grass, she realized that she viewed Charley in a different light since he'd grabbed her and kissed her when they were alone. If she had let him . . .

No. She was overwrought, imagining things. She couldn't be afraid of Charley. Look at him! Even now, he was taking care of things for her, adjusting the screen door so it wouldn't bang shut. Though his demanding mother Mattie was here, Charley was helping Betsie, tending to her house like it was his own.

She froze. The recollection flooded back, crystal clear. *It will be good to fix up this house when it's ours. . . . My own children, my own wife,* Charley had said. *My own farm.*

The food she'd forced down congealed in her stomach. Her parents weren't even cold in their graves before Charley had taken over. Maybe Betsie, Sadie, and Abijah still lived on the premises, but she felt sure that in Charley's mind, this was the Yoder farm now and he was the master, with Mattie rocking and knitting—no, spinning a web like a bloodthirsty spider.

Betsie shuddered. She wanted to bolt from the house and never stop running, but instead she stood up quietly and made a polite observation about how late it was getting, how tired she and her siblings were. Charley responded with grave courtesy and even Mattie surpassed herself by keeping her mouth shut and just patting Betsie's hand.

When they were gone at last, Betsie urged Sadie and Abijah to get some sleep, promising to follow after she'd closed up the house. She trailed listlessly to the kitchen door, but Charley had beaten her to it; the door was locked. As she turned from it with a growl, a dark lump on the floor caught her eye. A spider? She shivered and leaned for a closer look. No, it was a clump of earth that Charley, in his inspection of his new property, had missed.

She snatched at the broom, grateful for something to do, but as she drew the broom across the floor, the dark lump didn't move. Annoyed, she scrubbed harder, but the dirt was stuck tight.

Betsie cast the broom aside with a clatter and dropped to her knees beside the table, Yes, it was dried mud, all right, but a table knife would loosen it. She put a hand on *Dat's* chair to push herself up, grumbling to herself about heedless people with dirty shoes who walked all over clean floors—and then it hit her. Somebody had tracked in mud from the cemetery. This clump of dried earth was newly dug from her parents' graves.

She bolted to her feet in a split second, recoiling from the sacrilege in horror and running from the room. As she clawed at the doorknob to open the front door, she spotted the *Biewel* on the side table. She willed herself to calm down and picked up the heavy worn book, recalling how much *Dat* had loved it. With a deep breath, she held it protectively in front of her and braved the kitchen once more.

"It's just dirt," she told herself over and over. When she'd cleaned up the mess, she closed the damper on the stove and lit a candle. She sat at the table and pulled the big book toward her. Timidly she opened it, instantly confronted with margin notes written in *Dat's* hand.

As she turned the pages, she thought about what first *Dat*, then *Mem*, and then Lovina had believed. Salvation wasn't a proud crutch. To these dear ones, it was life itself, a reason to give up everything they'd ever loved and believed in and start anew, forgiven and free.

Sheila's dear face came to mind. What a change had come over that sweet girl since Betsie met her. Her faith had grown by leaps and bounds, and strangely enough, she believed the same as *Dat* and *Mem* and Lovina, though she was only a young English girl.

Sheila's friend Debbie, Mrs. Keith, and even the pastor at the revival—they believed, too. In fact, Betsie had begun to wonder if everyone in the world believed the same, though she knew now that wasn't true. It had to be a coincidence that she met people who knew the answers she needed to hear at precisely the right time.

Or maybe the good Lord was sending these people across her path, believers who prayed for her and instructed her in the truth. Was it too much to believe that He cared about her, yearned for her, loved her?

She paged through the Bible until she found *Dat's* favorite verse, Romans 10:9. She thought of all the times the family had sat around the kitchen table and listened to him read that verse. Tears spilled over as she realized she would never hear his rumbly bear voice again. "That if thou shalt confess with thy mouth the Lord Jesus, and shalt believe in thine heart that God hath raised him from the dead, thou shalt be saved," she whispered.

She'd lost so much, but God was still here, loving her. He was everywhere. She didn't need to leave Plain City to follow Him. She knew that now. If only her parents had realized this, they might still be alive, but how thankful she was that they had ultimately accepted Jesus' sacrifice before death snatched them away. It was enough, she decided. She knelt beside the table on the clean floor and bowed her head.

"Amen." Peace filled her soul. Sorrow would be her companion for a long time to come, but she knew that one day when she went to heaven, she'd see her parents again. Sweeter by far was the thought that she would see her Savior. She smiled through her tears.

Wait until she told Sheila! How happy that *Schnickelfritz* would be to hear her good news. Charley, on the other hand . . . she shook her head in wonder. Sheila had been right all along. It had been Michael from the very moment she met him. When Betsie's great crisis, the death of her parents, had come, Michael was the one who had looked deep into her soul and offered real compassion, real friendship—real love. He was the person she wanted by her side for all the days of her life.

But Michael could wait. Plenty of stormy days lay between now and the day she could share her heart with him, she realized. For now, she would keep her salvation a sweet secret. Her Amish friends and neighbors, not to mention her sister and brother, would never accept her decision. No, it was up to her to provide for Sadie and Abijah's welfare, to keep a roof over their heads. If that meant living a double life for a while, so be it. She'd seen her parents shunned for showing what they believed. She wouldn't make the same mistake.

And what about Michael's faith? He'd seemed on the cusp of a big revelation, but she decided she could wait to find out about that. After all, she was already sure of his heart.

First things first. Betsie knew she had another relationship to nourish, a relationship with the One who would never leave her or forsake her. And for right now, for always, that was enough.

How I Met "Betsie"

BACK IN 2005, a sign in Plain City, Ohio, caught my attention: Harness Shop, Closed Sunday. At the time, I was writing historical fiction about the Underground Railroad, and I knew that long before the Reverend John Rankin had aided slaves as they escaped to freedom, he'd worked with leather in his father's shop, crafting harnesses and even his own wedding shoes.

What an awesome chance to get some firsthand experience! I dialed the shop, excited.

"Hello, may I speak to the harness maker?"

"That's me. Rachel."

Surprised, I blurted, "Uh, I want to learn to make harnesses. Can I watch you sometime?"

"Yes!"

"Okay . . . when can I come?"

"Tomorrow!"

No time like the present, I guessed. "Okay. What time?"

"Come in the morning. Knock on the door." And she hung up on me.

Though a bit perplexed at the odd conversation, there was no stopping me now. The next morning, I grabbed my camera and stuck a legal pad in my purse before setting off for Plain City. It was a miserable January day, overcast with cold wind and sleet, but I was on a mission.

Standing to the north of the house, the harness shop had white siding and a tin roof. I knocked on the door and a lady with a drab-colored green dress and a head scarf invited me inside. She said her name was Rachel Miller and this was her harness shop. I examined the interior, dim in the gray winter light. A stove heated the room and a calico cat snoozed in the lawn chair beside it.

"Let's get to work," Rachel said. She briskly showed me the rolls of leather, the equipment she used, shiny brass buckles, thread, stain, and tools for cutting and shaping. She took up an edger and shaved a leather strap, smoothing the raw edge nicely.

"Now you!" she exclaimed. She slapped the edger into my palm and folded her arms, ready to observe me.

"Me? I'll mess it up!" I protested.

"I'm not worried." Obviously Rachel thought I should learn by doing instead of by watching. Bemused, I tried to follow her example and failed miserably. I apologized for my sloppy work.

"Oh, that's all right! You'll learn!" Rachel was nothing if not enthusiastic.

She bustled to the next work station, but my attention was captured by a roll of leather. I dug out my camera and snapped a picture. The flash illuminated the dim shop.

Rachel almost jumped out of her skin. "What was that?!"

And then it hit me. The phone difficulties, the musical accent, the dim shop, the hustle-bustle manner, the shock over a simple camera flash . . . Rachel was Amish!

After I promised that I would photograph only materials, Rachel spent the rest of the morning "teaching" me to make harnesses. As we visited, I learned that she'd grown up milking cows at four in the morning and making hay in the sweet hot sunshine. She informed me that she and her sister were two of nine remaining Amish of Plain City (as of today, only five practicing Amish remain).

I last saw Rachel when I delivered the resulting newspaper article and a copy of my first book, *Across the Wide River*. Sadly, Alzheimer's disease has since ravaged Rachel's memories, but her can-do spirit is embodied by Amish harness-maker Betsie Troyer, star of my Plain City Peace series.

BOOK CLUB DISCUSSION QUESTIONS

1. It can be challenging to write with authority about the Amish because many readers are very familiar with the Amish lifestyle. Contrary to many online resources, however, the Amish generally do have pockets in their clothing. Joe Keim, ex-Amish director of Mission to Amish People, remembers that shirt pockets weren't allowed for the men but pants pockets were, one on each side although not on the hip. A small hidden pocket in the front of the pants could carry a pocket watch. Coats, vests, and Sunday jackets all had pockets inside. Women's dresses were allowed to have one pocket under the apron, about the size of a post card. Their coats, too, had inside pockets. Can you imagine going through everyday life without the convenience of pockets in your clothing? Do you wonder, like Sheila, if God frowns on details of dress like shirt pockets, or whether He really favors patch pockets over hip pockets? What clothing items did your parents or school principal forbid you to wear when you were growing up? How did these rules make you feel? What conservative clothing views that we cling to are really just cultural and don't have a biblical basis?

2. When Sheila was impatient to hear news of her brother Michael, Betsie insisted on opening the package carefully so she could save the brown paper and reuse it; "waste not, want not" in her mother's words. In Life with Lily by Mary Ann Kinsinger and Suzanne Woods Fisher, Lily's Amish mama washes and reuses store-bought bread wrappers to use with the baked goods she sells. In my childhood, bread wrappers helped slide stubborn

shoes into overshoes or snowboots. Discuss some creative ways to recycle and upcycle. Can you recall some ways your grandparents pinched pennies? What value is there in frugality?

3. It may seem strange, but conventional good manners and other niceties (like table napkins!) are not much valued in many Amish households. Among the Swartzentruber Amish, for example, practicing good manners has even been called proud behavior and thus disdained. What about your own experience? Were you raised to say, "Yes, sir" or "No, ma'am" to your elders, especially teachers? Were you taught that it's impolite to point? Was "Shut up!" a bad word in your household? How would you explain the purpose of good manners to a child or someone unfamiliar with your household customs?

4. Michael feels sure he will find peace at The Farm, a commune-style settlement in Tennessee that still exists today. In the early '70s, Farm members took vows of poverty and owned no personal possessions other than clothing and tools. During that time, Farm members had a strong pro-life policy and did not use artificial birth control, alcohol, tobacco, man-made psychotropics, or animal products. They did, however, use marijuana. Farm residents made their own rules. With what you know of the Ordnung, the unwritten rules of the Amish communities, can you find any similarities between these two seemingly different lifestyles? What is the appeal of each?

5. Betsie believes she will find peace in Plain City, the place where she grew up. Do you have a special place where you can escape stress? When you wish you could "go home again," where is it you'd like to be and why?

6. In a letter to Betsie, Fannie Troyer quoted Mark 10:28–30. In this context, these Bible verses may seem unfeeling or even cruel. Discuss the meaning of these verses. What have you had to give up to follow Christ? In what situation would you share these verses with another person?

7. Betsie has a complicated relationship with Charley. Some of the difficulties stem from his mother, Mattie. As a result of her

domination over her son (which he finds difficult to change, lacking a father as an example), he overcompensates by taking charge and perhaps overstepping his boundaries at other times. Have you ever found yourself in this situation, either in the position of authority or as an underling? How did you change the pattern?

8. Communities vary, but many Amish tend to shy away from physical contact like casual hugging. Also uncommon is the use of the word "love" to describe a feeling between two people such as Charley and Betsie. Instead, according to Saloma Furlong (http://salomafurlong.com/aboutamish/2012/08/an-amish -handshake/), her community said, "I think a lot of him/her." Are you a "hugger" or do you shy away from a casual embrace of greeting or farewell? Were you raised in a publicly affection-ate family or one that was more reserved? Identify different ways that family members can express love for one another.

9. In *The Bargain*, Betsie thinks of her brother Abijah as a little boy. When he shows up at home in *The Bachelor*, she's sur-prised to see he's getting to be a man. And he seems to be inclined to fight to have his wishes heard, and yet despairs of it accomplishing anything. Whether you are the "baby" in your family, or someone else is, discuss the dynamic that creates in the family. Can you identify a turning point at which that youngest child asserted their adulthood?

10. Poetry is an important link between Betsie and Michael. Samuel Taylor Coleridge, a noted poet (1772–1834, The Rime of the Ancient Mariner and Kubla Khan), is attributed as saying: "I wish our clever young poets would remember my homely definitions of prose and poetry; that is, prose,—words in their best order; poetry,—the best words in their best order." Name or recite a favorite poem, or share one of your own. Is there a poem you memorized in childhood that you can still recite?

11. At my childhood church, our Sunday school class once played a game where there were two "fake" Christians and one "real"

Christian on a panel. Players could ask any questions they liked and then they would guess which one was the "real" Christian. A couple of kids left the room and teachers told the rest of us which part we would play on the panel. To my dismay (despite praying, "Don't pick me, don't pick me"), I was chosen to play the "real" Christian; I'm sure my teachers thought a good girl like me was a safe bet. Talk about panic! Although I was raised in the church and usually in attendance, I wasn't sure I could convince the kids asking the questions that I was a "real" Christian. Why? Because at the time, I wasn't! Sure enough, the game backfired because I couldn't come up with a good reason for people to go to church on Sunday instead of listening to a Christian radio program. "She didn't convince me," one of the boys insisted.

As a new Christian, Sheila shares her faith, as she understands it, readily. Do you regularly share your faith in Jesus Christ with others? Have you ever had to verbally defend your faith? If so, did you welcome the opportunity or shy away from it? What did you say? How do you apply the instruction in 1 Peter 3:15?

12. Many Amish groups believe that being assured of one's salvation before death is not possible. When Betsie loses both of her parents, she at first believes she will never see them again, not even in eternity, because they had left the Amish church. Betsie is reassured by Sheila and, strangely enough, by Bishop Jonas that her parents are in heaven. What do you believe the Bible teaches about assurance of salvation? What Scripture passages support your beliefs? How do you offer comfort when someone loses a loved one?

CHARLEY'S FAVORITE AMISH MONSTER COOKIES

3 eggs
1 cup white sugar
2 teaspoons baking soda
1½ cups peanut butter
½ to 1 cup chocolate chips
1 teaspoon vanilla
1 cup brown sugar
1 tablespoon Karo syrup
½ cup oleo (or margarine or butter, softened)
4½ cups oatmeal
½ to 1 cup M&M's

Mix everything together and bake at 350°F for 12 minutes.

Note: You can tell this is a real Amish recipe—whack everything in a bowl, mix it up, and bake, done that way for generations. Let me translate: Combine all the ingredients except the oatmeal and mix well. Lastly, add oatmeal. Dough will be stiff. Drop cookies by tablespoon onto ungreased cookie sheet and flatten with the bottom of a cup. Bake at 350°F for 12 minutes.

Yield: Four to five dozen. Happy baking!

CHARLEY'S FAVORITE HAM AND POTATO SOUP WITH MACARONI

3½ cups peeled and diced potatoes
⅓ cup diced celery
⅓ cup finely chopped onion
¾ cup diced cooked ham
3¼ cups water
2 tablespoons chicken bouillon granules
½ teaspoon salt, or to taste
1 teaspoon ground white or black pepper, or to taste
5 tablespoons butter
5 tablespoons all-purpose flour
2 cups milk
⅓ cup of dry elbow macaroni, cooked

Combine the potatoes, celery, onion, ham and water in a stockpot. Bring to a boil, then cook over medium heat until potatoes are tender, about 10 to 15 minutes. Stir in the chicken bouillon, salt and pepper. In a separate pot, cook macaroni according to package directions and drain. Set aside.

In a separate saucepan, melt butter over medium-low heat. Whisk in flour, and cook, stirring constantly until thick, about 1 minute. Gradually whisk in milk so as not to allow lumps to form. Continue stirring over medium-low heat until thick, 4 to 5 minutes.

Stir the milk mixture into the stockpot, and cook soup until heated through. Stir in cooked macaroni and serve immediately.

SWEET-AS-SHEILA
ICEBOX PICKLES

7 cups sliced cucumbers
1 cup diced green peppers
1 cup chopped Vidalia onion
½ cup water
½ cup white vinegar
2 cups sugar
2 teaspoons sea salt
½ teaspoon celery seed
1 tablespoon mustard seed

Mix water, vinegar, and sugar. When sugar is dissolved, add celery seed, mustard seed, and sea salt. Pour over pickles and refrigerate for a couple of days. Pickles will be ready to eat and will keep for up to a month in the refrigerator.

Pickles like these were a fixture at carry-in dinners in my childhood church. Mmm!

COMING WINTER 2016

BRIDE

BOOK THREE IN THE
PLAIN CITY PEACE SERIES